LIFTED UP

LIFTED UP

a novel

Guy Morgan Galli

Covenant Communications, Inc.

Cover illustration by Dave McClellan

Cover design copyrighted 2003 by Covenant Communications, Inc.

Published by Covenant Communications, Inc.
American Fork, Utah

Printed in the United States of America
First Printing: March 2003

10 09 08 07 06 05 04 03   10 9 8 7 6 5 4 3 2 1

ISBN 1-59156-179-5

ACKNOWLEDGMENTS

I am indebted to the many friends and family members who took the time to read early drafts of the work and give valuable feedback. A special thanks to Carol Holmes for taking a good story and turning it into a better one through her insightful editorial and storyline critiques. To the staff at Covenant, especially my editor, Angela, for their patience as I learned the business of publishing. Above all, I am grateful to my wife and children for suffering through nights alone while I banished myself to the basement to work on "The Book."

Coventry Carol

Lullay, Thou little tiny Child,
By, by, lully, lullay.
Lullay, Thou little tiny Child,
By, by, lully, lullay.

O sisters too, how may we do,
For to preserve this day.
This poor youngling for whom we sing
By, by, lully, lullay.

Herod, the king, in his raging,
Charged he hath this day.
His men of might, in his own sight,
All young children to slay.

That woe is me, poor Child for Thee!
And ever morn and day,
For thy parting neither say nor sing,
By, by, lully, lullay.

CHAPTER 1

The bright Judean sun bathed the ancient city of David with a warm embrace that seemed symbolic of God's love and care for His favored people and their city. The hint of a breeze left over from the cool night before was evidence that spring had not given up its hold on the land. When summer finally set in, any cool air born of the night would be gone by midmorning. But not today. This season was the perfect time to be alive in the promised land.

From atop the stairs connecting the Temple's meeting hall with the streets below, I had a complete view of the magnificent city that was Jerusalem. To my right rose the streets of the upper city where the wealthy of the city gathered and lived in opulence and splendor. In the far corner, walled in and guarded by a dozen men, was the palace of our king, Herod. Its riches put the other estates and gardens to shame by comparison. On my left was the walled-in business district with its seemingly endless flow of money, and beyond its outer wall, keeping a constant vigil over the land, was the Mount of Olives. Unfolding below me was a maze of small houses and shops, arranged and connected in chaotic clusters along narrow streets and blind alleyways, the section of the city I called home. The clay and brushwood roofs squared off the gentle rise and fall of the hills upon which they were built and reminded me of children's toy blocks.

Populated by craftsmen and laborers of all kinds, the lower city was looked down on by those with power, wealth, and authority. To them, its name implied more than its geographic location relative to the Temple. But the lower city held a special place in my heart. The sounds and smells that filled the streets were evidence of hard work and skills passed down for generations and mastered to the point of fine detail.

Those with similar skills lived and worked side by side. There was a street for butchers, one for those working in metals, and yet another for those skilled in carpentry. And those were only a few streets among the dozens dedicated to other specialties, crafts, and foods. It was from here, with tired and calloused hands that toiled from sunup to sundown, that Jerusalem was built and supported.

Poverty was a common thread connecting those who made up the rich tapestry of the lower city. But for most, there wasn't time to dwell on being poor. Life was simply enjoyed and traditions were carefully passed down to younger generations. But the most appealing element of the lower city was the faith of its people. Perhaps this, above all, attracted me to its streets and kept me there. They were a good-hearted people, and their love of God was evident in their humble generosity to their neighbors.

A hand rested on my shoulder, startling me out of my reflections.

"Congratulations," Joseph said. Joseph was a fellow student at the Temple. I had never really been properly introduced to the young man who had quickly become a leader among the other students in the class, his sights set on power and influence. He had only moved to the city not quite a month earlier. I had not had much to do with him.

"Thank you," was all I could think to say.

"You are fortunate this day to have received the nomination. You must be proud."

"Scared is closer to how I feel," I said. "This is a heavy responsibility. It is not something I can take lightly."

Joseph smiled and nodded, looking out over the lower city. "You don't still live down there, do you?"

"Why wouldn't I?"

"I recall hearing that your wife comes from a wealthy family," he said. "It seems odd that the daughter of a wealthy merchant would choose to live in such . . . conditions."

It was not his concern why we lived there, but I answered him nonetheless.

"It is a choice we have made not to rely on her family's money," I said. "We will make our own way in this world."

He chuckled lightly. "As I live, I cannot understand why you remain living in such filth and poverty."

"The streets are clean and our house is not lacking. What more do we need?"

Joseph came alive at the question. "Status, respect, power. Down there is no place for our kind, no place for a scribe of the Law. You cannot hope to gain what is important in life, living among . . ." He searched for the right word but couldn't find it.

"Who?" I said. "Those who look up to us? Those who petition our services and our prayers in their behalf? Are we better than they?"

"Of course not," he said, although the look on his face suggested that he didn't believe it. "But things are different now. Those old men in there," he gestured toward the Temple, "they don't understand what is required to move forward in these times. Talent and ability will only take you so far."

"They'll take me far enough," I said quietly. "Is there something you want, Joseph?"

He shook his head. "You are a strange one, but I can see why the council agreed on your name. You are faithful, even if you aren't the wisest of men."

"Am I to take that as a compliment?"

"Take it however you wish. You are the council's choice."

I wondered if he was jealous. He was older than I was, but age had little to do with decisions such as these.

Joseph bowed slightly at the waist. "If you'll excuse me," he said. He walked across the bridge connecting the Temple to the streets of the wealthy upper city, catching up with some other students as they returned home. Joseph was not alone in his criticism of my uncommon decision to live among those that were common. My choice to live in the lower city had been criticized by my young colleagues at the Temple since the day I married and moved there. But rich or poor, living in abundance or lacking, I had always believed my life would be fruitful and, God willing, full of service—a life to make a difference.

With the extraordinary news that threatened to burst my heart with pride and joy, I shrugged off the conversation with Joseph and made my way down the stairs, across the market square, and then hurriedly toward my refuge. It was the only place in all the world I wanted to be at the end of the day—home.

The way home seemed shorter today and I made the journey with a light step. Today my life was going to change. Tomorrow I was going to be a new man, with a new place in the world, and a new assignment from God to fulfill. My years of study and prayer at the Temple school were going to be put to the test. And if I passed, my life and the life of my family would be blessed forever.

As I traversed the steep roads and loosely cobbled steps on my way home, I began to plan how I would break the news to my wife. To be chosen for such an honor, and at my young age, was not the sort of news one simply announced. It would take building up to. It was a dance, so to speak, that would end at a precise moment and when the time was right. As I came around the corner, deep in thought, I was met by the unexpected sound of my name.

"Simon!" a sweet voice called out. It was my wife, Deborah. She was the prettiest woman I had ever met when I took her to wife. Five years later she still was.

Our house shared a small courtyard with six other houses. Like most everywhere in the lower city, the common area had its own cistern and fresh water for cooking or laundry, a small corral for our animals, and a small area with patches of wild grass as a play area for the children. There in the middle of the grass was Deborah, down on her knees, holding our beautiful young son by his hands; she was helping him stand.

"Joshua," Deborah said to the child, "show your father what you can do!" and she let go of his hands.

Joshua stood there, not quite sure what he had done worthy of repeating. Then, with a sparkle in his eyes, he remembered and leaned forward. He teetered on his tiny feet for a moment, stepping forward just before he fell. With a jerking motion he thrust out his other foot, again catching himself the instant before falling. Then he stopped, poised in a stiff, carefully balanced stance. He squealed and looked up to my astonished and approving look. I wanted to speak but couldn't find the words. My baby was walking!

Deborah's hands were never far from Joshua during his every move, and they quickly swept him up when his strength and balance left him. I rushed to her side, and together we covered him with kisses and words of praise. I couldn't believe it. My little boy was growing up so fast.

"He surprised me this afternoon," Deborah said. "One moment he was standing at the cistern, holding himself up like he always does; the next thing I knew he was falling into my arms. He must have taken two or three steps by himself."

"It seems like just yesterday that we presented him to the Temple priests," I said proudly.

I helped Deborah gather the baskets of clean clothes and carry them home. Deborah was almost floating on air she was so happy and proud of her son. *Our son. Our miracle. Our gift from God,* I thought.

"Come," I said. "Tonight we will dine in the city."

Deborah stopped at the door. "Do you mean it?"

I nodded, my smile conveying the deep love and the appreciation I had for her. The excitement on her face was briefly replaced with a dark concern.

"Can we afford it?" she asked. "Money is scarce, and I know we can't—"

I gently put my finger to her lips. "It's not every day our son takes his first steps. If there ever was a day to celebrate, this is it."

Deborah's face again lit up, and with her free arm she took me around the shoulders and neck and pulled my lips to hers. I felt truly blessed of the Lord.

* * *

The evening was without blemish as we dined on the finest food we could afford and were waited on by servants as if we were of the royal house. But the hours slipped past quickly, and we soon found ourselves hurrying to reach home before night settled in over the city. Not that there was any religious or legal reason for being home before dark—in fact, Jerusalem by lamplight is a marvel to behold—but we could hear the rumblings of a storm to the south, and ominous clouds were beginning to drift our way. As we walked, we could see that others had spotted the storm and were closing their stores and shops early. Rain is not plentiful this far inland, but in the spring and fall, when the skies are prone to heavy and sudden cloudbursts, the sun-baked clay of the streets can turn into spontaneous streambeds, channeling the water into swift currents. Although they are seldom dangerous, it is still wise not to be caught unaware in such paths.

We reached our door just ahead of the first drops of rain. While Deborah dressed Joshua for bed, I quickly set to work building a fire to ward off the cold that would otherwise stay the night.

"Rabbi Eleazer returned from his teachings at the synagogue in Galilee this afternoon," I said, my small fire growing.

"Is your old teacher well?" Deborah asked, sounding preoccupied with Joshua's bedtime routine.

"If he lives to be a hundred he could not be more kind or wise." I had always loved Rabbi Eleazer. He had been a friend of my father's for as long as I could remember, and he had been my instructor when I began my elementary studies in the synagogue. For five years, until I was ten, he had opened the Torah to me and taught the words of the prophets from his heart. I was saddened when he accepted an offer to teach among the northern cities and villages, for I was worried that I would never find another teacher and friend like him. He would visit Jerusalem from time to time and always stopped in to see my father. I wanted to believe he stopped by to see me too.

When my father died, Rabbi Eleazer gave the eulogy. I was seventeen and well on my way to following in their footsteps—becoming a scribe. Though he lived far to the north, Rabbi Eleazer made it a point to inquire of my teachers as to the progression of my studies, and when he could, he would offer words of praise and encouragement. He became a second father to me.

Deborah emerged from the baby's room, jostling me from my thoughts. Joshua was in her arms, ready for bed. From the crook of her arm, Joshua leaned over to me for his good-night kiss.

"He is growing up so fast," Deborah said with a mix of pride and sadness in her voice.

"He will grow to do great things," I said before my wife took him off to bed. Then I kissed his forehead and blessed him as fathers do, with a soft caress and the wish for the best gifts of God to fill his life.

She returned a short while later and began immediately tidying up the house before bed.

"Rabbi Eleazer came to visit us at the Temple today," I began again.

"Did you invite him to dinner?" Deborah asked, busy picking up Joshua's wooden blocks and other toys.

I shook my head. "He left just before the ninth hour for business in Gaza."

"Jerusalem is not exactly along the route from Galilee to Gaza," Deborah said, implying that she knew there was more to my story.

"He stopped by the Temple to present the name of a former student to the council of elders, one to be ordained a scholar."

I paused, hoping she would hear the words I did not speak. Deborah was attending to the clean laundry and stopped in midfold. She looked at me expectantly. Her eyes asked the question, which was answered by my smile. She dropped the clothes and ran to me, throwing her arms around my neck for the second time that evening and squeezing tight.

"I knew you would be chosen someday," she said, tears of happiness flowing as she began to choke on her words. "There is not another with more faith and love in his heart. I will be married to a rabbi! God be praised and thanks given."

"As I said, if there ever was a day to be celebrated, this is that day," I said, as we fell into each other's gentle embraces.

* * *

Some time into the night I first heard them. I had been dreaming of lying on a shaded patch of grass overlooking the city and her Temple. Haunting, formless, far-off sounds entered my dreams and chased away the pleasant images. In one terrifying instant my soft bed was replaced with rocks and shards of broken pottery cutting into my back. I sat straight up from the nightmare, instantly awake.

"What's wrong?" Deborah murmured, only half awake.

I did not know and stretched my neck out into the darkness, listening. Apart from the steady patter of the rain outside, I heard nothing. I threw back the bedcovers, stepped to the shuttered window, and looked out. Nothing appeared disturbed. Up and down the street all was quiet; even rodents and stray cats had taken shelter from the storm. But I could not shake the feeling that there was something amiss.

"What is it?" Deborah whispered, becoming more alert.

"Shhh." I thought I heard someone crying. Whether or not it was just the wind I couldn't be sure.

But inside I was sure.

I stepped quietly to the adjacent room and for a moment my heart eased its fearful pounding. There, safe and warm in his cradle, was our little Joshua, wrapped snug and sleeping soundly. He still looked proud; he had taken his first steps that day. Too young for words, his wide-eyed squeals had expressed his sense of great achievement. We had waited many years for his arrival, and now he was the love and center of our lives.

Off in the distance thunder cracked the sky, as if in protest of some violation, some crime veiled by the cloak of night, and my uneasy feeling returned.

"Come to bed," my good wife beckoned. "All is well."

I wanted to believe her, but I couldn't shake the sensation of foreboding, and as I turned back toward warm blankets, my feet resisted and took me instead to my coat of lamb's wool hanging at the door.

"Where are you going?" Deborah asked, propping herself up on her elbow and looking at me. She wasn't pleased. But how could I explain the feeling that the world was somehow off balance?

"I don't know."

"The rain . . ." she protested.

"I know . . . I'll be back in a little while. I've just . . ." *What?* All I knew was that I had sensed that something was not right. Hardly a reason to venture out in weather like this. But I had to, that much I did know, and I closed the door quietly behind me.

The rain was cold, and in no time my coat and night garments were soaked through to the skin. I wandered through the streets of the lower city, keeping to awnings and overhangs—anything that would shelter me from the elements. During the day these streets were alive with merchants and travelers, but at this hour the shops were all dark, having long since been closed for the night.

Satisfied that all was well, as Deborah had insisted, my common sense returned, and I had started back home when a frozen javelin of fear pierced my heart. The distant but sharp sound of wailing had distinctively reached my ears. The wind had died down, and I could hear it clearly. Crying. And now there was more. Screams too . . . distant but getting closer. My training at the synagogue and love for those I served at the Temple quickened my pace through the narrow streets to find the source of such pain.

Movement down a side street caught my eye, and I followed it. At the intersecting street I peered out. At one end a young woman was crouched low, partially hidden behind some old baskets and heaps of garbage. Had she caused the movement I had seen, or was she hiding from it? Before I could determine whether she needed my help or not, she dropped even lower to the ground and tried to push herself into the wall, as if the stones might envelop and hide her.

I too ducked out of sight as a soldier, dressed in the full armor of Rome, passed by where she was hiding. He paused and looked down the street, searching. He looked straight in my direction and would have seen me if the street had not been so dark, but then he moved on.

Until a child cried out.

I wiped the rain from my eyes to see better. Cradled in the woman's arms was a small bundle. She quickly put her hand over the child's mouth, but it was too late. The soldier knocked away the street debris and pulled her to her feet. The woman burst into hysterical tears, screaming and begging him to stop.

What does she fear? I wondered. My uneasiness spilled full over into dread as the soldier snatched the babe, and pushed the struggling mother to the ground. He then produced a knife, and with a sharp downward thrust, sunk his blade deep into the blankets.

I could scarcely comprehend the horror my eyes had beheld and suddenly I needed desperately to void my stomach. "Merciful God . . ."

The soldier let the bundle fall into the arms of the weeping woman and wiped his blade on the dark-stained rag at his belt. From up the street, two more soldiers joined him, devils in the darkness, their knives also drawn. They exchanged a few words, appeared to regroup for a moment, and then one of them kicked in the nearest door and forced his way inside. The other two did the same to the houses on either side.

I became aware that these three soldiers were not alone. From every street and every direction, it seemed, doors were being forced open. Screams sliced through the rain and cut me to my very center. The cries now echoed, mingling with one another to form a most unholy choir. There must have been an entire army out. But why? What had we done to warrant this attack from Rome? What anger stirred such crimes? For what ungodly purpose were they—

Deborah! My sudden thought was followed immediately by another. *Joshua!*

In my panic I turned and stumbled over a large vessel of water. It fell over and shattered on the cobbled street. I did not care if I had been heard. Now was not the time to hide. I scrambled to my feet, and with a fear I had never before known, I ran—to my home, to my wife, to my son. The soldiers were making their way through the city from the south. Our home was near the west wall, so there was hope that I could reach Deborah before they did.

I burst in through the door. "Get Joshua!" I yelled.

Deborah had been waiting up for me and jumped to her feet.

"What is it?" she demanded. "What's wrong?"

"Now, woman!" I cried so forcefully that in terror she was quick to obey me. I had never spoken to my wife in such a cutting way before; but never had our lives and our child's life been in so much danger.

"We must leave here," I said, more to myself than to Deborah. I fetched her sandals and mantle as she emerged from our room, little Joshua swaddled in a coat of sheepskin.

"Where are we going?" she managed to ask.

"The hills," I said, draping her coat around her shoulders. "The caves. We can hide there."

"Hide from who?" Deborah asked.

Shrill cries from only a few streets away silenced her question. She started to shake uncontrollably. Over the screams we could both hear shouted orders in Latin.

"What . . . what are they saying?"

My Latin was poor, but I understood most of the words. "They are searching for children."

Deborah pulled Joshua tight and backed into the wall, just as I had seen the mother on the street do. "Not my Joshua . . . God in heaven . . . no . . . ."

I steadied her by the shoulders. "Which is why we must not be here when they—"

At that moment the front door was kicked in. Filling the frame was a giant. In an instant, I took in the Roman soldier from helmet to leather boots, and acting without thought, I grabbed a small stool and swung. The soldier was not expecting anyone waiting at the door, and the wood connected firmly with the side of his face. He toppled, stunned, to the ground.

Deborah screamed.

"Move!" I commanded. "Now!" But she would not, or could not. I pried Joshua from her clutches and stepped over the soldier into the rain.

The city was alive with the sounds of death. Every falling raindrop accompanied a cry or wail that stung my heart. I wiped my eyes and peered up and down the streets. Which way to run? Did it even matter? There were exits leading out of the city either direction. And then a better idea. I would go to the Temple instead. The Temple priests would provide sanctuary and protection. The Temple with its guards and walls would be safe. If I could reach the Temple everything would be all right. With Joshua securely in my arms, I took the street north, up the hill and toward the stronghold of the Lord.

But what of the others? I could not let them suffer while I escaped. These were my friends and neighbors; I could not let death reach them without giving warning. Pounding the doors as I ran, I awoke as many as I could, crying out that their children were in danger. Lamps were lit and several doors opened, but I had already moved past. I hoped that my words and actions would be heeded in time to prevent what I knew was happening elsewhere in the city. *Why is this happening?* My thoughts were a desperate blur.

As I neared the top of the street, twenty or thirty men on horseback rode up and dismounted. My way to the Temple was blocked. They started down the streets doing what the others were busy doing on the other end of the city. Then one of them saw me. I dashed my way down the streets, taking the narrow alleys when I could, trying to lose them in the maze. *If I can just make it to the wall, to some of the stables, I—*

I was spotted again. A chorus of shouts rang out and I could hear at least two soldiers, maybe more, converging on my location. I bored through the night, but they closed in at every turn, and in the end there was no place left for me to run.

A grip as strong as an eagle's talon seized me. I was thrown into a wall and fell to the ground. More hands ripped Joshua from my clutches. My fingers quickly found a rock and I swung wildly at one of my captors. The stone struck the side of his young face, and he dropped to one knee, a deep gash torn into his cheek by the rock's sharp edge. Freed for the moment, I quickly turned my desperation to the remaining soldier—an animal in uniform, I thought—now holding my son.

I had never been a violent man. My heart had known nothing but peace and compassion, and before that night I had never struck another. But now I had felled two. My hands shook with a strength I had never before known. It was strangely intoxicating. At that moment I believed that no force on earth could stop me. I was Joshua's father, and I knew that Joshua and I were going to make it to safety; if I had to go through every soldier in the city, I would protect him. Then the giant I had left unconscious across my threshold reappeared, joining his Roman brothers. I could see the humiliation and rage that boiled inside him. My confidence crumbled like dry sage, and in one horrifying instant I knew that all was lost.

With a seething yell, the giant soldier rushed me, pinned me to the wall, and began throwing his fists like mallets into my face and midsection. There was nothing I could do. Through the pain, between crippling blows, I watched as the other helped his young comrade—the one I had cut—to his feet. Then he handed Joshua to him, as if the "honor" of the kill was now his. I tried to break free of the unrelenting assault, but could scarcely lift my head.

"What do you want with him?" I cried. "You cannot do this!"

I was forced to my knees. The young soldier clumsily held the sheepskin bundle and drew his knife. I briefly noticed his waist cloth. It was wet from the rain, but clean. Was this his first kill of the night? Could he be persuaded to show mercy? I opened my mouth, but could not make the sound. *Please!* I wanted so desperately to cry. *Please do not do this! Oh, God, please . . .*

The young soldier raised his blade but hesitated as the others urged him on. He looked down at me and our eyes met. He *was* young—no longer a boy, but not quite a man, being made to do the things of monsters. He raised his knife high—

"Dear God! Joshua!"

And with a sharp blow to the back of my skull, a searing white pain flashed before my eyes. My scream died out and was lost to the void. My world went utterly dark.

* * *

It would be years before I heard any explanation for what happened that night, but even then it was rumor and speculation at best. Herod was at its center, that much I was sure of, and my fate and the fate of my son were shared with hundreds of others. Those of us who fought back that night were condemned and punished under Roman law—for rebellion against the Empire—and sold as slaves along its coasts. Most of those originally with me could not adapt to life as slaves and died, or took their life within the year to hasten their eventual and humiliating deaths. I did not, however. A fire was lit inside me that would become a perpetual flame—bright enough and hot enough to keep me alive. I never forgot, and I never forgave. My life for the next thirty years would follow a very different course than all my rabbinical training had led me to. The man I was died with Joshua that day, and reborn in his stead was a new man, whose every action, whose very thoughts, were consumed with one thing.

CHAPTER 2

"Revenge."

Jacob stirred, breaking his long gaze over the hill's ridge and the vast waters of the Great Sea that lay stretched before us. "What?" he asked.

I didn't answer him right away. I, too, was mesmerized by the vivid colors that painted the evening sky. From our coastal mountain outlook the shores of northern Africa stretched as far as the eye could see in each direction. At regular spacing, fishing boats began heading for land as the night approached.

"The name of the ship," I eventually finished. "*Vindicare* means 'revenge' in Latin."

Jacob nodded but he wasn't listening. I wondered what reflections were preoccupying his mind as his old eyes searched the horizon.

"I do not believe I have ever seen the Great Sea look as beautiful as it does tonight," he said. Then it looked as if his thoughts shifted to the reason we were there. "We should have seen it by now."

Though neither of us would let our concern show to the others, I knew he was right. A hundred reasons for the ship's delay plagued my mind. It should have been here already. Lives had been put in danger to bring us word of its closely guarded schedule. So where was it? It must come tonight. Too much depended on this. We would not get another chance. It was too late to alter our plans, too late to turn back, and much too late to fail.

"It will come," I said with as much certainty as I could, and I left him as I had found him—alone and deep in thought.

I, too, turned to my thoughts. There had once been a proud time in which the whole of Israel had not forgotten that to establish and keep a land for our inheritance required service and sacrifice. But over time the thirst for freedom had been replaced with the mere request to be left alone to worship as we pleased. Conquered over the centuries by half a dozen empires, we were allowed to pray and conduct ourselves only if we did as our masters directed. Tribute was required and subservience demanded. In return our Temple and faith were left alone.

As Israel cowered under Rome's might, prophecies were repeated in secret—prophecies of being set free by some future messiah and king. But now many doubted that day would ever come. Waiting had not produced our freedom; something else had to be done.

Wherever there were communities of Jews free to gather and worship, there were those who possessed the religious zeal to speak out against our foreign invaders. Men and women of this conviction were common throughout the land, but those who we trained with and brought into our trust were not mere students of the Law, or even the religiously fanatical. We welcomed only those who had tasted of revolution and who had not turned away from the feast. These were the kind we sought out and invited to join our ranks over the years.

The Roman Empire had many enemies and only a handful of them posed an outside threat. Most of Rome's enemies were living and breathing within the boundaries of her empire. A conquering army cannot hope to occupy nations by force, by shedding blood and burning cities, without continual resistance. Soldiers, therefore, were stationed in every province and city, their swords and armor a deterrent to any and all thoughts of revolution.

But still protests were staged, and not all talk of revolution was conducted in private. There were others who combined their voices to make a noise, but none were as loud as the Jews. Ours was not a social or political revolution; we were not interested in some cause to effect change in the senate, or to demand lower taxes or more favorable trade conditions. We were God's people fighting to be free.

The five of us had made camp in the wooded hills that overlooked the great coastal city of Apollonia. The ancient Greek city was the seaport of the Roman province of Cyrenaica and the power seat of the Roman Empire for two hundred miles in either direction. It was a city whose people and streets we knew well and the stage upon which our carefully scripted drama would be performed for all of Israel—and the world—to watch. Many a battle had been waged here over the years, but never anything like what we planned to do this night. The stakes would forever be raised if we succeeded. We would cease to be merely a mild annoyance or discomfort to the great Roman Empire. This act would serve as an inspiration to other zealots years after our deaths, and would be a crippling blow to the Empire along the north coast from Egypt to Carthage—not a loss of life, but of something more important to them.

Every preparation for tonight had been done in secret—even our friends and families knew nothing of our plans. But if other men had known what we plotted, they would have called us mad. Terribly outnumbered and ill-equipped, we were an unlikely army of five. We each were as different in home and upbringing as we could be, but differences are soon put aside when uniting to a common good. While most Jews did not support Rome's presence and control, there were few in number that had the courage to speak out against them. Fewer still who would act. If Israel had had an army then, as it had in centuries past, Jacob and I would have been numbered among its generals.

Jacob was my oldest and most treasured friend—as natural-born a leader as there ever was. Despite his age, he continued to lead raids and strikes against Rome's hold on the north shore of Africa. He had told me once that he had been born into money, but that as a boy he had lost his father and his family fortune by the wax seal of the provincial governor. With one illegal decree, his life, once destined to be one of riches and prestige, became instead one of poverty and social outcast. In recent years, his strength and reserve had served to balance my fits of excitement and temper. He was the only man alive I completely trusted my life to, and though his beard had grayed, his heart was still young and willing.

Phillip, by contrast, was young in years, but his soul was aged by the lonely weight he bore. He had never married. His parents died when he was just thirteen, leaving him alone with only a brother. When his brother had been convicted of thievery and sent to the slave colonies of the Empire, Phillip began to search for him. It had been ten years now, and still he continued his search. I doubted, though, that he believed he would ever find his brother alive. Phillip sat atop a fallen tree, running his fingers over his arrows one at a time; he was giving them a final check before grouping the long wooden shafts in their quiver. He was a gifted archer and had used this ability to strike from a distance dozens of times over the years. Tonight, though, would prove to be his greatest challenge yet. This ritual with his arrows, I knew, was a form of meditation that would sharpen his mind, allowing him to focus when his skills were needed.

Then there was Levi—proof that courage and determination knew no age. A boy of just sixteen years, he had seen more action against Rome than men three times his age. He had lived his young life knowing his father only from a name etched into a grave marker. When his mother became ill and died, he became an orphan at the age of eleven. Jacob had found him, starved half to death, and had tried to give him a home with him and his wife, but Levi refused. Turning to God with an almost fanatical devotion, Levi believed that God would provide for him, and his faith and conscience became the group's. Jacob and I had taken a special liking to him over the past year, including him in all of our strikes against the Empire.

Cleophas was the fifth, and the newest, member of our little brotherhood. As I looked on him now I saw that he had not moved from the last time I saw him, but remained fixed on the knife he was whetting to a razor's edge. His story was a tragic one, but not unlike the rest of our tales. His sister had died a slave in a Roman brothel. Listening to him speak of his sister, innocent and undeserving of her terrible fate, I had sensed the need for vengeance that burned in him. He was prone to sudden outbursts, but he was loyal to the cause and accepted the guidance of our leadership. In one way or another, we were all men who suffered at the hands of Rome, and we felt a special kinship. Our pain was more bearable when we were not alone with it.

I walked through the small clearing and, with my foot, began to cover the last embers of the afternoon's fire with dirt. "If any of you have reconsidered our plan and want out, speak up now," I said. "There is no shame in choosing life over death."

Cleophas stopped what he was doing long enough to test the edge of the blade with his thumb. "Everyone dies," he said. "It is *how* we die that separates the brave man from the coward."

"There it is!" Jacob called out. He had spotted the ship, the great *Vindicare*.

With a mix of dread and excitement we moved to the overlook and watched in awe as the Roman galley made its way toward the city from the distant horizon, white sails taking shape from the dark waters as the mighty hull cut through the water. Even from this distance I could tell it was moving at a great speed. I had been told that a total of a hundred oarsmen, synchronized with a slow and steady stroke, propelled and powered its maritime might, and despite its size it could outdistance any ship built anywhere in the world. As it drew closer and crossed into the wide bay, the sails were furled and the oars put to the deep water.

"Look at the size of it," Levi said in fearful awe.

On the ground, scores of soldiers suited in their best military display began to line the dock and shore at full attention. In no time the galley was expertly guided and anchored at the end of the pier where a hundred torches drove off the approaching night. It was a military show to the letter; the ship unloaded her captain and crew with a rigid and orderly execution of duties. A few moments later the slave oarsmen were led out, manacled and chained together. This was not common practice, I noted, since most galleys had slave quarters for them to stay in. But this was an unusual galley with an unusual freight.

"She'll dock there for the night," I said. "It is too late to unload her cargo. Besides, the governor will insist on supervising the whole affair."

I leaned over to Phillip. "How many are stationed aboard?" I asked.

"A dozen up top," he said, seeing the faraway details as only an archer could. "With at least another hundred along the shore and securing the streets."

"A *hundred* men," Levi breathed.

"A hundred men or a thousand," Cleophas said calmly, "makes no difference. Kill them one at a time, and it doesn't matter how many there are."

Jacob had left us and hiked farther up the hill. From higher up he continued looking intently out to sea. I left the other three and joined him. "What is it?"

"You can just make them out," he said, his old eyes still as sharp as any young man's. "I count seven ships."

Already the night sky had begun to blend with the dark waters, but I could see them too, anchored farther out in the bay. "No doubt a deterrent to those who would steal her treasure," I said.

"But we're not stealing it," Jacob said. A thin smile crept briefly into his expression and left as quickly. "It is a feat even the great Judas Maccabeus would think impossible to accomplish."

"Perhaps," I said, as the memory of his faith and brave action swelled deep inside my chest. "But he would be proud that we were trying."

The stories of Judas Maccabeus have inspired generations to action. Even now, nearly two hundred years after his followers lived and fought, we spoke of those times at every opportunity we had. They were the examples and guides to all those who loved freedom.

Those times had been dark for Israel, not unlike today. All of Judea had been under the rule of Antiochus, the Seleucid king of Syria. To strengthen his hold on the land, he turned Jerusalem into a Greek city, gave it Grecian laws and government, and helped himself to the Temple gold. When the city protested, he ordered a ban on the Torah and decreed that anyone following the Law, including circumcision and the keeping of the Sabbath day, was to be killed. The Temple was desecrated with pig's blood and then used for worshiping the Olympian god Zeus. Many Jews chose death over being guilty of violating the Law.

Then, in a small town about a day's march north of Jerusalem, the king's officers tried to break the spirit and will of the townspeople. They set up a sacrifice to their pagan gods and demanded that the local priest perform the ceremony. When he refused, a deserter of the faith came forward. He would have completed the ritual if the priest had not struck him down and killed him first. Then the priest spoke the words that would inspire a nation to revolution and freedom: "Let everyone who is zealous for the Law and supports the covenant come out with me!" His name was Matthias, and with his five sons, one of whom was the brave and daring Judas Maccabeus, they united a country and a faith and won our independence.

From their mountain caves and hideouts, they moved across the Judean countryside, striking hard and fast at the Syrian power that choked a chosen people and their nation. A cry to arms was sounded, and for the first time in over four hundred years, the people answered. We could resist and take back our land, our city, our families, and our dignity. Israel was no longer the lamb—she was the lion—and in short time, Judas Maccabeus stormed the city of Jerusalem itself and recovered the Temple, purifying the sanctuary and restoring the House of God.

Oh! How I wish I could have been there, I thought. A proud smile came to my lips, as it did every time I thought of the Maccabeans and their fight, and for a moment I forgot that the freedom they took decades to achieve had been traded in a day to protect the title and power of a wicked king. My smile faded and was replaced with firm determination and resolve.

I put my hand on Jacob's shoulder. "Come, we'd best get moving."

* * *

As the last traces of day dissolved into night, we left the cover of the hills and made our way to the water. There, Phillip continued on toward the city—his crucial part in our operation would be performed elsewhere. The rest of us slipped into the cold water.

Rome was as vigilant as a serpent protecting its nest; she had stationed soldiers along the coast and throughout the city in great numbers. The farther away from their prized treasure, the fewer the soldiers. With cloud cover shielding the light from the half-moon, we were, for all purposes, invisible. Ever so slowly we swam parallel to the shore, using the few rocks just off shore for cover. Above us on the road, the military presence was progressively stronger as we neared the pier, but the soldiers' eyes were either trained inland toward the city or far out to sea, and we reached the dock undetected.

We had spent more than an hour in the cold water by then, and though our tired and worn-out bodies cried for rest, there was no time. Willing our bodies to move, we pulled ourselves hand over hand along the support beams of the underside of the dock, toward the Roman galley anchored at its end.

The planks above us suddenly shook and rained a long day's dirt as a dozen soldiers made their way from the ship to the shore. Levi stiffened and held his breath. I rested my hand on his shoulder.

"Second watch," I whispered.

Levi breathed easier once they had passed and the watch was staffed. At the end of the pier, we paused in final preparation. The plan was simple: steal aboard and sink the *Vindicare*. The deep waters of the bay would forever be its grave, rendering its precious cargo beyond anyone's reach. But how does one sink an impregnable and heavily protected Roman galley? The answer was just as simple: fire. Like the fire that Elijah called down from heaven to consume the priests of Baal, ours would also strike at the enemy of God's people. Though our fire would not come from the sky, but from flint and tinder. First, however, we had to get on board unseen.

With confirming glances that bespoke the blessings of God and the wishes of good fortune to each other, we again set to the water— Cleophas and I to the near side of the ship, and Jacob and Levi to the other.

The information we had about the ship was incomplete, but it told enough that we could prepare for its arrival. This ship was designed unlike any other in the Roman fleet and had been built for one purpose—moving and protecting Rome's most valuable assets. Its thick walls and many armaments made the ship nearly invulnerable. The stronghold of the transport was a windowless room set below deck in the middle of the ship. Half a dozen men would be guarding its one and only access. The ship was the first and only of its kind. And this, its maiden voyage, was to usher in a new age in maritime travel and warfare. Faster, stronger, without mercy: these were the mottos of Rome, embodied in this single vessel. On deck a company of Rome's most feared soldiers—the Praetorian Guard—stood ready to defend against an army from land or sea. A hundred men could not hope to storm the ship. But four men just might.

The clouds had built in size and shape, and there was now a threat of storm. The light breeze that would normally sweep down from the coastal mountains now pushed its way through the city and out to sea. The bay waters were no longer calm, pitching and tossing the anchored ship and throwing us into the hull with brutal consistency. We moved along the underside of the leviathan, keeping as far out of sight of the men on deck as possible. Finally we reached the lower row of oar ports. I pulled from my belt a short rope and a hook and readied them in my hands, kicking desperately to keep my head above the rise and fall of the waves. With a sure grip, I tossed it through one of the small ports on the first try. It would have been mere luck if not for the many hours Jacob and I had practiced such a throw in just such water. Preparation for the mission had been long and exhausting, but everything about this night had to be exact— there was no room for error.

I pulled myself up as quickly as I could. This was the single moment when we would be exposed to Rome's watchful eye. The port was only a few feet above the water level, but if any of us were spotted, the night would end in our prolonged and painful deaths.

My fingers took hold of the port, and I pulled myself up and peered inside briefly. It was empty and dark, just as it should be. Thrusting myself inside, I quickly reached back through and pulled Cleophas up and inside with a single pull. He landed on the wet floor and lost his footing, tripping over some of the many oars laid out over the slave benches that filled the hull. The noise was minimal, but we both froze and listened for any sign of alarm.

When we were sure no alarm had been raised, I stepped lightly past the rows of benches to the door and pushed gently, looking out. There was only quiet darkness.

I hurried back to the center of the room and knelt at the base of the interior wall. Just on the other side was the belly of this monster and, within it, the cargo Rome was taking such precaution to protect—an entire year's worth of gold and silver coins for the provincial governor; payments for his tribunes and soldiers, and enough to fund the daily government expenditures. The pungent odor of the newly treated and sealed wood filled our senses even above the stench of slave labor. It hurt my head to breathe the air. The empty benches were scarcely visible by the dim light filtering through the oar ports, but for a moment I could only stare at them. In my mind's eye I could see the galley slaves, the men who had manned the oars across the sea, their dirty bodies disfigured from days of work and neglect, their broken spirits manifest in empty stares as they pulled and propelled the enormous ship to the rhythmic pounding of slave drum. Their only exposure to the world around them was the occasional look out one of the portholes. No homes. No families. No love. No hope. I was reminded that the terrible risk we were taking tonight was for them, and those just like them enslaved throughout the world by the Empire's mighty sword.

From around my shoulder I removed a watertight goatskin pouch and emptied its contents: six small vials of oil, some wool, a piece of flint, and an iron striker. I unstopped two of the vials and began pouring their contents on the wall and floor. As I stretched and pulled the wool thin, I noticed that Cleophas was not at my side. He was standing at the door.

"What are you doing?" I demanded with all the power a whisper could carry.

"A handful of those coins on the other side of this wall would free a hundred men and their families!"

"We did not come for their filthy money."

"You would deny them their freedom?"

"We've discussed all this before."

"There was no discussion," he spat out. "I suggested it, you said no."

"We stay with the plan!"

"It's your plan, not mine. I will not turn my back on our brothers!" His voice was rising in stride with his emotions. "You do not know what it is like! I cannot face them knowing that I could have bought their freedom, and with Rome's own money!"

Cleophas did not know that I understood all too well what a slave's life was: not able to come and go as you please, as is your God-given right, but to be required to give an accounting all your days of your actions, your speech, even your thoughts. To be a slave was not to be human any longer. And if you lived, if you survived with any sense of self-identity intact, you were never the same. Cleophas could not be more wrong. I *did* know. But that did not change the plan.

"You will not get past the guards," I said, foolishly relying on logic to convince him in the throes of his emotion. "Will you simply ask them to step aside?"

"The fire should distract them. And if it doesn't . . ." He pulled back the folds of his shirt to reveal his knife.

"You will die before reaching the first post," I said, again trying to persuade with facts. "I cannot let you do this. It takes only one to give the alarm and all of us are hung out on crosses by the week's end!"

Cleophas looked me over with disgust. "What they said about you was right," he spat. "You don't have it left in you. You're a soft, old man."

I leapt to my feet and took him by the shirt, pressing him against the wall. At fifty and five I was every bit as strong as he was, and I had no trouble holding him there. I spoke in a furious whisper.

"I was fighting Rome well before you were even born! If I could, I would slay them all as they slept! We tried that! It didn't work. For every *one* we slew, *ten* more took his place."

I relaxed my grip but still held him fast.

"We are about to send this ship to the sea floor, and with it the means to run the Empire for a hundred miles in either direction. Rome will not easily recover. Many in her ranks will lose heart when they see what we have done. They will abandon their blind allegiance to the hollow power of which Rome boasts. Others in the city, friends loyal to our cause, will rally to our side; either way our enemy weakens and we grow stronger. It is that strength that will free us, not a little pressed gold. Rome will no longer be able to ignore us, and if the price is high enough, perhaps they will give up and leave. You speak of freedom—you don't know what freedom is! You would risk the freedom of thousands, or a nation, for a few friends and their families. There is a better way."

"*Your* way," said Cleophas, and he struck my hands, forcing them away and bringing his knife to bear, its thin point at my breast. I stepped back.

"Light that oil," he said, gesturing with the blade, and then he disappeared into the darkness that was beyond the door.

I wanted to scream with frustration! He would get us all killed. It had taken months to plan this and get here. Now we had as much time as it took him to reach the corridor guards to finish it—maybe to the count of twenty. It was not enough time, but what choice did we have?

I returned to the wall, finished placing the wool, and began striking the flint. It sparked onto the wool but it wouldn't light.

Someone suddenly cried out in Latin, sounding an alarm. I heard Cleophas cry out for help, but the scrape of a sword being pulled from a scabbard was followed by his abrupt silence.

I ran to the door. I knew I had to slow the guards before they discovered what we were doing, but the door opened out and the bolt and latch were on the outside. There was no way to lock them out. I believed I still had time to light the fire, but if they reached it before it spread sufficiently throughout the room, it could easily be put out. I surveyed the dark room—there was nothing but benches and oars. Then an idea came. I would have to act quickly if it was to work. It was a desperate idea, but I had no alternative.

I went through the room frantically tugging on the benches until I found one I could use. They were all nailed down, but this one had a little give. I stood over it, gripped it firmly on each side, took a deep breath, and pulled. My legs, arms, and back all strained as the bench came free from the floor. The noise was considerable, but that was the least of my concerns. From the floor I took the wet rope we had used to climb in, then carried the heavy bench to the door. Leaning it against the wall and propping the long wooden seat across the doorframe, I looped the rope around the latch on the outside of the door and tied it around the bench, cinching it tight. I tested my reverse lock by pressing on the door. The bench held the door closed. I knew the wet rope would not hold against a blade for long, but it didn't have to.

Voices outside were getting closer as they traced Cleophas's route down through the ship. At the wall I continued the long strokes of flint on iron. Sparks briefly lit up the room like small flashes of lightning, but the wool still would not light. A thundering clatter of several armed men reached the door abruptly. My body tensed instinctively and started to move to action when I remembered my lock. They pulled on the door, but the bench and wet rope held it shut.

"You in there!" a voice commanded. "Open this door!"

I struck the flint again, and again, and again.

The wool caught fire—sputtering a weak flame. If it died, my fight was over. Not just for tonight, but forever.

"By Caesar's throne, you will open this door!" they called, tugging on the door. And then the first of them began cutting on the wet rope.

I gently blew on the tiny flame, jumping back just as the oil and newly treated wall caught fire and erupted in flame. I fell back to my haunches, instinctively trying to distance myself from the sudden fire and intense heat. It was beautiful and fearsome all at the same time. A moment passed before I could shake off the spell and get to my feet. Wasting no more time, I took four more measures of oil from my pouch and smashed them open on the floor, the ceiling, and down the long stretch of benches.

The pounding on the door intensified with the rising flames and the suffocating heat that seemed to draw the air from my lungs. I coughed and could not replace my spent breath. My eyes stung but it hurt worse to close or rub them. My vision blurred, but I managed to find Cleophas's pouch and threw his oil at the door, sending fire underneath and farther into the ship. The soldiers yelled as the floor under their feet caught on fire. I paused briefly to take one last look at what Rome had not thought possible, then dove back through the porthole and returned to the cold darkness of the sea.

CHAPTER 3

I swam as far as I could under water. When I surfaced, I turned and watched the fire. Like fingers, it reached out from the oar ports and cupped the mighty warship in a deadly embrace. The fire was now out of control. Boats were launched from the shore ferrying dozens of soldiers to the distressed ship, inadequately armed to fight the flames with weapons of war. On the shore, our sabotage had created a chaos I had never before seen. Calls were being made for buckets to carry water to the distressed ship, but it was of no use. Even if they could have found every barrel and bowl in the whole Roman Empire, it would not be enough to reverse our victory. I could only imagine the dread and horror that would assault the governor when he was awakened with news of the fire. The unthinkable was happening, and there was nothing an entire army of soldiers could do.

Then it was as if heaven joined our battle as fire began raining down from the sky. Phillip's timing was flawless. Many of the frantic soldiers stopped in the midst of their panic and watched with fearful awe as a single flaming arrow sailed in a perfect arc from some unseen rooftop overlooking the bay. The arrow hit its mark and exploded in a pool of flame midway along the pier. Three or four soldiers unfortunate enough to be on the pier were sprayed with fire and jumped into the bay for relief. Then a second arrow lit the sky and fell to the wood planks closer to the galley. Another sailed overhead, then another, and another, each cutting off any hope of salvation for the valued ship.

Then the rain of arrows stopped, and I thought I might have heard Phillip cry out in his defense. His part, we all knew, was perhaps the most dangerous. Where the four of us had each other's help if things went wrong, Phillip was alone in his duty. Once that first arrow sailed out and cut through the darkness, it would be mere minutes before soldiers would spot him and find him. He would not be taken captive, of that I was certain. Phillip had no real wish to die, but he had no fear of death either—therein was the source of his quiet strength and determination. He had prevented any unraveling of what we had done and sealed the ship's fate. He was a hero to Israel's cause and deserved the rest of heaven.

The fire was spreading through the ship faster than I had anticipated and was now unquenchable. Pieces of the transport broke off and hit the water, filling the air with vapors of steam that shrouded the galley in a hellish mist. It was beautiful.

I continued to swim as much of the way as I could below the surface, coming up only when my lungs screamed for air. In those brief moments I scanned the water, looking for Jacob and Levi and hoping they had gotten away in time.

It seemed for a while I would never reach the shore, but eventually I emerged in a concealed inlet that lay opposite the heavily guarded docks. Looking back out over the sea, I tried to pierce the night, watching and waiting for any sign of Jacob and Levi. I had almost given up hope when I saw them and my heart felt release.

"What happened back there?" Jacob demanded, still struggling out of the reeds that hugged the shore.

Before I could answer, Levi noticed that I was alone. "Where is Cleophas?"

Answering Levi's question would also answer Jacob's.

"He went after the gold."

"Is he . . . ?" Levi couldn't finish.

"A patriot and a hero," I said, for Levi's sake.

"And Phillip?" Jacob asked.

I shook my head.

There was a moment of silence for the loss of our brothers, intermingled with a rush of pride and accomplishment. On the other side of the bay, the fire was now complete, illuminating the entire shoreline in yellow and orange. Desperate but futile attempts were still being made to control the fire. Already two of the masts had collapsed, and the stern was partially submerged. The rest of the galley would sink shortly. The wind had picked up and fanned the fire into a wild inferno. The blaze was beyond anything anyone could do to control it.

"A mighty blow was struck against Rome this night," I said. "Israel is closer to being free."

We took a final moment to view our handiwork and then hurriedly donned sandals we had concealed there earlier. Though our every muscle felt washed of strength, the three of us made the short climb to the road. The safety of the city streets was now only a few hundred feet distant.

No elaborate plan had been made for our escape. With Rome's attention drawn to the burning ship in the bay, we had planned to simply make our way quietly through the city, much the way we had come, and back to the safety of the hills. But as we approached the first street unseen, we passed a soldier running the other way from an adjoining street. He was surprised at our meeting and paused in confusion. We took advantage of his hesitation, breaking into a swift dash. When he saw the light from the fire on the other side of the bay, he took pursuit. He was young and had the speed of a gazelle, it seemed, for in no time he was upon us. He reached out and caught Levi, pulling him to the ground.

Jacob and I stopped and returned to our young friend's aid. The soldier had started to pull his sword from his scabbard, but Jacob reached him before he could free the blade and tore him away from Levi.

The soldier may have been young, but he was no fool. Three to one was not the type of fight he was willing to engage in, and after a tense pause he quickly retreated.

The soldier wasn't more than an arm's length away before Jacob grabbed his leather tunic and spun him around, driving an elbow into the young man's exposed face. The soldier screamed out in pain as his nose broke. But the soldier wasn't finished fighting back. He managed to land a couple of strong fists into Jacob's torso though not enough to weaken Jacob's hold.

I was checking to see if Levi was all right, and we both looked over in time to see Jacob wrest the soldier's helmet from his head and smash him across the face with it. The soldier dropped as if dead.

Jacob hurried to join us.

"I do not envy him when he wakes up," Jacob said. "Are you hurt?"

Levi shook his head. "No. Which is more than I can say about him."

Just then Levi alerted us to movement back down the street and pointed. "There's someone back there!"

Jacob and I turned around in time to see a shadow disappear around a corner. A moment later a shrill whistle was sounded.

"There'll be more here any moment," I said.

"We can't continue the way we were going," Jacob said. "The fastest way out of the city is a clear path to the mountains, but men on horseback could cover that distance in no time."

"There's more than one way out of the city," I said. "We must elude them."

"I know the city better than either of you," Jacob said. "Follow me."

Two more soldiers appeared at the far end of the street and immediately began running toward us.

"You there! Stop!" one called out in an authoritative voice. But surrender was never an option. We followed Jacob down a maze of streets. I did not think it possible for the soldiers to follow us. We darted around corners and ducked down streets one might miss even in full daylight. Each of us had spent time in the city, but Jacob spent some of his childhood here working with his father at the docks and seemed to remember every side street and alley, every abandoned shop, every hole to hide in.

Just as I thought we had escaped, Levi lost his footing on some small rocks while rounding a corner. He took a dangerous fall. His feet continued in a different direction than the rest of him and he tumbled and rolled into the alley wall. His hands went immediately to his ankle and his face twisted with pain. Jacob stopped and returned, kneeling and carefully feeling Levi's foot and leg. Levi winced several times but never once let the pain escape his lips.

"It's not broken," Jacob said, "but he won't be running anytime soon."

A few streets over we could hear the sound of our two pursuers.

"It's not possible they could have followed us!" I said.

"They are either very skilled or very lucky," Jacob said.

I looked at Levi in his injured condition.

"We can carry him," I said, kneeling next to Jacob and reaching out for the boy.

"No, you two go," Levi managed to force out. "I will only slow you down. I can find somewhere to hide. They won't find me. But if they do . . ." He paused, producing a dagger. ". . . they will not take me. Perhaps I will even take one or two of them with me." He tried to smile bravely, but terror shaped his wide eyes.

Jacob and I looked at each other and almost smiled at Levi's dramatic bravery. "Oh, you'll die, my young friend," I said, "but not tonight."

"Levi's right, though," Jacob said. "The mountains are too far for us to carry him. A hundred men would overcome us before we could reach safety."

I stood and closed my eyes, locating our place in the city with my mind's eye. The run had disoriented my sense of direction, and for a moment I was lost as to our position. With a bit of concentration I recovered it, and realized right where we were and what had to happen next.

"Take him to Joachim," I said. Joachim had been a mentor to Jacob and me in earlier years. He had once been a powerful ally and good friend as we matured in our skill and focus against the powers of Rome, but ill health had taken him in recent years. "He can hide you both."

"And you . . . ?"

"Will see that you do not make me a liar," I finished.

"Be careful," Jacob said.

"Am I ever anything but?"

Jacob nodded, then scooped Levi up and carried him away, no small task even for a man as big as he was. I knew Joachim still harbored no love for the Empire in his heart, and as a tanner he had plenty of places to hide them. But his home and shop were still many streets away. Jacob and Levi would need some help to make it—a little diversion, something to draw the soldiers' attention and grant a little time to my friends.

The narrow alley was lined with refuse and debris abandoned by craftsmen and laborers long since moved on. It provided everything I needed.

Climbing in beneath some old beams leaning up against the wall, I put my back against them and toppled the heavy wood across the way, ensuring Jacob's escape. The crash, though, shattered the still spring night. Even the most inept Roman could find me now, and I could hear the soldiers closing in. Picking through the scattered wood I found a broken piece of timber that would serve me well; it was long and thicker at one end—a natural club. I swung it around a couple of times. The balance could not have been better and it looked strong enough. It was perfect.

I waited where the alleys intersected until I could hear the soft scratching of my pursuers' leather and armor. As their approaching footfalls became dangerously close, I started out down another way, careful to make enough noise to be followed, but not enough to arouse their suspicions that they were being led into a trap. At a wide, secluded intersection, I ducked around an adjoining corner, moved to the shadows, and waited.

The first Roman burst into view at a dead run and met with my wood, delivered at full force across his face. He was lifted off the ground and his head hit the cobbled street beneath him before his feet did. His helmet was the only reason he would draw breath again.

With no time to waste I repositioned the club in my hands and spun around, gaining momentum for a like blow to the second soldier. Fast as I was, he was somehow faster and raised his sword in time to parry my attack. I could tell this soldier was a seasoned combatant, and he quickly threw himself into the fight. His sword was a blinding whirl of steel that almost ended the fight as quickly as I had started it. His blows were swift and strong, and I wondered, briefly, if he had fought in the arenas before joining Rome's military ranks. He struck and moved like no soldier I had ever encountered, and it seemed that my head had been specially chosen for a prize. It *was* a prize, I quickly realized. Promotion, honor, and riches awaited the man who could bring me to Roman justice, and it took every skill and trick I had ever learned to fend off his blade.

But the question of my skills soon became the least of my problems. The piece of wood I was using, my only defense against the onslaught of sharpened steel, was beginning to crack and splinter under the relentless attack. As strong as it appeared to have once been, it became clear to me in one frightening moment that the salt-sea air had worked its corrosive magic on this old piece of wood. It was no match against steel.

With precious little time left I pulled back and swung with every bit of strength that remained. One last attack. I had no other choice. The thought briefly lit in my mind that if the soldier simply stepped aside I would end up off balance and on the ground at the end of his sword. But he did not move to accommodate my energy. His military training took control of his actions, and he stood his ground, meeting my attack with his. The wood broke in two as I knew it would, but as it did, it jarred the sword loose from his hands. The soldier was momentarily stunned—a warrior without his weapon—and I drove my shoulder into his midsection, taking him to the ground before he could recover his blade. We fell into the wall, knocking over a tall earthen jar of water. The dirt road turned to mud beneath us.

He was strong as we traded fists and kicks, and both of us struggled to get control of the other. Then the balance of events shifted and I knew the fight would soon be mine. From deep inside me an anger took control of my hands, and I erupted with a bellowing yell. Everything around me changed. One instant I was locked in mortal combat with a soldier in the back streets of Apollonia; the next I had returned to that night thirty years before in Jerusalem. For a moment this soldier's face became the face of the one who had taken my son, raised his knife, and . . . But this time I was not helpless. I had dedicated my life to never being helpless again. Over and over I pummeled the parts of him not protected by metal plates. "Murdering heathen!" I accused between strikes. "Animal!"

My fists struck fast and hard, fueled with thoughts and emotions that seemed loosed from a floodgate. Their empire was a disease; the Romans insects, moving in swarms, devouring entire cultures and growing fat on the lives and lands of others. *They use their iron and steel to take what they want,* I thought, *and when we resist, they kill or make slaves of us! When their appetite is satisfied, they toss us the unwanted spoils and punish us when we do not grovel and give thanks for their benevolence.* "But no longer!"

By now the soldier had ceased resisting. I didn't care. It had been too long since I had experienced the fight—the anticipation, the danger, the speed at which it all seemed to be happening. I had nearly forgotten how good it felt. The pain—to know you were alive, to know that you were free—and the power. *Especially* the power; to know that you were at no one's mercy. It was a strong wine and I was drunken with it. I scarcely noticed the blood covering my hands as I hefted a large stone over the unconscious soldier, prepared to send him to his pagan hell.

"The dogs of the desert have more worth!" I hissed.

Before I could release the weight, I was shoved from behind. The stone fell but missed its unconscious target. I fell to one knee and spun around to welcome my new attacker to the fight. What was one more?

But it wasn't another soldier. It was Jacob.

"This is *my* kill!" I yelled in fury and tried to push him away. "Mine! Do you hear me?"

But Jacob was every bit as strong as I was. He grabbed me and pinned me, helpless, up against the wall. He wore a look of confusion and shock, wrapped up, as it were, in disappointment. His lips moved, but I could not hear the words he spoke over the sounds of death beating loudly in my ears.

"You must not do this!" I finally heard Jacob say. "It is enough."

Between heartbeats I could feel the heat leave me, like the setting of the sun, and a cold chill rose from my feet to the base of my neck. It was an awful feeling. I looked over at the soldier and saw not the face of the young soldier that cursed my nights and times of silence, but another man, bloodied and unconscious, clinging to life with every shallow breath. What had I done?

"The streets are filling quickly," Jacob said. "We must leave now."

I could hear the sounds of a city being awakened with the news of what was happening in the harbor. Rome would soon have a thousand eyes watching the streets. We would need to hurry.

"Is Levi . . . ?" I asked, my head beginning to clear.

"He's fine," Jacob said. "It is you I worry about. Come!" Together we slipped easily through the dark streets and out of the city.

CHAPTER 4

The hills south of the city were heavily wooded and made for an easy escape once we reached them. The night sky had begun to sweep away the last torn fragments of the evening's clouds, ushering in a calm and quiet night. Bright stars and a half-moon painted the hills and trees with a soft, gray light. The hot south wind from the desert was replaced with a gentle breeze blowing in from the unseen ocean, rustling through the fronds of the date trees and swaying the long grasses and sage. All was at peace except for the telltale smell of smoke and ash from the fire now miles behind us.

When we had gotten safely beyond the limits of the city and its outlying posts, Jacob found a small patch of grass and fell into it, exhaling loudly and staring up at the stars. I, too, found a soft spot on the hill and sat down, pulling my knees in close to my chest. The sensation of rest was almost too much for my old body to take—I feared I would be unable to stand again before sleeping. Every muscle complained of overuse and reminded me that I was not as young as I wanted to believe I was.

"God smiles down on us tonight," Jacob said.

"Perhaps," I said. "But that is all He does."

Jacob sighed. "Is it too much for you to acknowledge a miracle when you see one now and again?" Jacob, though not the most devoted of followers, still had a thin foundation of faith supporting his thoughts and actions. But tonight he spoke of things he knew little about.

"A miracle?" I said. "Is that what you call Phillip's death? Or Cleophas's greed that almost got all of us killed?"

"They died doing what they believed in," Jacob said. "There is no dishonor in that."

"But they died. There was no miracle in their deaths."

"And the ship?" Jacob asked, his tone still pleasant and friendly and without the slightest hint of offense or criticism. "Can you forget that tonight we did the impossible? Can you not even entertain the thought, even for a moment, that God was with us back there?"

"I counted five as we set out," I said, "not six."

Jacob said nothing for a while and continued breathing in the tranquil night air as if it were a banquet spread before him, and he, famished.

"Do you ever think we're getting too old for this?" Jacob asked.

"Old?" I said. "Too old for what?"

"This," he said. "The fighting, the late-night strikes, the remote desert raids, everything. Don't you feel it?"

"What are you talking about?" I asked.

"Tonight," Jacob said. "You and I both know that neither of us thought we'd be going home tonight. Oh, we boasted of our plan and our strength, said what the others wanted to hear—maybe even what we wanted to hear. But tonight we were going to our deaths, and we all knew it."

I had never seen Jacob so somber. "Is that what you wanted?" I asked. "To die back there?"

"It is what I was prepared for," Jacob said softly. "Without drawing attention to it, over the past couple of days, I said all my good-byes—to my wife, my friends. I made peace with God . . . " He trailed off. Then, "You may not be able to acknowledge God's help, but I cannot ignore it. Not anymore. We're alive, and there's a reason for it, I'm sure of it."

"You are sure of nothing."

"How else can you explain it?"

"Why must there be a reason behind everything that happens?" I asked, my voice rising with my pulse. "Am I to believe we each are so important that God reaches down from heaven with His mighty finger and controls all that happens to us?"

"Guides, perhaps, more than controls," Jacob said.

"It's bad enough hearing this nonsense from those young and naive," I said. "There is no plan for each of us. For a nation, for a kingdom, perhaps, but as for you and me—we are on our own, to choose our own fate. To blindly trust in something that is not there is like ignoring the light and following each other, lost, in darkness."

Jacob seemed to think on this for a moment, then asked, "But which of us are lost, and which of us are found?"

I had never heard Jacob speak like this, and was tiring of it quickly. "You are beginning to sound like someone I do not know."

"And I am afraid you may be returning to one I used to know," Jacob said.

"Explain yourself," I said impatiently.

"You almost took that soldier's life when there was no need," he said, his words sharp and to the point. "Until tonight I thought I had seen the last of your anger swell up in you and burst forth like that. You were in no danger; your fight was no longer in defense of your life, or even to allow our escape."

"What is his life to me?" I countered.

"To us, to the battle we fight? Nothing. Whether he lived or died, I don't care. It's *you* I worry about."

"You sound like a woman with all this talk of worry," I said, feeling tense about where his words were headed.

"I haven't seen you like that in years," Jacob said.

"I know."

"What happened?"

Unable to control it, I saw portions of the fight play out before my eyes. I recalled the soldier's face, changed in an instant to one of thirty years earlier, and those same feelings stirred deep inside me once more. I pushed them away and shook off the images. "I don't know."

Jacob paused, as if to tell me he didn't believe me, but didn't press the question. He suddenly clapped his hands over his head and rolled up to his feet. He stood and stretched, yawned like he hadn't slept in days, and then offered me a hand up as well.

"Tomorrow then? Midday meal?"

I nodded. Such meetings had become somewhat of a tradition following a strike. It would be a time to reflect and learn from our mistakes; though tomorrow, it would only be Jacob and me. We would talk to Levi in a day or two.

"Sleep well, my friend," he said, then turned and started toward his home in the neighboring village. I watched him until he blended with the night and then continued on my own way home.

Jacob had been a good friend for more years than I cared to count. A better brother I could not have chosen. From the beginning, Jacob had always been at my side when the stakes were high. His words about giving up the fight troubled me though. I was forced to admit that most men our age filled their days with grandchildren or gathered together to tell stories of deeds in younger days. They were not usually in the lead of every attack and raid.

As Jacob made his way down the winding path, I wondered if he spoke the truth. As much as I refused to admit it, we were both slowing down, and just when the fight was quickening its pace. Jacob would deny it, but he had begun favoring his right leg and stepped with the trace of a limp. He blamed it on the weather, or a misstep he had taken the day before, or anything but the cause: old age. And he was not alone. I looked at my hands. I was loath to admit it, but over the last few months I had noticed the slightest tremor in them when left idle. I squeezed them into fists, as if to defy age itself.

When we were twenty years younger—taking our first steps down this path of action in a world filled with too much talk—not once did our thoughts turn to old age. A long life is not usually companion to the sword. In the beginning, Jacob and I had helped organize a small band of men who were no longer satisfied just waiting to be delivered by our silent God, and who possessed the strength of character to make a stand against our pagan oppressors. It seemed a lifetime ago. Our little group had quickly gained support, and soon after we formed, we had our first taste of rebellion along a deserted highway as a Roman caravan made its way to the sea. It was a miracle that any of us survived. Back then, uprisings and attacks had not been a concern in this corner of the Empire, and the Romans were ill-prepared to fight us off—a mistake they had not made since. But our hopes had been cast and forged that day. We *could* fight back. Israel's long history of captivity could come to an end, though the price was high and could only be paid with a willingness to lay down our lives. If

God would not send His promised Messiah to deliver us, then we would deliver ourselves. Others had fought before and more would continue to struggle until, God willing, our nation tasted the delicious fruit of freedom.

I quietly stole through the streets of my home on the river. A large city for the north desert, it was a small village in comparison to some of the larger coastal cities. Being some distance from the sea, it was of little importance to the Empire, and we were largely left alone. The streets were quiet, as they should have been at that hour. The sun was still some hours away. The wet, cool air had started to settle and condense, covering the streets and shops in a blanket of dew. A chill ran the length of my back, and I pulled my wet clothes tighter around me, as if they could keep me warm. Down dark streets, dark windows seemed to bespeak the peace of deep sleep.

At the street before mine I stopped suddenly. A dog barked, then all was quiet again. I paused and listened for a long moment. All seemed as it should be, and I sped to my small house and gently bolted the door behind me.

I had not so much as taken a deep breath when my peace of mind fled. Someone else was there, in the room with me. My first thought was that my intruder was a Roman, here to exact punishment for my crimes, past and present, against the Empire. I immediately dismissed that thought. Soldiers were not known for their stealth and surprise. A more likely scenario took shape. I had stumbled upon a thief in the act of a crime. I moved swiftly to the club leaning in the corner near the door. One who made a secret profession of doing what I did could never be too careful.

"You'll find nothing here but a crippled life full of pain," I said, raising the heavy wood back over my shoulder. "Show yourself and I may let you live. Choose to hide in the shadows, like the thief and coward you are, and you will beg me to release you from your pain."

In the dim light I could see the figure of a man seated at my table. The intruder spoke calmly. "Deep down, I'd hoped to have found the house abandoned and you moved on, but luck has never been mine to command."

I knew that voice. I was sure of it.

"Who are you?" I demanded, gripping the wood tighter.

"Where are my manners? Mother would be disappointed," he said, and then with no apparent feeling, gave the traditional Jewish greeting. "Peace be with you . . . Father."

The figure struck some flint and lit a lamp on the table. In the soft light, I could see the features of a strong, young man. His face was long and had gentle features I recognized. I dropped the club to the stone floor. Could it be?

"Lexi?" My son.

"Lexi is a child's name," he said dismissively. "I have not been a child for many years." Standing to his full, impressive height, I could see that Alexander was now a man.

For the next moment neither of us knew what to do or say. I could not take my eyes from him. He had my build, tall with a strong, wide back, and he resembled me in my younger days. From ear to ear he wore a short, trimmed beard. I didn't like it. It made him look older than he was. Or did it? How old was he? Eighteen? Nineteen? He had been four or five last I'd seen him.

What was I to do? Was I supposed to throw my arms around him in an embrace of father and son, or just clasp his hand? Was I supposed to welcome him at all? Was I to offer an apology for my being absent from his life for so long, or demand one from him? For a moment I wished it *had* been a thief or soldier I had stumbled upon.

His eyes flicked to my shirt, and he noticed the blood from my earlier fight with the soldier. His already distant expression turned to disgust and shame.

"Is there no other way with you?" he asked.

I did not have to explain or justify to my son my actions of the night. His tone was one of condemnation, and it was carried with disrespect. I wanted to strike back with words of my own, but I was still overcome with surprise and stupor at my son's sudden arrival. A question was formed and uttered before I could contain it or save it for later, or not at all.

"How is your mother?" I asked, regretting the words as they left my lips.

He did not answer right away. When he did, it was with guarded emotion.

"She is well. She has us to support her."

I would not turn away from his hard stare. I knew he was trying to hurt me—punishment for being absent in his life—but I returned his look, determined to make a stand against his attacks of words. After a few moments, it was Alexander that turned away.

"And your brother?" I asked.

"He is with me. This is his first trip this far north."

"He is here?" I looked around the dark room.

"He is busy overseeing the last of our preparations before we set sail. But enough of this. You need not feign concern for the family you abandoned so long ago."

"It was your mother who left. Do not forget that!" I said reflexively. "It was she who returned to Jerusalem." I knew this night would not end pleasantly. My son had come to fight.

"And why would she have stayed?" he asked, clearly having anticipated this very conversation. "To remain second in your life, behind your hatred? To watch her husband, the father of her children, be consumed by rage and acts of violence?"

"That is your mother talking," I said. "Those are her words, not yours."

"But it is how I feel!" Alexander lowered his voice. "It is how we all feel."

I felt a tremor begin in my legs, then work its way throughout my body and limbs. Who did he suppose himself to be? Though a man in years, Lexi was still a child, nourished by lies told to him since his youth. "You would stand here, in my house, condemning me, blaming me for you and your family's ills?" Son or not, I wanted him out of my house that instant. But then a look about my son gave me some pause. I could see that Lexi was not enjoying the conversation any more than I was and did not want to be there at that moment either. I swallowed my impulse to throw him out, and when I felt it settle in my belly I said, "I do not think you crossed the deserts and sought me out to give me a lesson on fatherhood."

"I am here only because of Hannah." His tone became impersonal, businesslike. He was on an errand.

"Hannah?" My oldest. My daughter.

"She begged me to stop on our way."

"What is it? What is wrong?" Terrible thoughts flooded my mind, and fear must have shone through on my face. The occasions were far apart when I paused to think of my Hannah, or any of my children for that matter. But if it were urgent enough to send a resistant brother, her news must be of the gravest sort. Alexander must have realized what I was thinking, or at the least anticipated my reaction, and just shook his head.

"A child grows within her," he said, with the glowing pride of a brother. "The Lord has heard her prayers and now blesses her womb." His eyes darkened. "And though I cannot understand it, she wishes you to know."

"A child? When?"

"Her time approaches. A week, perhaps two; no more."

I reached for a small bench and sat down before I fell. My Hannah, my little girl—a woman now, with a child of her own. I did not understand what I was feeling. This was wonderful news, but my heart ached. For the first time in fifteen years, I think it yearned for something more than the cold, harsh life I nourished.

For the moment I forgot my offense and my impulsive thoughts to send Alexander away; instead, I welcomed him to stay further.

"You'll stay the night," I informed my son. "I insist."

He shook his head. "We sail at first light. There is still much to do."

Not wanting to spend the remaining brief moments with Alexander in the dark, I lit a few more lamps around the room.

"You are here on business?" I asked, surprised that he would let anything take him away at this important time in Hannah's life.

"Extending the route west, past Egypt for the first time, and looking for contacts to the northern deserts." My son's voice did not convey the slightest warmth or real desire to share this news. He delivered the news matter-of-factly, a reluctant accounting of his actions and whereabouts.

"You are continuing in your grandfather's business, then?" I said, choosing to ask questions rather than sit in uncomfortable silence.

"Not just continuing," he said, this time with a hint of excitement. "We are expanding into exports as well. Olive oil, balsam, and wheat. Business is good. We are also nearing a deal to open a route east to the Orient. The caravans are many that stop in

Jerusalem. Ours would travel with the others until it became wealthy enough to venture on its own."

"Your grandfather must be very proud to see you take and prosper his trade," I said, feeling a bit more at ease with my son. "How are your grandparents?"

"Dead," he said, cool and remote once more. "Going on seven years now."

The ease I had begun to feel vanished with his blunt and insensitive words. I had always loved Deborah's parents. They were honest and caring people and had been like a second father and mother to me. Did Alexander know this? Was his every word that night meant to hurt me? For an instant I did hurt for their loss, but now was neither the time to mourn nor inquire further. I abruptly changed the subject.

"And where does this business you are on take you?" I asked.

"Syracuse, Carthage, and then Rome."

"Rome?" I could feel the rage seep back into my chest, constricting it, making it difficult to breathe. The thought of my sons, my own precious flesh and blood, working with Romans sickened me. Did their mother never tell them, or had they so soon forgotten?

"I cannot allow it," I said.

"You cannot allow what?"

"I forbid you to travel to Rome or to do business with them. You would bless Rome with the goods Israel has to offer? They are unworthy of anything we have."

"I am taking nothing that is yours. Business demands we go. Besides, we have been trading with them through contacts at Caesarea for some time now. Dealing with them directly will expand our trade and increase our profits. It is a matter of business, nothing more."

"Is money worth more than your sister?" I voiced the bitter thoughts.

"What do you mean by that?"

"Hannah will need the support of her family during this time. This is her time of need and you would leave and take Rufus with you, for what? A little money? You are wrong to leave her!"

"You, of all people, should not speak of not being there when you are needed!" he yelled back.

"I will not be spoken to like this!" I roared. "I have decided. You cannot go!"

"You command no one, least of all me!"

"I am your father!"

"You are no one's father! Not anymore."

His words felt like stones slamming into my chest. So that was it? To them it was like I never was. I had chosen to stay behind to do what I knew was right, but I always considered them my family still. It seemed that I was mistaken. My role and my position in the family were all for naught.

Alexander gathered his belongings from the floor and stepped toward the door. "Peace be with you," he said, the intended irony clear in his tone. Then he was gone, and I was left alone.

Sleep would not come for the remainder of the night. The hard words I had traded with my son refused to leave me. Nothing I could do dismissed them, nor could I think of anything to replace them. When my attempts to sleep failed, I climbed to the roof, as I often did, to wait for the sun.

It took some time, but as the sky shook off its cover of night and let in the light, my feelings smoothed somewhat and I was able to think more clearly. For years I had pushed away thoughts of my family when they arose. It was less painful not to dwell on happier memories. But my son's visit had made it impossible to hide from my reflections. There, speaking louder than any ill words spoken by Alexander and myself, was the simple call of my daughter. My Hannah. I tried to tell myself that she didn't need me, as my son had said, but a small voice inside refused to believe it.

When the sun broke free of the hills I returned inside to change from my damp, bloodstained clothes and prepare for Jacob's visit later that day.

Jacob arrived at the promised hour with a tangible excitement about the previous night's work. But I could not join him in his enthusiasm. I went about preparing the meal with hardly a greeting when he arrived. Jacob noticed my somber mood and asked what was wrong. Before he arrived I had decided that I would not share what had happened in the night, but at his question I could not hold back and told him of my unexpected visitor.

"Your *son?*" Jacob choked on his drink and started coughing. When he recovered somewhat, he said, "How long have we known each other, and not once did you mention a son."

"I saw no need," I said, which was the truth. "They made their choice long ago, and I, mine. They left the year before we met."

Jacob looked at me cockeyed. "Are you . . . ?"

"Married?" I nodded.

"Other children?"

"Three . . . four."

Jacob belted out a hearty laugh. "Well, which is it? Three or four?"

If anyone else had laughed, I would have made them a cripple.

"She bore me four." I didn't feel like telling him any more, and he had the sense not to ask.

"Separated all this time," Jacob mused between mouthfuls. "You never once mentioned her, or your children. Tell me about them."

"What is it you want to know?" I asked reluctantly.

"Their names would be a start."

I found strength from a deep breath. "It has been a long time since I have thought of them."

"But you do remember their names, don't you?" Jacob laughed again.

"My oldest, a daughter, is named Hannah. She would be three and twenty, maybe four and twenty now, if I am not mistaken in my accounting of the years. My boys are Alexander and Rufus. They were young when they left. Lexi was only but four or five years, and Rufus was a babe in arms. It was Lexi that came to visit me last night."

Jacob finished his bite. "Those names are not Hebrew names— for your boys, I mean. The names sound almost—"

"Greek," I said flatly. "I know."

"And the other one?" Jacob asked.

"What other one?" The words were painful for me to speak.

"You said you had four children, yet you only speak of three."

I took a constricted breath. "My firstborn died as a child."

"I am sorry to hear that," he said, and I could tell that he was.

"And your wife's name?" Jacob asked after a moment.

"Deborah," I said. "I haven't spoken her name since she left."

"All these years married and living on opposite sides of the world. It seems odd that you never divorced her."

"On what grounds?" I said. "My hatred of Rome? My desire to see all of Israel free? If those were reasons to put a wife away, many a Hebrew woman would be left without a husband."

"Ah, your words are true," Jacob said. "So you still love her then?"

The question was abrupt and I didn't feel like answering. Instead, I ripped off another piece of bread and studiously ignored Jacob. But he was just warming to the subject.

"How is it that in all these years we have never spoken of your family? It is like you are a new man to me, a stranger I am meeting for the first time."

"As I said, I saw no need to tell you, or anyone. It is not a source of pride and accomplishment."

"So why are you alone?" Jacob asked.

"She did not understand. She could not—"

"No, not the reasons she left. The reasons you stayed—the reasons you fight. You and I have been fighting longer than anyone we know still living. We have searched out and recruited hundreds of loyal men and women to fight, and always we ask these questions of them. Their reasons for fighting are more important than their willing words and hands, and reveal who they are on the inward side. Perhaps it's ten years late, but today I am asking you."

Jacob said nothing more to lead or prompt me to explain further, but his silence was a scream compelling me to answer, to tell someone, for the first time.

"I left Jerusalem in chains. A slave."

"A slave?" Jacob was startled.

"Stripped of all rights and forced to work the coastal mines and quarries."

"You were not born into slavery?"

"No."

"What was your crime?" Jacob asked, knowing that slavery was often a sentence for crimes against the Empire.

"Striking down two Roman soldiers."

"You are fortunate they did not kill you."

"Most days I wish they had."

"And what of your wife?" he asked. "Was she . . . ?"

"A slave too? No. The crime was mine alone."

"You were married before it happened then?"

"She followed me over the sea and across the deserts. She never left my side," I said, and we finished the meal in silence. When Jacob had eaten enough and drained his cup of wine, he asked, "What prompted a visit from your son?"

I hesitated to answer him. The news still seemed so strange to me, I could scarcely comprehend it myself. "It seems I am going to be a grandfather."

Jacob laughed in delight. "Miracle of miracles! Today I learn you are not only married and a father, but a grandfather as well! It is a happy day." Jacob paused, searching my eyes, "But you are not happy."

"The news is wonderful, and I am pleased and proud and will find happiness in it soon enough, but . . ." I stopped, unable to put my conflicting emotions into words.

"Finish," Jacob said. "Ofttimes it helps to sort our feelings if we voice them."

"I am haunted by the memory of the last time I saw her," I said. "Hannah was so young and was hurt by the conflicting decisions Deborah and I had made. She had no control over our fights; she had no control over our silence; she had no control when we went our separate ways. For her to share this news with me, after all I have done . . ."

"So when are you leaving?" Jacob asked.

"What?"

"You are going to Jerusalem, are you not?"

"How do you know this?"

"Come now," he said, "do not take me for a fool. There is more weighing on your mind than a visit from a wayward child with a message to deliver. The news shared would seem to me an invitation to return. From your daughter at least." When I didn't answer immediately, Jacob took the moment to perform some quick calculations in his head. "Jerusalem is not exactly a neighboring village," he said. "It is seven hundred . . . eight hundred miles away. Most men's life travels are not a fraction of that." The magnitude of my quickly made decision had clearly surprised him.

"I've made the distance once before," I said flatly. "I plan to return to Apollonia in the morning and take the first ship that sails to

Alexandria," I admitted. "If I can, I will find passage to the shores of Caesarea. If not, I will join a caravan."

"It will not be safe in the city," Jacob reminded me. "What we did last night will have the governor frantic to find us."

"I know, but I have no other choice. It would take too long overland across the desert, and I refuse to be captive here, hostage to my fear of being caught. Besides, the sooner I leave, the greater the distance I can put between me and the authorities."

Jacob nodded, then said, "Assuming you can actually slip aboard a ship and make your way to Jerusalem, have you considered that your reception may not be warm? Have you given thought to what you will say? Will your words be, 'Good day, wife, I've returned,' and there will be embraces and tears?"

"I am going to see my daughter—not Deborah," I said.

"Who lives under the same roof as your wife. Her reaction to your visit cannot be ignored."

"Yes, I know. It's likely to be anything but pleasant. Still I must go. You will not convince me otherwise. I've decided."

"I did not intend to dissuade you from doing what you think you must, only to help you make a wise decision. You must answer for yourself: what good can come of it after all these years? You live your life here, and your family a very different one there. Is it worth the pain to return now?"

"Sleep has not come to me, and I fear it will not be my companion until I do this. You must understand; Hannah was just a little girl the last I saw her. She was seven when her mother left. The boys were too young to understand what was happening, but the look in Hannah's eyes that day has returned to haunt me—I cannot drive it from my mind. She looked so sad, so confused. This is the first news I have received from them since then. I did not even know she had wed, though I expected it by now—she was so beautiful as a child. Yesterday, and all the days before it, I was so sure I made the right choice to stay and fight. But now . . ."

Jacob took a bite of cheese, washed it down with a swig of wine, and wiped his mouth on his sleeve. "A daughter's love is strong, but is it strong enough?"

"It will have to be," I said.

"Then you must go," he finished.

I started to clear the meal away. There was a brief stretch of silence and then a rueful chuckle from Jacob.

"I hope there is room aboard for *two* old men." He smiled.

I stopped and looked at my friend, confusion written across my face. "What?"

"You did not think I would let you go alone, did you?" he said.

"You do not need to come with me."

"True, you are no longer a child," Jacob said. "Call it . . . a rest, if you must. No one is more deserving of time away than me. Except, perhaps, you. Besides, after last night, Rome will be combing the streets and asking questions and I would rather not be around when they are answered."

"And what of your wife?" I asked.

Jacob tried to smile and traced the rim of his cup with his finger. "She seems happier when I'm away."

A strange silence followed. I had met his wife only half a dozen times in the many years we had known each other, but each time I could feel the distance, the tension in their relationship. They were unhappy in their marriage. Like Deborah, she did not approve of his actions against the government, but unlike my wife, she remained with her husband. They had never been able to have children, and they were each miserable in their partnership. But, I always thought, at least they were together, which was more than I could say.

"But . . ." I tried to object again.

"Go to your family. I will visit mine."

"You have family in Jerusalem?" I had never heard him speak of any family there. Though I had no reason to be, I was surprised to find I was not the only one with secrets.

"A brother." The corner of his mouth raised. "A patriot for our cause." From beneath his shirt he produced a pendant. It was his family seal. I had seen it several times but had never examined it closely. It was the six-pointed star, carved with intricate detail into a small stone. In the center were the Hebrew markings of his family name. "Carved by our father," Jacob said. "Gifts to my brother and me when we were boys. It would do me good to see my brother again after all these years."

"And what of Levi?" I said, still unsure whether I wanted company on this trip.

"Perhaps he will come with us," Jacob said. "I know it is difficult for one man to accept another man's offer for help or company, even when friends. But there will be no more discussion. I have made up my mind to go. If you decide now not to go, then I will make the voyage alone. There is nothing you can do to convince *me* otherwise," he said, mimicking my words earlier.

I felt a huge weight lifted by his show of friendship.

"Thank you," I said. "You know you have always been like a brother to me."

Jacob poured himself the last of the wine, then stood to leave. "If you will excuse me, I have some preparations to make. Tomorrow promises to be a busy day."

* * *

It did not take long for me to pack what I needed. I didn't have much. My house was sparsely furnished, and I had collected nothing of real or even sentimental value during the past many years. I did not think I would be missed. I didn't have many friends in town and only rarely spoke to my neighbors. I was known as somewhat of a hermit, a peculiar old man that young mothers told their children to stay away from. It had taken some years, but I had finally convinced myself that I liked being alone.

I worked, when I could, as a carpenter, though not a very good one, and made only enough money to buy food and keep my house and shop in good repair. What money I did not spend was put in an earthen jar, hidden in a corner of the workshop, and forgotten. Until now. It was a meager life savings, but it would be enough to buy passage to Jerusalem.

A feeling possessed me that I was looking upon my home and workshop for the last time. I walked past my workbench and sawhorse, running my fingers slowly over the worn, soft wood. In the early days, Jacob and I had used the room for our secret meetings as we complained, planned, and gave strength to each other. As we became more daring and extreme in our measures, more remote locations had to be found. But for a time, this shop had been the center from which the ripples of action against Rome extended. And now I was leaving it. *But not forever,* I kept telling myself. Somewhere inside, though, I truly questioned whether I would return. Was it hope? Not exactly. Just an anxious feeling that I was going at all.

I took one last look at my cluttered workshop. My tools still lay where I had last used them. There had never been any real order as I worked, and it was a wonder I found any work at all. As fastidious as my leadership of men was, one would think I would be better organized at home.

The sun was setting, and I lit a lamp to go through the house one more time in search of anything else I might need or want to take with me. The rooms used by the children had remained empty since the day they left. Not for any sentimental reasons. I had just never found the motivation to fill them. In one of the back rooms, in the corner and covered by twenty years of neglect, the lamplight fell on a small, wooden chest. It was stained, and the wood had warped with time, but it was mostly intact.

I hadn't seen it in fifteen years, but I recognized it immediately. My knees became weak, and my heart began to beat wildly. I suddenly felt afraid. But as troubled as I was by its sight, I was also drawn to it. I brushed off the dust and spiderwebs. Carved on the side of the box, between crude images that were meant to be flowers, was a name: Hannah. It had been a gift for her fifth birthday to hold her dolls and the treasures she had accumulated during her young years. It was the only thing she wanted. As I pulled it out into the light and opened it, I was struck with a consuming feeling of guilt for leaving behind painful memories all these years past.

Inside were the crumbled remains of a burlap doll and a homemade wooden spinning top. But what captured my attention were the rocks and stones. Until this moment, I had forgotten how Hannah had collected them, both the "pretty" ones and the "shiny" ones. One rock in particular caught my eye. In the corner was a round, black one with streaks of white that, I suddenly recalled, was Hannah's favorite. A real prize, she had believed. It was supposed to give one good luck. I held this last stone up to the light and wiped a layer of dust off it. Perhaps it would bring me luck, I thought, deciding to take it with me and then blowing out the light.

CHAPTER 5

All of Apollonia was talking about the destruction of the *Vindicare*. Word reached our ears even before we reached the city. A small group of shepherds had left their flocks watering at the river and gathered near the roadside, sharing the incredible stories they'd heard over the past two days. Jacob and I pretended to be in from the country and ignorant of what they spoke. They were eager to tell their tales. One of the shepherds had heard that a hundred desert raiders had swept in from the mountains and stormed the shore in hopes of stealing the ship's treasure. Just what that treasure was, he didn't know. The fire had been started in the fight and had driven away the would-be thieves. Another was told that the captain of the ship had set the fire himself, in retaliation for being shorted on pay for his men. A third shepherd, Greek by his accented words, had heard something else.

"Fire from the heavens," he said, "raining down on the Roman ship."

"Fire, you say?" I said, looking at Jacob and trying to conceal a proud smile.

"Because the God of the Jews is angry," he offered in explanation. "Of course, this was told to me by a Jew." He laughed, and the others joined him as if in on some private jest. The levity I had felt moments ago was swept aside by confused anger.

"Are the words spoken by Jews so easily dismissed?" I said. "Explain your doubt of the Jew's story."

Two of the shepherds stopped laughing and looked to the third for a response. The old Greek had a look of frailty but did not show the slightest worry at being confronted. He continued to smile in mild humor.

"I see that you have taken offense at my words, and I apologize. They were not meant to discredit the Jews' religion or show disrespect to them," he said. "Only, we have heard enough of their 'One True God and His Will and Law.' In a world of hundreds of countries, thousands of cultures, and millions of people, to the Jew there are only two kinds of people: Jews and Gentiles. They think the world was created for them, and that they are the center of it. For them to say that their Hebrew God caused this destruction to the governor and his ship is the result of a misguided idea about their 'chosen' relationship with their God. One can believe them as much as one can believe anyone, but I find their perspective . . . peculiar."

His fellow shepherds relaxed as he spoke, and moved closer to him in support.

"But you have not heard what *I* believe happened that night," the old Greek continued.

"And what is that?" I said, insulted further by his attempt at apology.

"That the ship, built by inept Romans, sprung a leak, and the night watch, drunk on cheap wine, tripped over a lantern; in their panic, they could not have found water if they'd fallen overboard." He barely finished before bursting into laughter, soon joined by the others.

Jacob couldn't help himself and started to laugh with them. A moment later I was too. Few things in this world unite men like mutual hatred and disrespect.

We parted friends and left them to their flocks, making the short walk to the city proper in little time. As Jacob and I blended with the crowds of the busy streets and marketplaces, many more wild stories were traded like trinkets and passed off as truth. The ship's demise was on everyone's tongue, and it took a strong will not to speak of our involvement and brag about the deeds we had done. The praise would feed our egos, but the risk—the danger that would befall us—was simply not worth it. We moved through the streets without speaking a word of it to anyone.

Joachim was not expecting us. He hurried us inside, bolting the door behind us. Without a word to either of us, he pulled the shutters closed and moved the drapes over the windows of his tanning shop. The stench was almost enough to bring an old man to his knees.

"You should not be here," Joachim said, his stern voice just above a whisper.

"It is good to see you too," I said dryly.

"If they knew you had returned . . ." Joachim trailed off, unable to think of a suitable punishment the authorities could impose.

"But they don't," I said.

"How is Levi?" Jacob asked.

"Huh? Oh the boy. He's fine. He is resting in the back. Come."

Joachim led us to the back room, and as we stepped down the stairs, I desperately longed for the comparatively fresh air of the shop. It took a moment for our eyes to adjust to less light. The room had two windows placed high on the wall near the ceiling, and a small door that led to the courtyard in the back. All around us the skins of animals were stretched across wooden frames. There was a heavy, dead odor that filled the room; and the flies—a hundred for each man, at least. I could see why Joachim's wife left him, and my heart went out to Levi. I hoped he would forgive us for leaving him here.

On a couch in the corner Levi propped himself up. His face was lit up, though I could see he was still in pain.

"How are you, boy?" Jacob said.

"I owe my life to the two of you," Levi said softly.

"We're a family, Levi," I said. "We take care of our own."

"How's the ankle?" Jacob asked. He stepped over and examined it, feeling for evidence of broken bones, but not finding any. "You'll be up in a week or so, but don't strain yourself. You'll need to start slow. Use a crutch and build the strength back into it. Time can help it heal, but it won't do everything. You'll need to take care for a while. With a little luck, you'll not have even the slightest pain in a month or two."

Levi smiled, welcoming Jacob's concern and fatherly attention. Levi without a father and Jacob without a son. They had forged a special bond that, though unspoken, was as strong as any father and son's. I suddenly looked away, uncomfortably reminded of the sons lost to me.

"You three pulled off quite the operation the other night," Joachim said. "The whole city is in a commotion."

"We could tell," I said, welcoming the return to business. "It seems that everywhere they speak of Rome's misfortune."

"Misfortune? This is beyond any misfortune, accident, or bad luck. The governor has called in every tribune, every centurion along the coast to vent his rage. He is determined to find those responsible and punish them with every means available to him. Guards are posted in triplicate around the imperial palace, the meeting halls, the arena, and at every port from here to Ptolesuais. Every soldier has been drafted into services, every conscript enlisted, and a recruiting effort has begun that will likely attract a thousand more."

"Until they learn there is no money to pay them," I said, chuckling.

"He is not employing them for protection," Joachim snapped. "The governor is not at all worried about a repeat attack. He may be a politician, but he is not a fool. Where else would such an opportunity present itself? No, the governor is looking for you. He would have your heads. In fact, he has offered a price for them. A poor man would be made rich for a lifetime for what is being tendered."

The three of us, confident and proud a second before, now looked at each other in consternation. None of us spoke as the seriousness of our situation settled on our minds.

"Do they know who did it?" Jacob said.

Joachim shook his head. "But they will. Every man loyal to the Empire, or to gold, is being asked questions. And not of the general sort. Already half a dozen extremists have claimed responsibility for what you five did, but the authorities are looking for those who haven't."

"No one was in on the plan except the five of us," I said, trying to think if that was true.

"One word, one comment, one question gone unanswered," Joachim said, "and they'll find it. You may have kept a perfect confidence, but what of the others?"

I turned to Levi.

"Not a word," Levi said, his fear stronger than his courage at that moment. "I swear by heaven, I told no one."

Jacob spoke up. "We've been too long together to suspect each other." I knew he was right.

"Phillip's best friend was silence," I said, thinking aloud. Then I stopped abruptly.

"What is it?" Jacob said, getting to his feet.

"Cleophas spoke of freeing some of his friends with money stolen from the ship. He said that he could not face them knowing that he gave up the chance to buy their freedom."

"That doesn't mean he told them," Levi said.

"But I'm not convinced he didn't," I said.

"If there is a chance he did," Joachim said, "then you must act as if it is so. At least for a while."

I couldn't believe what was happening. I had known that the consequences of such a bold attack would inflame the wrath of the provincial government, but I assumed it would be conducted blindly, as it always had been. Now I wasn't sure of much. In fact, the only thing I was convinced of at that moment was that Cleophas *had* talked of our plans.

"I never should have brought Cleophas into this," I said.

"Nonsense," Jacob said. "Cleophas was right for the assignment. You know that. We all do. If he kept a tight tongue then there will be nothing for the governor to find. If he did not, lamenting over decisions we cannot undo solves nothing."

"You understand now my outburst when I saw you at my door," Joachim said. "You were fools to return, albeit ignorant fools."

Joachim reached over to one of his skins and adjusted some of the cords holding it taut. "This was no desert raid or treasury robbery. If you slew a hundred men the governor would not be more enraged." Joachim's tone suddenly changed. "Now, I do not think he will find you, and when he doesn't, he will be laughed at by every governor from here to Rome; when they are done laughing, he himself will be executed by Tiberius for the loss. But before he goes, he will take out his anger on the people. This will have consequences that reach beyond Apollonia and her neighboring cities and villages. Your actions will be felt throughout the Empire."

Joachim moved to another stretched hide, his head lowered as if in deep thought.

"If this were a game, the first move and first victory would be awarded to you. But the next move belongs to Rome, and they will play to win. Not only to win, but to annihilate."

Jacob moved to my side. "What the governor or the emperor does is not our responsibility. They are free to crawl back to Rome and leave us."

"If they push," Levi added in his youthful way, "we will push back. They will not find us silent or submissive. There are too many of us. If it is war they want, it is a war they'll get."

"No, no, no," Joachim said, his old voice gruff and tired. "I did not mean to place the actions of another on your shoulders, and I am not a prophet of doom. All I am saying is that we must all go to ground if we wish to live to fight another day."

We all shared glances, each pair of weighted eyes meeting briefly with the others. When Jacob's met mine, it was as if I knew his thoughts. I pulled him aside.

"We cannot bring Levi," I said quietly. "His injury would raise too many questions. He'll have to stay. He will be safer here than anywhere. Joachim can watch out for him. If you are having second thoughts about going, I would understand."

Jacob looked at Levi quickly and then shook his head. "No."

"Going?" Levi said. "You are leaving?"

"Yesterday, without knowing the grave state we were in, Jacob and I decided to take the first ship that sails for—"

Joachim interrupted, clearing his throat loudly to drown out my next words. "It is best if we do not know when you leave and where you plan to go."

I nodded, now on guard with even the words I used with friends. "This is why we came back."

Levi looked at us, loss and sadness animating his entire face, and I saw that Jacob wore the same look. Without speaking a word, the two of them were saying good-bye.

"You might find leaving difficult," Joachim said. "Rome has restricted travel at all ports, both merchant and cargo ships."

I suddenly decided I'd had all the bad news I could take for one day. "How is it that you know all this?" I asked.

Joachim smiled. "I am an old man, and I have ears. There is much to be gleaned by keeping one's mouth closed and ears open."

I tried to smile back.

Joachim clapped his hands. "But if you are determined to go . . ."

"We are," I said firmly.

"Then you will need some help getting on board unnoticed," Joachim continued. "Come with me."

Jacob helped Levi to his feet and we followed Joachim through the store and up the back stairs to his home above.

"You wait here," he said, then disappeared into one of the side rooms. He returned holding a pile of fringed clothing. He threw it onto the table.

"You can take these," he said.

I knelt and picked through the heap. When I saw the multicolored mantles and tunics, I realized what my old friend was suggesting.

"No," I said, shaking my head. "We will not do this."

"Do what?" Jacob asked.

"But Rome is looking for men," Joachim said, ignoring Jacob's question. "You will pass by without a second look."

I held up one of the articles of clothing to show Jacob. It was a floor-length mantle, black, with patterns of green, red, and orange running the length of it. The fringe on the outer edges, long enough on the bottom to cover the feet, was of the same colorful design. Jacob reached down and pulled out a matching veil and head cover. Levi snickered in the corner.

"You want us to dress as women?" Jacob asked, looking dubious.

Levi could no longer contain himself and laughed out loud.

"There are many who know you have no love of the Empire," Joachim said. "If even one of them spots you here, today, so soon after this happened and leaving the city, you'll certainly be detained, interrogated, and then executed, whether or not they find proof of your involvement."

I could see his logic, and I had to applaud his creativity, but . . .

"But women?" I asked, hoping to hear a better plan.

"Two Jewish women, properly veiled, could buy passage and board with hardly a word spoken. The men standing watch will probably even help you with your bags," explained Joachim.

"Disguised as women . . ." Jacob said, his words trailing off as his mind played through the deception. I could not believe he was able to accept the idea so willingly.

"And when you are safely away," Joachim said, "you can shed the clothes and discard them any way you see fit. In fact, I would consider it a favor to me if I never saw them again."

"Whose are they?" Levi asked.

"My former wife's," Joachim said, and then cursed quickly, "may all her hair fall out."

Jacob looked up and nodded. "I believe this just might work."

I looked at the woman's dress in my hand and shook my head back and forth.

* * *

We looked ridiculous. But as uncomfortable as I felt wearing women's clothing, all went as Joachim said it would. As we neared the shorefront, the presence of Rome became conspicuous and menacing. Men were stopped without cause and interrogated as to their business and purpose there. Witnesses were called in to confirm identities, and any suspicious activity, innocent or not, was met with force enough to handle a riot.

Rome's presence had never been as strong. From behind our veils, we were disappointed, but not surprised, to see more than a few men we had thought loyal to Israel's cause conspiring with soldiers in their search through the city. Money possesses a power almost unmatched in this world; friendships are betrayed and birthrights sold for a few coins. Such men didn't deserve to be free. And with such shifting loyalties, they never would be. Jacob and I had each dedicated many precious, irreplaceable years to our nation's freedom. In a single moment, and with the exchange of a few coins, that work could be undone. *Freedom has a price,* I suddenly thought, *but it is not in denarii and talents, but in tireless work, selfless dedication, and blood.* Many of those selling their integrity this day also complained about Rome and her laws and taxes. All compassion I had for them ceased.

We passed by the guards and soldiers without hesitation. I felt ashamed to be covered in garments meant for a woman, but as I watched Jacob's eyes, I believed he actually enjoyed parading through town in his new clothes. We were hurried aboard an empty grain ship destined for Egypt, and were even given preferred places on deck for our journey. The soldiers posted at every plank and dock looked beyond us and through the crowd, searching for men they would never find.

The ship was free of Roman influence, and when we were each confident that we were unknown to any aboard, Jacob and I ducked behind a stack of crates, stripped off our female outer garments, and pitched them overboard. They were lost almost immediately as the heavy material became soaked with seawater and sunk into the depths of the Great Sea.

"I'll wager Levi and Joachim are laughing even still," I said. "When we return, remind me to thank Joachim in a generous way."

"Oh, I don't know. I thought the colors accented your eyes very well," Jacob said, then laughed.

"We will never speak of it again," I said. "Now let's find another corner of the ship to set up in."

Jacob put his arm around my shoulders and squeezed. "If you ever fall on hard times, I think we've discovered a hidden talent you could use," and he laughed jovially again, making his way over the crowded deck.

The freighter was larger than most, and of Greek design. I had heard the captain say it could carry three hundred tons of grain as it traveled up and down the coasts of the Great Sea. The hulls were wide and flat to maximize cargo space, which also provided for maximum occupancy on its return trip. In pursuit of the ever-elusive greater profit, ship captains learned early that although grain traveled one way, the ships had to return. Human cargo, though not as valuable, padded the loss on the return trip. Passage was expensive, but given the choice of an overland route, the price was well worth it. At Alexandria, the human cargo would be emptied and replaced with stacks of wheat and barley, and tall, clay amphorae filled with wine or oil. It was a profitable business to be sure.

A business, I now knew, my sons were learning well.

The days were long on deck, with little more to do than spend time watching the desert coast slip past or participate in the several games of chance that had sprung up in every corner of the ship—the wager of money on the roll of a shaped die, or the casting of lots for any number of worthless trinkets or baubles. But if the days were long, the nights were longer. Near as we could count there were a hundred and thirty aboard. Many of them were from the far reaches of the Empire, and some, by their behavior, looked to be hiding or in flight. It was these men, especially old men like us, one did not turn one's back to. One who did so might find himself minus his purse, and swimming to his destination. For protection we divided the night and slept in shifts, but even then the sleep was not sound.

That first night as I drifted in and out of a restless sleep, I questioned my hasty decision to leave and return to Judea. On the open sea there is little to do but eat and think. Joachim's words repeated in my ears. The land we had left would feel the consequences of our victory, and as new battles were waged, I would be on the other side of the world. It didn't seem right, but I knew it was. If we had stayed, we would be constrained to hide while injustices were committed in order to search us out. The screams and pain would reach our ears by one means or another, and Rome knew it would be more than we could take. They would expect us to strike back, and they would be right. Joachim was wise in his old age, encouraging us to leave. But still, it was difficult to leave, knowing that the fight would be waging and I would be absent. It felt as if we were running away, though I knew that was not the truth.

But what is the truth? What am I doing? Always these questions.

According to the captain, the trip would take four days, thanks in part to a strong wind from the northeast. On the evening of the third day I found Jacob leaning on the deck rail watching the sun sink below the horizon. The brightly colored sky, reflected on the crests of the water, was a beautiful panorama of reds and oranges, though it stirred a certain melancholy in my heart. By the somber way Jacob held his head on his sunken shoulders, I knew what he was thinking about. *Levi.*

"You miss him," I said.

Jacob didn't answer right away, but I could see in his windswept face that he did.

"I've taken many young men under my wing, been their mentor, their inspiration to fight back, to struggle for freedom," he said. "But never did any of them feel like a son, like the child I had wished for."

"I knew you loved him," I said.

"You did?" Jacob looked honestly surprised.

"We could all see that you cared for him. I think he looked to you as he would his father."

"He'll grow to be a fine leader of men," Jacob said. "Join that with his faith in God, and Rome will have a worthy adversary to contend with."

"Joachim promised to care for him," I said. "He will be fine without us."

"Yes," Jacob said, taking in a deep breath as if the thought pained him. "I know."

As old friends are wont to do, we let silence pass between us until the last embers of twilight were snuffed out by the heavy blanket of night. Then Jacob spoke.

"When did they leave?" he asked.

"Who?"

"Your family."

I inhaled deeply, as if to draw strength from the night breeze. This was all happening too quickly. A week ago I would have believed I had forgotten about them, pushed them far from the life I'd chosen to live. I hadn't thought of that day in years, yet now, as the winds filled the dark sails, I was helpless to think of anything else.

"I wonder if Deborah felt the same way when she left," I said.

"What do you mean?" Jacob asked.

"Three days ago, as we pulled out of port at Apollonia, I felt no remorse, no sadness in leaving. I . . . I don't know exactly what I expected—some sense of attachment, some pain, some loss as I left behind the only home I have known these last thirty years." I paused and looked far out to sea. "I can only believe Deborah felt the same way. She didn't even say good-bye."

"Oh, come now," Jacob was quick to say. "You're speaking nonsense. No one can make a change of that magnitude and remain unaffected. How did *you* feel when she left? Her feelings were surely similar if not the same."

"You don't know my wife," I said.

Jacob laughed, "I didn't even know you *had* a wife until a few days ago."

My thoughts raced back through the years until they stopped on the face of an elderly man I had known during my last years as a slave and then after I had been freed.

"Did you know Rabbi Eli ben Joseph?"

"I do not believe so."

"You would have liked him. He was one of the strongest voices against Rome—a voice that seemed to call to my most inward feelings. I would spend hours at the synagogue, listening to him speak of freedom and courage. His words were like a fire that warmed me during those cold years spent in servitude. Then, later, he was a guide when I had paid the price for my freedom. In public, he spoke the words of the Torah and recounted the stories of faith and inspiration. But in other times, times away from the watchful eye of the Empire, he would speak of action against our oppressors. He had a special gift for words, and there wasn't a single man who could listen to him and remain unmoved."

The memory of my mentor still sparked reverence in my heart, though, oddly, reservation as well. He was, after all, a man of his word, a man who was true to his integrity at all times. He was a great man in his own right, but very different from another great rabbi that had inspired and tutored me in my youth. Their conflicting viewpoints troubled my heart, so I did what I had grown accustomed to doing when faced with unpleasant or clashing thoughts—pushed them aside in hopes they would just go away.

I took a moment to reflect on all I was telling Jacob. Never in all my life had I opened up to anyone about feelings such as these. I wondered if being distant from the land that bound me as a slave was loosening my tongue. The sensation of opening up was more than a bit uncomfortable, but I didn't want to stop.

"Deborah didn't approve of my devotion to the rabbi and his 'inciting' words, as she called them. She would say that there was enough hatred and anger in the world without encouraging violence in the name of God. But what she didn't understand was that it wasn't violence for the sake of being violent. Violence is a language, spoken by the great oppressors of the world—a language I would need to learn if I ever hoped to make a difference."

I stopped suddenly as a far-off thought clambered to be remembered. I had once had a desire to make another kind of difference in the world. But that dream now lay in an unmarked and forgotten grave.

I let my thoughts drift for a while, like the gently rolling sea. "We started staging protests, denouncing Roman law and government, which escalated to throwing stones from afar at the marching ranks of soldiers, but we were far from being a threat to them."

"And you failed to get their attention," Jacob added, seeming to know where the story was going.

"We eventually did, though, and the magistrate sent troops to quiet our demonstration. When we refused to disband, words were quickly replaced with weapons and blood was shed. I returned home a new man. The line had been crossed; the course I knew my life must take had been set. I knew Deborah would be less than understanding, but I misjudged how strong her feelings were. She helped dress the wound in my side I had suffered from the fight and then told me that I had to choose between her and the family, or this fight. She seemed to know that it had only started, and she refused to have her children exposed to the risks she believed my actions would create. I tried to explain my reasons for doing what I knew was right, but my words fell on deaf ears. She was gone by the next Sabbath, without so much as a farewell."

"It must have been a hard choice," Jacob said.

"I can't remember her saying very much about it during those few days before she left," I said. "And Deborah was not one to cry."

"Not for her," Jacob said with an air of disgust in his tone. "For you."

"No. It wasn't hard. The choice was simple. If she was not with me she was against me. We were each better off that way."

"And your children?" Jacob asked. "Was it better for them?"

The painful image of Alexander, and the feel of his sharp words, flashed in my mind and heart, cutting through to my center. But just as quick came the soothing balm of the message he brought from Hannah. It was all so confusing.

"They knew no other way with me as their father," I confessed. I was grateful for the cover of night—Jacob would not be able to see the pain expressed now in my face as I thought of them.

"Hannah was born while I was still in bondage," I continued. "All three of them were, actually. This is why my sons have names that are not of Hebrew origin. Born to a slave, they were property as well. God be thanked that the master of the house where I lived and worked was of Greek descent, not Roman. We were free to name the girl anything we wanted, but the boys' names he chose for us. I had no other choice but to give them the names chosen by our master. Those years, though, could have been worse. Working in the coastal fields gave us great stability. The master of the house allowed us to live together as a family. Two years after Rufus was born, I had saved enough to purchase our freedom. A year later Deborah had left and taken my children with her."

"Tell me of Hannah, then," Jacob said. "Her memories of you must be better than yours are of her."

"I can't imagine that they could be." I gazed out over the water, seeing clearly the picture of my little girl fifteen years ago. "She was a happy child. To see her without a smile on her lips and a giggle in her voice was rare indeed, though I scarcely took time to notice. My days were spent working in the rock quarries, and the nights were filled with rigid silence when I wasn't fighting with Deborah. We had . . . differing views on the world and our place and role in it. Hannah seemed to know that there was something missing in my life—some hole that she tried to fill. If ever there was a father unworthy of a child's love and care, it was I. Her sweet attention and simple words of love and support fell upon deaf ears and were not once returned. Though we lived under the same roof, each day was a new attempt to find her daddy, and each night I remained lost to her."

I was beginning to doubt I had any memories I wasn't ashamed of.

"She showed her love day after day, but seldom did she let me see her cry. I knew she did, and even then I could not give her my love. I didn't mean to hurt her, but I did nonetheless. I just couldn't help it. I had no love to give her. The words I spoke, the feelings I had; they were just too strong to conquer."

"They must have been," Jacob commented. "For a child's love, I have heard, can conquer all. What could possibly persuade a man to ignore the pleas of his children? It must have been a terrible deed."

Jacob was as intelligent and perceptive a man as there ever lived. His suspicions about my past life, crimes, and pain had been aroused even before the day of Lexi's visit. His words now were an invitation to speak further of them, but it was an invitation I did not want to accept. Not tonight. Not now.

"It's getting late," I said, "and if I'm not mistaken the second watch is mine. Thank you for listening to an old friend ramble on about things of little importance. I bid you good night."

I left Jacob at the deck's edge and made my way across to our little corner of the ship. I pulled the blanket tight around me and briefly looked up at the brightly lit heavens before closing my eyes and straying cautiously into the world of dreams.

CHAPTER 6

The morning sea air was crisp as we cut through the placid waters. The night had passed quietly and had given me time to think through the many conflicting thoughts that had all vied to be heard the night before. As the sky began to separate from the dark sea, my resolve to see Hannah grew firm. My concerns and doubts, which were many, could not outweigh the simple call of my oldest child in her hour of great blessing. For better or worse, I felt I needed to press on and do this one thing.

As more light filled the sky and lent itself to our little ship, the still, huddled masses began to stir and wake. The children on board were first to rise and quick to begin playing and chasing each other around the ship. A few minutes later their parents rose to catch and quiet them as the ship was brought to life by the rising sun. By this, the third morning, the ship was beginning to resemble and feel like a village. Small pockets of men and women of shared cultures, languages, and faiths united to build relationships that would help them endure the short trip. There were even those with extra to sell to those in need; treasures were bartered, money exchanged hands, and almost everyone was happy. I watched with some amusement as a few of these impromptu merchants were already setting up their transitory shops and displays at such an early hour.

Jacob awoke early and joined me at the ship's prow just as the sun was rising.

"A peaceful night?" I asked.

Jacob shut his eyes in a painful grimace as the sun lit the sky in white brilliance and covered the water with a glitter as bright as diamonds. He shook his head.

I reached into my bag.

"Here." I tossed him a mango I had purchased from the ship stores and bit into my own. "You missed a good fight last night. On the far side. They were drunk. One pushed the other, the other hit back, and in an instant they were both wrestling around. It didn't last long though. Those scuffles never do. By the time the crew knew there was a problem, both men had passed out. It was quite amusing."

"How so?"

"Neither one had good form," I said between bites. "And I'm not talking about the wine. Even if they were sober, these men couldn't have hurt each other much."

"You should have given them a lesson, then," Jacob said, sleep not entirely driven from his thoughts and words.

"They wouldn't listen to an old man," I said, finishing the juicy pulp and throwing the pit far out to sea.

I was about to tell Jacob of my new resolve and the thoughts I had through the night, when suddenly a woman yelled out, "There it is!" All eyes went to a small woman leaning over the rail and pointing just south of the rising sun. In an instant as many as could squeeze shoulder to shoulder forced themselves to the ship's edge, waiting to catch their own glimpse of the famed seaport. Hands went to their eyes to block the reflection of the morning in the water, and one by one we all caught sight of the monolithic lighthouse that marked the entrance into the man-made harbor. It stood as a beacon to the world, enticing all those who traded by land or sea. The descriptions I had heard from sailors who had seen it firsthand did not do the architectural wonder justice. Twelve cylindrical structures, stacked one on top of the other, and each twice the size of a house, reached up as tall as a mountain, and at its peak burned a fire that could be seen even in daylight. It was amazing to behold.

Jacob stood up, holding to the sail's rigging with one hand and shielding his eyes from the sun's glare with the other; finally he saw what the commotion was all about.

"Have you ever been to Alexandria?" Jacob asked.

"No," I said, but I was not sure if that was true. Though I could not recall ever being there, the closer we sailed the more an uneasy feeling built in my stomach, challenging my memory.

Jacob reached down to help me up. "You must see this better, then," he said with an air of nostalgia. "It is just as I remember it."

Beyond our first sight of the lighthouse that marked the outer island, our view was filled with an immense field of green. I was speechless. I had never seen such fertile land, especially in such close relation to the white sands of the desert.

"It is here that the heart of Egypt beats," Jacob said. "When I was old enough, maybe six or seven, my father took me with him on one of his 'buys,' as he called them. He was a shrewd businessman. Even as young as I was, I remember thinking that whatever my father wanted, my father would acquire, and at the price he wanted to pay."

Jacob's words became heavy and more than a little sad. "He's been dead almost fifty years, and still I find myself missing him, even at my age. I guess some pains do not heal entirely with time."

Jacob was silent for a time, staring at the unfolding land, though I believe pictures and images of his father played before his mind's eye.

My attention left my friend and returned to the coastline and the city that seemed to grow in size and density the closer we sailed to port. Then a sight appeared that forced me to take a second look. The city seemed to extend itself right out onto the water. Reaching out from the shore, a line of square buildings seemed to be floating on the sea. I started to smile at the strange sight, but a dark picture and an even darker feeling shook my body, and I shut my eyes as suddenly it all came back to me. The unsettling feeling I'd had earlier was exposed as I remembered that I *had* been in Alexandria before, though I did not know the city's name at the time.

It had been night. Stripped down to my tunic and chained to what must have been a thousand other men, I had been forced to stand in a deep cargo hold because there was no room to sit or lie down. I remembered being confused and tired, so very tired. And sad. No, not just sadness. Despair. I couldn't remember much of the night before my journey, just waking up with a cut on the back of my head, my hands and feet in irons. No one had answers, and no one seemed to care. Through a portal I caught a brief glimpse of lights shimmering in the dark water, and then I saw the outlined shapes of a city built on top of the deep.

They were the same buildings I was seeing now. I turned away, and looked instead out to sea with such intensity and emotion that Jacob was concerned. But before he could ask me about it, and with a skill practiced and mastered through years of use, I buried the memory deep inside where it would never be seen or experienced again. I put my hand on his shoulder to gesture that I was fine.

"I'll be with our things," I said, leaving Jacob to be alone with memories of his father and their time spent together.

With skills of his trade, our captain deftly guided our ship through the narrow entryway to the bay and passed the other ships docked in the harbor. Within the hour we had set foot on the shores of Egypt.

We agreed that, in the interest of time, we would separate in seeking our choice of passage to the Judean coast. Jacob would manage the sea-going choices while I would look into an overland route. We would meet back at the docks in an hour.

Alexandria expanded from the water in the shape of a fan, the main roads reaching far into the rich Nile Delta like a net to ensnare anything of value and worthy of sale. Like so many other coastal cities dotting the shores of the Great Sea, Alexandria was built on principles of commerce and trade, but in some immaterial way it differed and felt unique. As I walked her streets, I realized it was not the city that lent this uncommon feeling, but the land she'd sprung from. Egypt had existed for thousands of years. Her cities and great stone monuments were aged when Joseph was sold into slavery and ancient when Moses led the children of Israel through the Red Sea. Alexandria, I knew, had only been built to its current size and magnificence about three hundred years earlier, but the land upon which it was built was older than any other known, and had lost more history than all the nations of the world combined could record. Egypt seemed to demand recognition and respect as I made my way along her shores and the streets of Alexandria.

The air was noised with a multitude of languages and dialects. At every shop and corner, men haggled and bartered for goods and services at such a volume that I was amazed any of them could hear or understand each other. Surrounded by this confusion of languages, I was struck with the image of ancient Babel, and there, as I turned to look back out to sea, was the lighthouse, a similitude of Babel's tower reaching a defiant hand to the heavens. It was an uncanny resemblance, and I paused briefly before pushing on through the crowded streets. In time my task was accomplished and I returned to meet up with Jacob.

Jacob was waiting in the shade of a store awning, sitting atop many bags of grain. He had taken the opportunity to buy a meal of boiled fish and a loaf of bread flavored with nuts and honey. He moved over and offered me part of his meal.

"What did you learn?" I asked, breaking off a piece of the tender meat.

"I did not think it possible," Jacob said, "but in all of Alexandria there is but one ship destined for Caesarea and permitting passage aboard."

This was less than great news, but given the circumstances, I would take it. "When does it leave?" I asked.

"It is overdue as we speak."

I moved to stand. "Then we must hurry."

Jacob reached out and took my arm. "No," he said.

"What do you mean, no?" I asked, trusting Jacob's judgment and sitting back down.

"I talked to a member of the crew," he said. "He spoke of a dream the captain had three days ago."

"A dream?"

"This I remember my father telling us when I was young. Sailors are a superstitious lot. In fact, my father was no different. Dreams and omens are taken seriously by those who live by the sea. The smallest things, like a crow or magpie on the rigging, for example, or ill words or blasphemies spoken before departing, could interrupt a voyage with delays or even cancellation. But of all the signs, dreams are heeded most."

"Of a storm or wreck?" I asked.

Jacob shook his head. "Animals, usually. Goats, boars, or, as I heard the captain saw, a bull. They are all bad omens that are interpreted to mean storms, shipwreck, or worse."

"I cannot believe that so much at stake can be dismissed on account of a fretful night's sleep."

"In the captain's dream, he was gored by a black bull. He is convinced a titanic storm is coming, and he refuses to set sail until the proper sacrifices are offered and accepted by the temple priests and the pagan gods they worship."

"How much longer will this take?"

"A day, a week, who knows? They have already been waiting three days. What is three days more, or three times three?"

"Well, we can't wait for their nonexistent gods to be appeased."

"Which is why I hope your news holds more promise than mine."

"Only slightly," I said. "Caravans leave every third day or so. Tomorrow, as chance would have it, is one of those days. But though we can leave in the morning, it will take nearly a week to reach Jerusalem."

"Do we have any other choice?"

We didn't, so the next hour was spent finding a room near the edge of the city—one not far from where the caravan was lodging for the night. As big as Alexandria was, we had a difficult time finding a room large enough for two for the money we had to spend. Two hours later we found what we were convinced was the last available room still big enough to suit the both of us, paid the innkeeper to secure the room, then left again for the busy markets we had passed up while looking for lodging. The next few hours were spent purchasing supplies for the long, hot journey ahead of us: a tent and bedding, dried and peppered meats, nuts, and skins for water. At one shop Jacob bought a roll of papyrus, a dozen thin reeds, and an ampule of ink made from lampblack and gum.

"What is this for?" I asked.

Jacob carefully fit his newly purchased writing tools into his shoulder bag. "Do you ever wonder if your life has made a difference?"

"You're not going to talk about miracles and being saved for some higher purpose again, are you?"

"I mean, when you're gone, will there be more than a few stories and a grave marker to testify that you once lived? What of your hopes, your dreams? What of your struggles and the lessons you learned from them? What will exist to tell future generations that you tried your best in the world in which you lived?"

"And writing on a few sheets and rolls will accomplish this?" I asked, more than a little annoyed at this new talk of Jacob's.

"I don't know," he said. "I haven't written it yet."

"Who will read it?"

He shrugged his shoulders. "Someone. Anyone. No one. That's not the point."

"Then what is?"

He paused, as if to collect his thoughts and plan his answer with great care.

"History may or may not remember us for deeds great or small," he said. "But in this small way I can say that I was here, that my life did have meaning, that it was worthy of remembering. It's hard to explain these new thoughts I've had. Am I making any sense?"

"No," I said, slapping Jacob on the back, "but that never stood in the way of our friendship before."

"Come, I'll buy you dinner," Jacob rejoined good-naturedly.

Not one to argue when it came to matters of food, I accepted the offer and followed him to the market square. I had never seen so many different kinds of food in all my life. Apollonia was a major city and had many cultural delicacies from the world over, but nothing compared to what was offered here. So unique were the foods that we even dined on the tail of alligator, though I was unsure whether or not it was forbidden under the Mosaic law. Jacob convinced me it wasn't, and we ate our fill of the strange beast. As the sun was starting to set, we returned to the inn, thrilled with the prospect of a good night's sleep on a real bed.

When we returned to our room there was a pitcher of wine and plate of bread and cheeses waiting for us.

"Did you order this?" I asked Jacob, lighting the lamps on the walls.

"It must have come with the room," Jacob said. "The innkeeper charged us enough."

Jacob delved into the complimentary food and poured each of us a glass of the wine.

"For the first time since we left, things are beginning to come together," Jacob said, drinking deeply from his cup. "You must try the cheeses. Fresher curd is not found in the morning markets."

I took the offered cup of wine, sniffed it, and took only a sip. "This wine doesn't taste right," I said. "It doesn't taste like wine I've ever had."

"Of course it doesn't," Jacob said. "This is Egyptian wine. It is fermented differently than at home. Besides, the grapes are special here. Don't ask me how, but they are. Now stop worrying and enjoy what is meant to be a welcome gift for staying the night—"

"Shhh!" I suddenly interrupted. "Did you hear that?"

"Hear what?" Jacob said. "Now you're hearing things too? Your lack of sleep on the ship must be playing tricks with your mind."

"I didn't imagine it. I heard something. It sounded like it was coming from just outside our door."

"We're not the only patrons of this inn," Jacob said, a bit more jovial than I could remember him ever being on so little wine. "Could you have heard someone with a room next to ours?"

"There it is again. Did you hear that scratching sound? It *is* coming from our door."

"Then why don't you open it and see who it is, hmm?"

Stepping lightly I went to the door and put my ear to the wood. I couldn't hear anything now, but I had been sure I had a moment ago. Taking up an offensive position at the door, I slowly unlatched the lock without making a sound and threw open the door, grabbing the figure waiting just outside. I spun him around to disorient him, and as he turned I could see that his hands were free of any sort of weapon. He was still spinning around when I slammed him into the wall and held him tight. It took me a moment longer to realize that something about our trespasser wasn't right. He was short and small of frame. I did not think a stiff wind would have trouble holding him down. When I looked closer at him I saw that "he" was actually a "she." A young she, at that. She was maybe twelve or thirteen years old.

"Who are you? What are you doing outside our door?" I was embarrassed that I had hit a girl, but I was even more upset that she had been listening in and spying on us. "Who are you? Answer me!"

She was terrified in my hands. Her whole body was shaking. "M-m-my father owns the inn," she answered.

"Why were you outside our door?"

She didn't answer but looked, instead, at the pitcher of wine.

"You brought this to us, didn't you?"

She just stood there, too frozen in fear to speak to me. I shook her in hopes of loosening her tongue.

"Answer me! Did you put this in our room?"

She finally nodded.

"There's something in it, isn't there?"

"Please let go of me," she said, starting to cry.

"You will answer my questions and then I'll consider letting you go. What is in the wine?"

"I—I don't know." She was sobbing now.

"Who told you to do this?"

"Please don't kill me," she pleaded.

"Kill you? We'll do no such thing. Why would you say that?"

"The man said—"

"What man?"

"I don't know his name," she said. "He bought the wine. He told me it wouldn't hurt you; it would just make you sleep for a while. He said you were criminals and he needed my help to catch you. He said he was here to arrest you. He . . . he gave me this . . ." A silver coin dropped from her trembling hand.

By this time Jacob had gotten to his feet and joined me at the door.

"But why were you waiting, child?" Jacob asked.

"I was to check on you from time to time," she said. "I was supposed to tell him when you were asleep."

"Where is this man?" I asked.

The girl had forgotten that I still held her wrists and hesitated before answering. A sharp squeeze reminded her.

"In the dining room."

Jacob started to sway and took a step back to steady himself. His hand went to his face, and he pinched the bridge of his nose. Jacob shook his head and tried to shake off the drug's effect.

"You're going to show me this man," I told the girl.

"No, please don't make me," she said. "I just want to go home. Can't I just go home?"

I shook my head sternly. "You are going to show us who asked you to do this."

"Must I?" she asked fearfully.

"Consider it a lesson in duty. You're going to do just what he paid you to do. We're just going to go with you. Do you understand?"

She nodded, and the three of us went outside and down to the inn's dining area. Several of the tables were filled, but no one seemed surprised to see the three of us.

"Where is he?" I asked. "Which table is his?"

"The one in the corner," she said, pointing to an empty table with a half-eaten meal that looked as if it had been abandoned in a hurry. "He was there when I left a moment ago."

"You wouldn't be telling us a lie, would you?" I asked.

"No, no, I swear. He told me to come back when I thought you were asleep."

The noise of shattering glass from the back room kitchen area startled us, followed by a shout for someone to get out.

"Someone's in a hurry to leave this place, and not by the front door," I said.

The girl pulled away from my grip on her arm and ran through the dining area and out the front doors. Jacob moved to follow her but I put my hand on his shoulder and stopped him.

"Let her go," I said. "Our fight is the other direction."

Together Jacob and I followed the commotion through the back room. The kitchen area was a small, crowded room in the back. The innkeeper, a tall, thin man, turned and yelled at us too, and started waving a knife in the air to emphasize his objection to his kitchen being used as an alleyway. Paying little attention to his ranting, we ran past him and outside. Down the back street, a dark figure turned the corner at a dead run. It was our man.

I could see that Jacob was still feeling the effects of the wine.

"Are you all right?" I asked. "Maybe you should stay here and wait."

Jacob shook his head almost violently. "Have you ever known me to shy away from a fight? I'll be fine."

We ran after him as fast as we could. Alexandria had a thousand places to hide, though I did not think he would find safe harbor in any of the shops set up and lit for the night's business. We could not see where he had run to once we turned the corner, but we only had to wait a moment before shouts farther down the street from one of the shop owners focused our attention. On we ran, Jacob falling a little behind, but still able to keep up. Men and women were all too willing to help us as we pursued our elusive spy, pointing in the direction they had seen the man run without our needing to ask a single question. He had knocked into many of them and had made quick enemies of more than a few. But despite our help from the local citizens, the man's speed was too great for us to overtake him on foot. We needed an advantage, and suddenly I realized we had one. There were two of us and only one of him.

We had run almost to the edge of the city in our pursuit. I began to recognize many of the streets I'd traveled earlier in the day in search of a caravan. Many of them converged on the main roads that fanned out from the bay. There were few shops out here, and the streets were lined with straight, high walls.

"We need to corral him down one of these side streets." My lungs were burning and I felt on the edge of exhaustion. "They all lead back to this one. You follow him and I'll run and meet him where the street exits. We'll die before we catch him this way."

Jacob was even more winded than I was, and could only nod his understanding and agreement with my plan. Unable to catch his breath, he started down the street where we had last seen our would-be assailant disappear. I looked around for something I could use against him and found a hand-sized stone that would do nicely.

I pushed myself to the limits of my endurance. My legs felt numb but somehow I kept running; though my lungs burned with every breath, I knew I could not let this man escape. Our very lives likely depended on it. I needed to know who he was and why he would use a young girl to do his work. At last I saw the side street's exit onto the main way and pushed myself even harder to reach it before our prey did. As I neared the corner I could hear the footfalls of a man running straight toward me. I repositioned the stone in my hand and raised it to deliver a disabling blow, then rounded the corner ahead of him.

I pulled back from the attack just in time, for the man running was not our dark-cloaked enemy, but Jacob.

"Where is he?" I asked, winded.

"You didn't see him?"

I shook my head and swallowed hard. "You must have passed him somewhere."

"Impossible. There were no side alleys he could have ducked down or hidden in. I'm sure of it."

I looked around, up and down the streets, and listened for any sign of him, but there was none. I was confused.

"Somehow we missed him," I said. "It's not possible, but he's eluded us."

"Why was he after us in the first place?" Jacob asked. "It seems like a great deal of trouble for a thief to go to for our meager purses. Surely there are more wealthy visitors in the city to prey upon."

"That's why I don't think he was after our money," I said. "He was after our heads."

"Why would someone want to kill us?"

"Not kill, necessarily. But capture. It seems that word has reached Egypt of the reward for our capture."

"But that's impossible," Jacob said. "No one knows it was us. And even if they knew our names, no one here knows our faces."

"That's what worries me," I said. "No one saw us board in Apollonia, not dressed like women. I just can't make sense of it."

Jacob suddenly went into a fit of coughing.

"Are you all right?"

"I'll be fine," Jacob said, bent over trying to ease the fit. "I haven't run like that since I was a boy, and even then I don't think it was ever that fast."

"We'll take it easy on our way back to the inn," I said. "Whoever he is, I don't think he will try anything more tonight."

We walked back to the inn, begging water from two shop owners on the way. Each asked us if we had caught the man we were chasing. They were momentarily disappointed that he had gotten away, then returned to advertising their deals and selling their goods.

When we got back to our room, we threw out the wine and cheeses before securing the lock on our door.

"We should sleep in shifts," I said. "I think it would be safer if one of us takes the watch."

"Always in shifts," Jacob sighed. "Just once I'd like to sleep the entire night."

"Why don't you take first rest and sleep off whatever was in the wine. I'll wake you after a while."

I didn't wake him, though, and let him sleep clear through to morning.

* * *

The caravan was making final preparations to leave when we arrived. I was not at all surprised to see some of the same faces from the ship now traveling with the caravan. They had, no doubt, also learned that there was no sea voyage to the coast of Jerusalem. Among those who now joined us were two Jewish families on a pilgrimage to celebrate the Passover under the shade of the Temple, three merchants bound for the shores of Antioch, and a desert Bedouin with a quiet demeanor and distant look in his eyes; he kept to himself as if to show that his business was his own.

The leader of the caravan, I had learned, was an old Egyptian named Shadid Ibn-Farukh. He was from an ancient line of desert sheiks who had changed with the times and gone into the business of leading caravans across the deserts. Ibn-Farukh looked to be near seventy years. Though his skin was tanned to a coarse leather from years of toil under the sun, strength radiated from his dark eyes, testifying that he was unquestionably a strong leader and a master of what he did. He shouted sharp commands to the men of his train, and not to his men only. As condition of our passage, all who were able-bodied were compelled to assist the drivers and servants. Jacob and I, though older than most, were still strong enough and were enlisted to help finish loading the wagons with sacks of wheat and other grains to sell along the way. The work was hard but not long, and at the appointed hour we were off.

We could not afford our own horses or camels, so Egypt and all her wonders played before our eyes from the back of one of the wagons. My eyes drank in the ancient land, while Jacob became lost in his writing.

The caravan was not a haphazard, spontaneous collection of camels and goods traveling the roads of the deserts. There was structure here that rivaled that of the sharpest military command. Led by the caravan commander, as he was called, the train was marched across inhospitable lands in quick time, and according to a schedule planned out months, or even years in advance. I was duly impressed.

As caravan sizes go, ours was a modest one with a modest cargo to carry, or so I was told. Seven camels with five mule carts were accompanied by Nubian men with skin of beautiful ebony, all of them as royal and regal as any men I had ever seen. Theirs was an impressive presence. Ibn-Farukh had taken command of the caravan at Aswan, just past the Nile's first cataract. Carrying skins of exotic beasts, and gems and precious stones from Nubia's legendary mines, the caravan was actually quite wealthy and, hence, well protected. The sheik had a dozen men accompanying him on the journey. These men would provide for our security, each riding a desert stallion and armed for heavy combat. Four of them, I learned along the way, were his sons. The others were members of his brother's family. The sheik was clever. Their presence along the caravan was strong, but not noticeable enough to draw special attention to it.

Our route took us in an arc across the Nile Delta and overland through the Sinai. What took Moses forty years, I thought with some amusement, would take us a couple of days. From there we would travel north, parallel to, but just beyond sight of, the shores of the Great Sea, then through the Gaza and Idumean Deserts before reaching the Judean hills and Jerusalem. The journey would take place in relays, as the distance was far too great for any one beast to make.

Set up along the route were a series of caravansaries, or inns, each about a day's distance apart. Generally built around a source of water, the purposes of these hostelries was to provide lodging and rest for the travelers and their animals. They were also used for protection. Usually built of stone, if available, or sun-dried bricks, these inns were a welcome sight to the weary with promises of shaded rooms and stables. But not for us.

We passed many of the caravansaries as we made our way across the Nile Delta. Our caravan commander refused to stop, but pushed through from city to city as if on an accelerated schedule, his only goal to reach the deserts and the long trek still before us. At Pelusium, the last prominent city before entering the barren wastes of the desert, we were forced to wait to connect with a small caravan making its way up along the Red Sea. The delay was only for a few hours, but it seemed that to Ibn-Farukh it could not have been worse if we had stayed a week. He sent men out looking for the caravan or any news of them, but could not rest with that. As he paced just beyond the high stone walls, he swore and vowed never to work again with this family that would detain one of his caravans. He had a reputation to uphold, and generations of trust to fulfill. As hard as his men tried, he would not be consoled.

For Jacob and me, though, the time was a blessing. The light of dawn was still hours away and the past week weighed heavy on our eyes. We had not slept well during our drive through Egypt. Because of the incident at the inn at Alexandria, and knowing that the assailant was still out there somewhere, we had continued to sleep in shifts and were always on alert when people approached the caravan as we passed through the cities and villages. It had been stressful, but now we took the opportunity to recline and relax under the roofs of the many rooms on the upper level overlooking the courtyard.

We were not the only people at the inn, and the many caravans bedding for the day filled the dusty pens. Drinking at the troughs, camels and other pack animals lined up side by side to replenish their spent stores by drinking from the warm but refreshing water drawn from the well, while others sat on folded legs as they ate hay and dried grasses. Men talked in a dozen different languages as stories were exchanged and friendships born. In many respects, the inn resembled a small village, similar to the phenomenon aboard the ship from Apollonia; and what village would be complete without the sounds of children running and playing?

From the half-wall that lined the upper floor I looked down over the yard. Children were busy at play. There were six of them, as best I could count, and their game of chase must have been one of some excitement, for each of them yelled in turn and then continued running over and around the resting animals. Busy with other duties, their mothers had turned them loose to run and play as they saw fit. I could see that two of the women were Jewish by their dress and manner, one was a wealthy Egyptian, and one was—

"No, no, no!" I yelled from the balcony, getting louder as I raced to the stairs and down to the ground.

The children froze in their play, frightened at the sight of an old man descending the steps and yelling at them when they hadn't done anything wrong.

But they had.

Before any of the other men and women could stop me, I ran to the scared bunch and separated the Egyption and Jewish children from the other one. The mothers dropped their work and rushed to their children. A few of the men stopped their business with the animals and looked on with more than a little apprehension.

"You cannot play with him!" I ordered, pointing to the Roman child who had been their playmate. The children were frightened even more, looking at their friend with new suspicions. The mothers reached us and quickly took their children from me.

"You must not let them play together!" I said.

The mothers and children answered only with confused silence.

At that moment Jacob was at my side. My yelling must have awakened him. "It's all right," he said, putting his arm on my shoulder.

I shrugged it off. "No it is not!"

"They were playing, that's all."

"They were blurring the lines," I said.

"What lines?"

"Between us and them."

"Simon . . ." Jacob said, trying to calm me down.

"This is war! Or have you forgotten that?" I said. "They are the enemy."

Jacob looked at the alarmed mother and child. "He's a child," Jacob said.

"Children grow up to be men," I returned.

Jacob looked at me, shook his head, and turned and walked away. The others at the inn all returned to their business as well, and I was left standing alone under the hot Egyptian sky.

* * *

The remainder of our wait was short, and the merged caravan got under way as the hot sun cooled and prepared the land for nightfall.

With the hindrance of civilization behind us, the caravan commander made better time than I had hoped or even thought possible. Of course, there was a price to pay for such speed. At times the old Egyptian resembled more a slave driver than the commander of a caravan as he set a pace that threatened to exhaust man and beast alike. But, Jacob was sure to remind me, in the business of trade, the less time it took to move the goods, the greater the profit. The quicker goods were delivered, the more money the caravan stood to make. It was no consolation to hear of the greater profits made at our expense, but I kept my concerns and complaints to myself as we seemed to race over the desert sands.

Resting during the hottest hours of the day, the caravan pushed through the nights along the familiar desert route with no apparent fear of bandits or robbers, exchanging beasts of burden as we passed the caravansaries instead of resting or seeking shelter. Fortunately, we had no ill encounters, and it looked as if our faithful pilgrims would reach the city in time for the celebration after all. Their tongues were still uttering thanks to God when our advance rider, a scout with the name of Quamar, returned on his horse at a dead run. It would seem that our good fortune was to be challenged by the most fierce and deadly of all desert predators.

"Sandstorm!"

We had stopped to rest until the sun passed overhead, and those of us awake to hear the warning scrambled to our feet and saw, out on the eastern horizon, the dark clouds just over the hills. Quamar immediately sought out the caravan commander.

"The next hostelry is too far. We cannot reach it in time," Quamar said.

Ibn-Farukh stood in his stirrups and looked in every direction, turning slowly and taking inventory of his options, which were few out here in the middle of Gaza.

"We will take shelter in those mountains," he said, ordering such to be done.

The mountains, as he called them, were little more than gently rolling hills several miles off toward the approaching storm.

"Even if we make it in time," Quamar counseled, "they cannot protect us."

"They can protect us better than the open," Ibn-Farukh said. "Take a new horse and find a canyon, a gorge, a dry riverbed—anything—and find it fast. We will follow."

The rider did as he was commanded and was gone again in moments.

Everyone was roused, and the desperate news of our situation was explained in concise detail; if we were caught out in the open, we would all die. Camp was broken, and the animals were hurriedly packed and loaded, then driven for the hills.

I had nearly finished packing our tent when Jacob took my arm.

"We are not alone," he said. "Look."

Behind us, on the road to the south, another small cloud of dust rose over the desert sands. The afternoon's heat distorted the horizon and prevented a clear picture of its cause, but soon enough I caught a glimpse of reflected metal and the color red.

The color of Rome.

"Do you think they are coming for us?" I asked.

"No," he said. "Why would they wait until now? It is over a day's ride to any major city. No, I don't think they have any interest in us."

"Still, I don't like it," I said.

"If they haven't yet seen the storm, they will," Jacob said. "They will also see the hills and make the same decision we have."

"We are going to be neighbors until the storm passes," I said, disliking the words as much as the idea of weathering the storm with a company of Roman soldiers.

Just then one of the caravan drivers rode up quickly on his horse, pulling hard on the reins and bringing the animal to a short stop.

"We wait for no one," he said, then he looked out over the desert as we had done. "We see them too. Now gather your things and get aboard one of the wagons, or be left behind to follow on foot."

The advice came across as a threat, spoken with a hardness that is born of fear and desperate times, but as we had no quarrel, we adhered to his order and joined our tents and supplies with those on the back of the wagon.

* * *

If the journey thus far seemed like a race, the stretch to the hills was a sprint. With every passing moment, the clouds grew in size and darkness. The wind had picked up by now, and the air seemed to carry on it the scent of death and destruction. Those who live in the deserts know and fear sandstorms, respecting their awesome and fierce power. Gathering strength as they sweep through the desert wastelands, they strike with great unpredictability and without mercy. A small sandstorm can cover a field with a deep layer of dust and sand; a large one can bury a small city. In either instance, to the man or caravan caught in its fury, the storm meant almost sure death.

We met Quamar at the foot of the mountains. The storm was nearly on top of us.

"The life of every man and woman here rests with your doing what I asked," Ibn-Farukh said, yelling to be heard over the winds. "What is your report?"

"There is a place where the hills meet," Quamar shouted back. "It is not much, but the ground is wide enough, I think, for all of us. It is just over that hill."

"Forward!" the old Egyptian shouted.

We made tremendous haste. No time was wasted as the tents were erected and staked into the rocky ground against one of the hillsides. All able hands were put to work covering the wagons, unloading the camels, and corralling the horses to best protect them from the blinding and suffocating sand.

The sun was blocked out almost entirely as we finished securing a large tent. At times I believed the woven cloth would rip and tear as the winds increased and whipped at our hastily made defense. But the ropes held, and the sand was forced to remain outside. Inside, the few children with us were frightened, but the soothing words and songs of their mothers put them at ease. We could do nothing now but wait out the storm in the dark tent.

Suddenly the front flap was thrown open. The women and children screamed, and in an instant the tent was filled with sand, stinging our skin and eyes like the bite of a thousand flies. When our vision cleared we could see our trespasser. With his leather armor and gold eagle plated on his sword scabbard, there was no mistaking him: a captain in the armies of Rome. Our unwelcome neighbor had come for a visit.

Sheik Ibn-Farukh and two of his men ran forward to confront our uninvited guest and secure the tent door again.

"What is the meaning of this?" Ibn-Farukh demanded.

The captain stood at attention. "By command of Caesar," he began, "you and your men are enlisted to build shelter for the soldiers of Rome to wait the storm."

"We will do no such thing!" the old sheik said. I sprang to my feet and joined with his men standing in defiance of such a command.

"You will help us or we will use your shelter, though I doubt there will be room enough for all of you."

"You have no right to do so," Ibn-Farukh said.

"I not only have the right," the captain said, his words becoming a threat as he touched the hilt of his sword, "but I have the means to do it. You will help us, or you will be forced to find another shelter. The choice is yours."

A choice, indeed, I would have said, if not for Jacob's firm hand on my arm. With all their military might, armies are still at the mercy of the elements, as are the lowliest of men. A sword does about as well against sand as it does against fire. This last thought brought a twisted smile briefly to my lips.

Better equipped to fight the sandstorm outside than an army, the caravan commander directed several of his men to go with the captain and build the Romans a shelter using whatever they could find in the wagons. I was suddenly aware that our tent was in one of the wagons. It was larger than most and, if discovered in the darkness, it would likely be used. I was enraged. In a way, I was providing protection for my longtime enemy. I wished I hadn't purchased it. I would rather bake in the afternoon sun or freeze under the stars than help one soldier bearing the insignia of the Empire!

"They cannot get away with this unlawful show of force!" I said as quietly as I could, taking a seat by Jacob. "This abuse of power must not go unpunished!"

"But what can we do?" he asked.

A dozen thoughts of action flashed through my mind. But Jacob's question raised doubts that I could rely on him for support of any action here in the desert. More can be done with two, but one is often sufficient. He had been acting strangely since Apollonia, and not at all like himself. I would need him back before long, but not tonight; I knew what I was going to do could be done with an army of one.

* * *

All traces of sunlight faded, and a small lamp was lit to give a flickering light to the dark expanse of the large tent. Outside the wind and sand continued their unfailing assault, though the most deadly hours had passed. Most of the men and women of the caravan took this time to catch up on missing sleep. Jacob, too, had joined with the mass slumber.

I had not.

As carefully as I could, I crawled to the tent's edge and, confident that no one's attention was focused my way, slipped under and out into the night. The sand lashed out at me and I promptly wrapped my kaffiyeh around my face and head. The night was dark as pitch for there was no trace of the moon or stars. There was not even a hint of light coming from anywhere. A tense feeling washed over me, and I was struck with the sense that this must be akin to hell—a fathomless existence without light, without warmth, and without hope. The only evidence of life were the grunts and nickers of the horses and camels. I tried to dismiss the feeling but couldn't. I was momentarily disoriented, lost in the darkness not ten feet from the tent and Jacob inside. Off balance, I was nearly blown over by the gusts of wind before finally shedding the defenseless feeling. Once more I was able to focus on the task at hand.

Earlier I had heard some of the disgruntled men talk of the Roman dogs' poor choice of a location to wait out the storm. Their camp was about a quarter mile to the south, in a hollow "no deeper than a heavy dew," as one of the men said. With that direction and distance, I set out against the wind.

My kaffiyeh kept the sand out of my nose and mouth, but it could not provide that same protection for my eyes. Shielding them was a futile exercise, for the wind was throwing sand from every direction. It felt as if the storm had found a target to unleash its rage upon and had called in its strength from every direction. I forced myself on, defying the wind, or Jacob, or God to try to stop what I was planning to do. The footing was soft and shifted under the accumulating sand. This trek would have been treacherous during full sunlight, but at night, under the wrath of a sandstorm, it teetered on suicide. Relentlessly, over the low hills and through the shallow valleys, I pushed my feet to take one more step, and then another.

For what seemed like hours I pressed on through the sea of sand that threatened to engulf and bury me if I stopped for even a moment to rest. I was beginning to doubt my sense of direction in the dark, and was preparing myself for the possibility that I was, in fact, lost, when my ears picked up a sound over the howl of the wind. I held my breath and could hear, again, the sound of horses, frightened and jailed in the dark. Relying on my ears to guide me, I followed their sounds until I saw the vague shape of their covered pen, like a hole in an already black sky. A small distance away were three more shapes, tents by the look of them, just visible against the sand hills behind them. They, too, were anchored securely to the deep sand and rock.

The soldiers live because of our help, I was reminded by my anger, *and the only thanks they offer is the end of a sword.* Tonight they would learn the consequences of such manners.

I slid down the small hill and into the horses' pen. They had constructed a small corral using a corner made by a small, steep incline and lances used in their military displays when they traveled from village to village. A pole in the center provided enough pitch to drape a cover over the pen. My presence was almost immediately felt by the horses, and they whinnied and began kicking wildly at being spooked even beyond what the storm was doing to them. Their sounds would not carry over the roar of the storm outside, but I did not know if the Romans checked on their steeds from time to time, so I set to work at once.

I moved along the tent's wall until I came to the makeshift fence rails and dismantled the gate holding the horses in. Then, feeling my way blindly in the dark, I found their reins tied to several stakes in the ground. One by one, I loosed the knots holding them bound and threw open the tent flap, slapping them on their hind quarters, sending them all out into the storm. In the confusion, two of them bolted into one of the soldier's tents, tearing it from the ground. The frightened curses of the soldiers was sweet music to my ears, and I dashed for the hill I had come down.

I paused for a moment to survey the damage I had done and, though I could not see what was happening below, the sounds of confusion and further cursing when they learned what had happened painted a perfect picture for me to take in. I knew the horses would not go far, but come morning, the soldiers would curse their ill luck and spend the better part of the day looking for them. Beneath my kaffiyeh I smiled, then quickly returned to the bedded caravan.

The journey back seemed to take only half the time, and I softly stole back into the dark, quiet tent. All was as I had left it, or so I thought, as I settled in to join the group in sleep.

"That was foolish, what you did," Jacob said softly so as not to wake the others. "Foolish *and* selfish."

My sense of accomplishment was immediately replaced with the feeling that I had somehow done something wrong. But immediately I felt I was being judged unfairly. These were the last words I ever expected to hear from my friend, and I was put straightway on the defensive.

"Critical words from a man who has lost the courage to fight."

"Was it worth the risk?" Jacob asked. "Whatever you did out there, was it worth the risk of getting lost, being taken captive, or even being killed?"

I did not have to see him to know he was shaking his head as he spoke, a further condemnation of an action he was unwilling to take part in. Jacob's words were bordering on betrayal.

"Fighting the enemy that enslaves our nation is far from selfish. There is honor in action," I said. "What is selfish is to sit idle and watch as others do what you will not."

"You loosed their horses and scattered them, didn't you?" Jacob asked.

I was taken aback. "How did you know?"

"We have been friends for too long, fighting at each other's sides. And," he confessed, "it is what I would have done."

"Then why this talk of foolishness and blame?" I asked. "If we were ever going to strike back at their insult and threats, the time is now. There will not be another."

"You have always been quick to take action. Sometimes, though, it is without forethought. Some things we do must outweigh others. We are here, hundreds of miles away from our homes, battling the desert in all her might because a daughter wants to see her father and share her blessing with him, and I wish to see my brother before the time is gone forever. Is risking your life, and mine, and everyone's here to slow down a few soldiers equal to giving that up?"

As much as I wanted to resist his reasoning and logic, I had not the words to reply.

Jacob continued. "I am sorry, but you have known me never to be anything but honest with you. I did not mean to attack your convictions. Do not forget they are mine as well. I only meant to challenge your judgment. Rome deserves everything we can do to her. I thank God for your safe return," he finally said and rolled over and went to sleep.

CHAPTER 7

The storm passed sometime in the night. A thick layer of sand three fingers deep covered everything. In places, drifts had built up to half the size of a man. But for all the sand, we appeared to have fared well, and with minimal damage. It was decided that we would not wait for the soldiers to return with our tents and materials. We cut our losses with an early start. By the first light of dawn we were packed, the camels and carts loaded, and on our way. There was time to be made up; the caravan commander was clear on this, and the new pace he set made the old one seem a slow walk. If he was not careful, I thought, he would run the animals to death. But the old Egyptian knew their limits and kept them just this side of exhaustion.

The miles passed largely in silence. Jacob was consumed with his writing, and I was left alone with my thoughts. It was an uncomfortable companionship as Jacob's words echoed in my soul and reached back through the years. Had my decision to stay behind and fight been the right one? It was the same question I had when I had first learned of Hannah's news, only now the answer was not as clear. I knew I would not have been happy accepting my fate under the rule of Rome. Even as Hannah and my boys were born to us, there had been something lacking in my life. I filled that void by fighting back. But now the question I asked myself as the miles passed beneath me was if I would have found greater happiness with my family instead of without them. Buried deep inside my heart was the answer—and the reason I chose the way I did—but it scared me to think of it, and I quickly left it alone.

The days and nights passed without further incident. Our route took us east at Azotus, up through the Valley of Elah, past the inn at Bethlehem, and through the rocky Judean hills toward Jerusalem. The mountainous climbs and valleys slowed our pace, and were a welcome relief from our time in the desert. Sleep was uneasy, and my anxiety grew with every passing town and village. Doubts circulated again in my mind and heart. It felt as if my head knew this journey was the right thing to do, something that I had to do, but my heart was still fearful of what might happen. This conflict consumed my waking thoughts, and even lent itself to a restless struggle with sleep.

The night before we were to reach the great city of Jerusalem, sleep finally overtook me, though I wished it hadn't. Images of thirty years ago flashed before my eyes without restraint and, with the vivid clarity only dreams can deliver, drew emotions from those unwanted memories of that night. I was alone in the house when the soldiers came. I looked around but couldn't find Deborah anywhere. Outside the soldiers were getting closer. I ran to Joshua's room and snatched him up. When I turned around, a lone soldier was there in the room with me. But this was no ordinary soldier. His face was horrific and I wanted to scream. Where his eyes, nose, and mouth should have been, there was only smooth skin. I tried to run past him but he moved to intercept me. Even without the use of his sight he seemed to know where I was and anticipated my every move.

The faceless soldier reached out for my son and me. Somehow I was able to elude his grip and escaped through the back room. When I turned around to see if he had followed me, the house had disappeared and I was standing outside in the rain. Instead of one soldier, there were now three of them, all looking fearsome without faces. I was surrounded by walls on every side of me. I pulled Joshua close, but in that instant he wasn't in my arms anymore. One of the soldiers had him, holding him with one hand, and in the other hand a knife. He didn't have a mouth, but I knew somehow he was smiling. He raised the knife high, and—

"No!"

I woke screaming and sat straight up. My bedroll was twisted in clumps and knots, and my clothes were wet with sweat. Jacob came running, and for an instant I mistook my friend for the faceless monsters in my dreams. I scrambled to my feet, crouching low and ready to spring into an attack if he moved closer. In a moment the ghosts of my past disappeared, and I was left again with the loss. Left again with the pain.

"What is it?" Jacob asked in a panic. "Snake? Scorpion?"

"Dream," I replied, the images still vivid in my mind's eye, but fading.

Jacob nodded a strained understanding, and left me to work through my distress. When my chest and hands stopped shaking, I gathered my sandals, threw a blanket over my shoulders, and joined him.

The sky was gray, and all but the brightest stars had fled the morning that was just over the horizon. Others in the caravan were already up, making preparations to enter the city later that morning. Just beyond the last tent stood Jacob, looking out toward the hills.

"You can just make it out," Jacob said, pointing. "There."

As we had set up camp the night before, we could only see a cluster of lights set against the dark hills. But now, as the land began to take shape and separate itself from the darkness, there it was, sitting precariously atop a rugged plateau of sloping limestone— Jerusalem. With its broad steps of flat-topped buildings and a maze of stone walls, it was the center of Jewish activity and law for believers in the One True God, and the gathering point for religious pilgrims true to the faith of their fathers. It was the last place in the world I had thought I ever wanted to see.

"Tell me," Jacob asked, "is the city as great as I have heard it described?"

This surprised me. "You've never been there?"

"When I was a child I accompanied my father once or twice, or so I was told."

"The city is great . . . or was, once." I turned and started back for my tent.

I didn't get five paces away when Jacob asked directly, "What happened here?" When an answer was not easily forthcoming, he pressed forward with his question. "When your wife and family returned, you could have come with them. A free man, you could go where you wanted. And Rome is certainly stronger here; you could be fighting alongside my brother instead of with me. Why could you not return? Why did you stay behind? I have been patient, waiting to hear what you have been speaking around but not addressing directly: your crimes, your time spent as a slave, the feelings that consumed you before and after your family left you. I will wait no longer. I am your closest friend. Tell me what happened."

The words froze in my throat. I had never had the courage, nor the desire, to speak them before, but I knew I could no longer hold them back.

"They took my son," I said, trembling with a flood of intense emotion. "They came in the night and they killed him."

Jacob stared, horror stricken—a new pain and confusion on his face.

"You wanted to know what happened, why I could not return. That is why. What happened there can never be undone. The city's name still brings me pain. I still have questions that will go forever unanswered. As far away as Bethlehem and the surrounding villages, they killed them. Herod's rage reached across the entire country."

"It was real, then?" Jacob asked.

"What do you mean?"

"I had heard tales that the Jewish king had committed horrible acts, to his family and others, but I did not want to believe anyone could . . . Were they all male children . . . ?"

"Mine was. To me, that is all that matters."

"I am sorry. I didn't know."

"No one does," I said softly.

"And you've kept this to yourself, holding it in since then?"

High above the gentle hills, a hawk spotted a group of sparrows and circled back. In ever-shrinking circles, it waited for the perfect time to strike.

"No," I said, finding comfort in watching the bird of prey. "I've been letting it out for years. With every attack, every single strike, I let a little bit free; a little is released. It feels good."

"Does it?"

The hawk seized the opportunity and dived into the mass of birds. When he took to the skies again, a sparrow was dead in his powerful talons.

"No."

There was a stretch of silence between us. Then Jacob put his hand on my shoulder and squeezed warmly. "Let us eat," he said. "You will feast with me this morning."

"Is that what you call it?" I asked. "Meal cakes and a handful of dried figs?"

Jacob laughed. "I doubt you have a more appetizing offer."

I didn't, so we returned to the camp.

The caravan got under way just before first light. The fields and hillsides were filled with sheep grazing on the sweet, wet grass, while not far away stood their shepherds—their ever-vigilant protectors and guides. As dawn steadily approached, lending ever-increasing light to the countryside, we wound our way, almost snakelike, through the hills and valleys on the way to the city. Even from this distance, still a few miles away, we could see the brightening sky reflecting off the gold and alabaster roof of the great Temple with increasing brilliance.

"It *is* magnificent," Jacob said.

"Just wait," I said. The sun was going to peek over the distant horizon at any moment.

"For what?"

I paused and waited. "This."

I timed my words precisely with the first rays of the sun as they struck the city. The gold atop the Temple was set ablaze and shone as if God Himself had polished it to a celestial luster. Moments later, the melodic fanfare from the silver trumpets atop the Temple wall heralded the new day.

"God be praised," Jacob offered, truly held in awe.

"When the sun reaches its zenith, there is not a soul within or without the city walls that can avoid taking notice of the House of our Lord."

"God must surely be there," Jacob said, overcome with the magnificence still several miles away.

"God?" I said. "Not likely."

"What do you mean?" Jacob asked, looking almost hurt by my words.

"How could He be?" I said. "Look beyond it. Can you see it?"

Jacob squinted against the sun and shook his head. "See what?"

"To the north of the Temple, you can just see it beyond the brilliance—Antonia."

"Antonia?"

"The fortress that sits touching the Temple courtyards. From atop its walls one can look down on the Temple. Have you never heard of it?" I didn't think it possible that one could not have heard of the mighty Roman stronghold in the heart of the city.

"And why should I have?" Jacob asked.

"It was built originally to protect and defend the Temple from her enemies," I explained, "it was later given as a gift to the Roman governor and his forces by King Herod. Now housed within its massive stone walls reside a thousand conscripts and soldiers, each with their gentile ways, and worshiping their pagan gods."

Jacob kept looking. "I still can't see it."

"It's there," I said. "You'll soon be able to, if you look hard enough. Its standards flying high above the Temple, placing their gods and their Caesar over our God."

"There is much evil in the world," Jacob said. "Is that which is good always at the mercy of that which is not? Cannot God dwell where He pleases? Or is even He bound by what men do and build? Who is more powerful? God or Rome?"

I thought of Joshua, held by Roman fiends, and my prayers supplicating his return. Who was more powerful then? Where was God when I had needed Him?

I did not answer his question, but continued on with the caravan as it pushed through the hills of Judea with an eye single to the great city of the Jews.

The roads were largely empty and served only to connect the small villages that dotted the mountainous hillsides and valleys. The occasional farmer, craftsman, or family seeking the greener pastures of neighboring towns were our only contacts. As we neared Jerusalem, the look of the land changed dramatically. Along the roads were set up all kinds of tents, organized in small camps, and not just for the night. Many looked as if they had lived there for weeks. As we plodded past them, we could see that they were already established in routine. The country had become an extension of the city as children played with each other, women gathered to cook and clean, and men engaged in their craft or trade to provide for their families. At one point along the road school had been called under the shade of a mature fig tree.

The caravan was moving slowly enough now through the hills and roads that Jacob and I walked alongside the wagons. The exercise felt good, since most of our time had been spent riding on the hard carts. As the road rounded a small hill and traversed a rather steep valley, Jacob noticed what looked like a camp down at the bottom of the ravine. It was unlike the camps we had passed thus far. The camp was located amid dirt and rocks, and had very little vegetation growing around it. It was as if they had specifically looked for the most barren and withdrawn valley to set up camp and call it their own.

"What is that place?" he asked. "It is too far removed from the road to be a camp."

I knew what it was at first glimpse.

"It's not a camp. Not like these, that is," I said, gesturing at the roadside tents.

"Who lives down there?"

"Lepers."

Jacob recoiled from the edge of the road as if he had just noticed a snake at his feet.

"Don't worry," I said, "they are far enough away not to be a threat. We are in no danger of infection."

"They truly live there?"

"They are not permitted in or around the city," I explained. "They are, to everyone, dead and unclean, and can in nowise touch the things that are holy. The Temple, the city, the wells: they are all forbidden to a leper."

"Are they common here?"

"No more than at home," I said.

"You may choose not to believe this," Jacob said, his eyes showing a look of weary fascination that never left the camp below, "but I have never seen the disease. Have you?"

"Once, when I was training at the Temple, when I was young," I said.

"Forgive me," Jacob interrupted. "You trained in the Temple? To be a rabbi?"

"It was a long time ago."

Jacob gently shook his head and clicked his tongue. "You become more complex and difficult to understand every day. It seems that there is more to you than you let on."

"I did not choose my fate," I said. "I did not choose to lose my son."

"I am sorry, it is just . . ." Jacob couldn't find the words to finish. "Please, continue. The lepers . . . you were saying . . . ?"

"We had taken a trip to the hills north of the city. It was well known that there was a colony of lepers living in the mountain caves there. It was there we learned and saw, many for the first time, this awful sight. It was horrible. Words cannot describe it. A worse plague could come upon no man. It begins with the hair turning white. What doesn't fall out is spotty and coarse, like an animal's. Then, the parts of the skin that are thin or exposed—the eyelids, the nostrils, the cheeks, the lips—fall off, or at the least become swollen and raw. The skin becomes as scales, and the joints of the fingers and toes are worn away, bare to the bone; or, if not bare, are gnarled and crusted with blood and other secretions. It is, as I said, the most utterly destructive of all of God's plagues given to men."

Jacob's wide eyes told of his revulsion as he listened to my candid description of the most despised men and women in all the world.

"Is there no cure?" he asked.

"None that is known," I said. "Some priests and physicians try special ointments or baths, or other fabled remedies. But they are just that: stories and vain hopes. To tell you the truth, there are not many who care for them. To the world they are dead. Even to their families, they can never return."

As we spoke, a man came walking along the road and bowed in greeting before beginning down the hill. Jacob reached out to stop him.

"Do not go down there," Jacob said. "They are lepers."

The man smiled. "I know. I minister to them."

I could see that he carried with him a basket of food and several skins of water.

"Do you not fear becoming one of them?" Jacob asked.

"Afraid? No. They are my people," he said. "I was a leper once, like them."

His words were obviously a lie. He looked healthy, his skin showed no marks or blemishes, and he walked and moved without the slightest show of pain.

"Impossible," I said. "There is no cure."

"Aaah," he said. "But there *is* one cure."

From below, several of the lepers noticed our caravan and began to climb the side of the mountain and approached closer to the road. "Tell Him that we are here!" some of them cried out. "Tell Him not to forget us!"

At one of the nearby camps of pilgrims a cry went out that the lepers were coming up. Immediately there were a dozen men and children standing at the road, throwing rocks at the lepers who had moved toward the top. Many of the lepers retreated back to their caves and camp.

"What do they mean, 'Tell him'?" Jacob asked the "cured" leper. "Who are they talking about?"

"Word has reached them that He has returned to the city," he said, "and they do not want Him to leave again without visiting them. It has been over a year since they have seen Him."

"Who?" I asked. "Who is here?"

The man looked at me strangely. "Are you new to this country?"

"We are Jews from the coasts of Africa," Jacob offered.

"Then you haven't heard of Him, or seen His following?"

"Whose following?" I asked again.

"Jesus," he said. "He is Shiloh; He is the Branch of David. He gives sight to the blind, heals the sick, and cures all manner of disease."

"Including leprosy?" I asked.

He pulled up the sleeves of his robe and showed me his hands and arms, all the while smiling gently at my disbelief. "Including leprosy."

His skin was as smooth as any man's. There were no scars, no marks, no discoloring evident of new skin growth. His skin was a healthy olive color. I could see no trace of leprosy or of any healing of the feared disease for that matter.

"What does that prove?" I asked. "Anyone could claim he had been cured and then show a healthy arm or back as proof. What you say is impossible."

"What is impossible for God?" he said, still smiling gently.

I had heard of wise men—healers who could treat small afflictions, or remedy an open sore or blister, or even stem the bleeding of a wound or cut; but what this man was talking about bordered on a miracle which, though I had to admit was possible, I found unlikely.

"Can he cure old age, as well?" I asked, pleased with my jesting remark.

"You are not a believer?" he asked.

"There is little left to believe in," I said.

The man smiled, much as I had a second before. "But there is always something, small as it may be. You may even have to look long and hard, but there will always be something to believe in."

I admired the man's faith, naive and faulty as it may have been, and reached into my bag, producing a couple of denarii. "Here, buy some bread and meat for your friends."

He accepted them with sincere appreciation.

"May God bless you for your generosity, and on your journey," he said.

I thought of the nightmare I'd had this morning, and many nights before that. "I'd settle for an end to the punishment."

The man touched his forehead as if to say, "As you wish," and then started the descent down the hill. When he was far enough away not to hear us speaking, Jacob asked, "What did he mean by 'Shiloh' and 'the Branch'?"

"Has it been so long since you have seen the inside of a synagogue that you have forgotten the meaning of these words?"

"About as long as you," Jacob said. "Not all of us were schooled to become rabbis."

I tried to smile at his attempt at levity. "They are titles given to one who will free our people, prophecies of a redeemer. It is a foolish hope against hope. It is nothing," I said.

The sheik drove the caravan on without rest over and around the mountains of the countryside. The closer we came to the city the more numerous and densely arranged the pilgrims' camps became. I questioned why there was such a multitude outside the city until we came over the hill and saw for ourselves the city gates. The valleys surrounding the city were an ocean of people, gently swaying to their own ebb and flow as hundreds and thousands waited to pass through the gates.

It was here that many of us parted from the caravan. Sheik Ibn-Farukh continued on to the caravansary just north of the city to conduct his business before moving on to the lands north and far east. Thanks were expressed and wishes for health and prosperity offered as we made our way down the hill to join with those below and wait for entrance into the Great City.

CHAPTER 8

Jerusalem is a city surrounded by high walls and is accessible only through a handful of gates. These entryways, guarded and regulated by the city officials, were seldom without a crowd of people wanting either to get in or get out. During a celebration or feast the waiting became much, much worse.

It took us three hours to reach the tax collectors at the entrance. Because we had nothing but tents and clothes, we passed through easily and with minimal tribute. But the sight that greeted me inside caused me to pause and wonder; in a sobering instant I knew why so many were camped beyond the walls.

If the city was to hold another soul, I was sure the walls must come down to accommodate it. In every direction, down every street, every courtyard, anywhere they would fit, men and women—many with their animals—were all in continual motion. We were pushed through and swept up in the river of people along the streets. A wave of nausea suddenly washed over me as the smells and confusion of the city overwhelmed my every sense. A look from Jacob told me he was feeling the same way.

"Come," I said after a moment, feeling slightly better as my senses slowly adjusted to the mayhem around me. I led him through the streets of the great Hebrew metropolis and center of the Jewish world.

Jews from every caste and country filled the streets as they made preparations to celebrate the Passover. There were Jews from Babylon and Persia, adorned in fine velvet and silk; others from the mountains, clad in tunics made of goat hair; and every class imaginable in between.

Fortunes were being made at the shops and posts that pushed into the streets, and as was common with crowds such as these, thieves flocked in from anywhere and everywhere, lying in wait to prey upon the weary religious travelers.

"I have never seen such numbers all gathered in one place," Jacob commented as we pressed through.

"Rome has good reason to fear us," I confided to my friend. "If Israel were to unite, no nation in the world could defend against it."

Jacob nodded. "They are only looking for one to lead them."

I clutched my bag tightly, and together we were carried along the narrow streets scarcely wide enough for three or four men, but crowded at least seven or eight men deep, pulsing, as it were, to the heartbeat of the city.

As we neared Jerusalem's upper city, the crowds thinned a little. Most of the homes here were new, built in the recent time of prosperity, but some were at least a hundred years old and were, by some miracle, still standing. One could travel a thousand miles in a few steps along the streets of the upper city. Here, the wealthy from the vast stretches of the world found residence and imported the features and feel of their distant lands and cultures. Walled gates, some two or three stories high, protected and enclosed the spacious courtyards and gardens with their fountains and private wells. Beyond the artistic buffers visible to passersby towered the palatial homes of the rich. Occasionally we would pass an open gate and were given a peek at the wealth and breadth of the inequality that fractured and divided people of the city.

"Where are the merchants?" Jacob asked. "With the money here, I would think the streets would be filled with those eager to make some real wages."

I shook my head. "Travelers and merchants find few occasions to visit here," I explained. "Money is to be made from the poor, those easily divorced from their meager earnings. Many of these homes belong to the priests and their families. They can live according to Jewish law, but also enjoy the riches and splendor Rome has to offer."

"You once lived here, then?" Jacob asked.

"No," I said. "Deborah did though—raised here her entire life. Her father was a traveling merchant and fared well enough to afford a home on the hill."

"Very well, indeed," Jacob commented.

"From the roof of their house you could see most of the city below, and even a corner of the Temple."

"Does she still live with them?"

"Who?"

"Her mother and father."

I shook my head. "My son informed me of their passing."

"It's hard to lose one's family," he said, and I knew that, in part, Jacob understood.

We walked streets that appeared at the same time familiar and foreign to me. Jacob asked question after question, inquiring about everything—from the history of the city to points of the Law and if they were enforced differently or with greater emphasis being so close to the Temple. But I was less than insightful, and he drew no more than a few words from me. I was preoccupied with memories I had almost forgotten, being away so long.

I remembered moving to the city with my family while at the end of my youth. We had lived in Jerusalem a full month before I first saw her. When I had made some friends from my schooling in the synagogue, we all ventured to the upper city to walk the roads of the rich and dream of fabulous wealth and daring adventures, as young men were prone to do. I was seventeen at the time and believed I had the whole world at my fingertips. Then in one awestruck moment I saw her, and I knew that my life was far from complete. I sensed that the part of my young life that was lacking would not be filled with anything or anyone else but her.

She was the most beautiful girl I had ever seen. Leading a cart from shopping in the marketplace with a woman who could only have been her mother, she walked right past us without even an acknowledgment of our raucous presence.

"Who is that?" I asked after she had passed. "Do any of you know her name?"

Every one of them did, and a couple of them even laughed at the naive question.

"Her name is Deborah," one of them said.

"But 'Shellfish' fits her better," said another, and they all laughed. Later I learned why.

Deborah was about the prettiest girl in all the city and had been the object of desire for many a young suitor. Despite their many attempts to negotiate her hand in marriage, none of them had been able to win her heart. The custom was that a father could compel a daughter to marry whomever he chose, but Deborah's father refused to require her to marry anyone she did not wish to. For this, I was told, her father was criticized by the other men of the city. "Shellfish," I learned, was the name she was called beyond earshot because it was said she had a hard outer shell and was to all men untouchable. But they were all wrong. I had only to prove it.

In addition to her beauty, Deborah was endowed with a fierce will, and stubbornness to match. When I first possessed the courage to stop her and introduce myself, she did not wait long enough to even hear my name. But she was not the only stubborn child in Jerusalem, and I refused to give up. Our early courtship consisted of my undying persistence in attempting to talk with her, and her refusal ever to listen. My friends teased me and ridiculed my seeming madness for her, but they could not understand. I had been smitten that first day I saw her and I knew that no other woman would do. If Deborah would only have me, I would stop at nothing to make her my wife.

Several months later, she consented to let me walk her home from the marketplace. Over the next few months, the buds of friendship blossomed and matured into a deeply profound respect and love for each other. Later, the decision was made, a bride-price negotiated, and the betrothal ceremony performed. After a year, we were married.

Now, nearly forty years later, we remained husband and wife only because I lacked the resolve to end it. Or was that not it at all? Could Jacob be right? Was there still some love there?

I abruptly stopped walking. Jacob had been talking to a deaf ear, but stopped too, and his gaze followed mine to a gated house and yard.

"Is that it?" he asked.

There it was. Deborah's house. And inside, my daughter. My Hannah. My feet felt like stone weights, and I could not discard the thought that this was all a mistake. What was I doing here? What had I expected? Jacob had been right to question my desire to return. What good could possibly come of it?

Jacob motioned to the end of the street. "Don't worry. I won't go far." I felt a quiver deep inside my old frame but nodded and continued on.

The house was large by most standards. Compared to its neighbors, though, it looked modest and from a simpler time that had all but passed away. The low, thick stone wall that enclosed the estate was dark and stained with a hundred years of standing watch. The heavy gate door was unlocked, and I stepped through slowly, as if expecting an attack by man or beast. But no attack came. Instead I was met by the small courtyard with its well-cared-for gardens along each wall; they seemed to invite me back. The temperature dropped as the deserts of Judea and the dusty city streets were left behind and replaced with the colors of a mountain oasis. The air was filled with the sweet fragrances of the tended flowers and vines that dressed the gardens.

The house was just as I remembered it. It stood as a memorial to superior craftsmanship and masonry, lost now to the fancy designs and ornamental whims of the rich. This was a house to stand the stress of time. Like the outside wall, the stones that constructed the house were dark with age but looked to be in good repair. I expected no less, knowing the fierce determination of their owner. Great oaken rafters overreached the walls as they supported the cement roof where summers were spent relaxing in the cool of the night. I had a sudden yearning for those days long dead and walked on.

The shutters were open, and from a draped window I could hear the scuffle of a busy kitchen as preparations were made for the Passover meal. It had been many years since I had really thought on the Passover. Celebrated each spring during the month of Nisan, the Passover was a special commemoration of our forefathers' delivery out of the cruel hands of Egypt. It was a time to remember God's promise to His children: "I will pass over you, and the plague shall not be upon you to destroy you, when I smite the land of Egypt."

I could not help but be reminded of the first Passover Deborah and I shared. We had been married almost eight months and still there was no sign of a child. Oh, how we wanted children. Raised ourselves as only children, we both wanted a large family and were eager to begin. But almost a year had passed, and our hopes waned with it. I offered prayers and sacrifices at the Temple before and after my studies, but still the ears of heaven were stopped to our pleas. That first Passover, when we set an empty place for Elijah, the guest who is expected but will come unexpectedly, we both secretly wished for a child to fill that place instead. It was a prayer that would go unanswered two more years. And when it was finally answered, a cruel God would deny our happiness once more and forever.

I felt an angry wave swell up inside, and I was forced to stop and breathe deep to quiet the powerful feelings.

I could smell the unleavened bread baking, masking the sharp odor of the bitter herbs that had already been prepared; above them all was the aroma of the paschal lamb, roasting slowly to tender perfection. Despite the normally inviting smells, my nerves were twisted and I felt sick to my stomach.

I reached out to knock at the door, but my hand hesitated and faltered, making only slight contact. It was a weak, embarrassing tap on the wood as my hand fell away. A long moment passed. Had they heard me? I feared my pathetic knock had blended with the other noises of the house, and I raised my hand to try again when the door opened.

A young man stood in the open doorway.

"May I help you, stranger?"

He was tall, almost my height, and I noticed the build of his shoulders and his strong arms and hands. He had the look of a craftsman about him; perhaps he worked in wood or leather. Complementing his size was an expression of kindness, even for a stranger that came on this busy eve of celebration. Was this the man who had taken Hannah to wed?

"Good traveler," he said again. "May we help you?"

My mouth opened but no words came out. What was I to say? Announce myself as his father-in-law? Say that this was my family? That I had returned after so long an absence? I had not planned for his greeting. It was supposed to be Deborah at the door. I had not anticipated the need for a proper introduction. Here was a stranger. And at the same time a son.

I could not find the right words, or any words, for that matter, and I could see in his eyes that his good feelings were giving way to suspicion. He looked back, over his shoulder, as if to ask for help.

"What is it, Matthias?" a soft voice called from within. No sooner had the words been spoken when there came a clang as an iron skillet dropped to the stone floor. Matthias took a step back as a hand rested on his arm.

It was Deborah. My wife.

The years had been good to her. Though her hair was now gray and her skin was beginning to show the wrinkled effects of time, I believed she was still as beautiful as on the day I had first spied her. But now, just as on the day she left, there was no warmth or a smile, only suspicion.

From one of the interior rooms I heard a sweet but tired voice ask, "Is it him?"

Deborah didn't look away but called back, "You need your rest, Hannah." Then to Matthias, "See that she stays in bed. She must not get up now that the pains have begun."

We stared at each other for what seemed like an hour, but could have been no more than a quick moment. As we stood there, the drafty silence fanned a fire of feelings I had hoped I would be able to set aside for Hannah's sake. They were too strong.

"Your husband comes home, and you have not so much as a greeting or welcome?" I said, in a voice as cold as Deborah's look.

"Welcome, husband," she said. There was no welcome in her words, but she opened the door, stepping to one side so I could enter.

Memories of the house returned immediately, as if thirty years had not passed. The house was built in an open style and had a central, spacious living quarter furnished with brightly colored rugs and wall tapestries. Above, a sometimes-open section of the ceiling and roof provided plenty of natural light for the house; today it illuminated a large wicker mat in the center of the room with place settings for the Passover meal. On either side of the room were wooden doors, and behind one of them, I knew, was my Hannah.

I motioned my head toward the closed room. "Was that . . . ?"

"Matthias," Deborah said. "Hannah's husband."

"I thought as much."

"He is a good husband to her," she said.

"Do they live here with you?"

Deborah nodded. "He is a carpenter. He just opened a small shop in town. Things are difficult for them right now. Work for a single carpenter is scarce in the city."

I understood the limitations placed on one man to find enough work and at a price to support himself and his home.

"He would do better in the country," I said. "Trade skills are always of more use in the smaller towns and villages."

"They know. I think they plan to make a move soon. They would have already except . . ."

"Except you don't want them to go."

"She's my only daughter," she said.

"Mine too."

Deborah held my stare as she wondered what exactly I was trying to say. She skillfully changed the topic of conversation.

"We have no room prepared for you," Deborah said at last. "I did not expect you."

"Through all else, she is my daughter," I said, my tone more critical than I had meant it to be.

"She will be pleased to see you."

"She is well?" I asked.

She nodded. Silence. We both looked away. Finally Deborah said, "Am I to say that it is good to see you?"

"You have never been good at lies," I said. "There is no need to speak them now."

She returned to the kitchen and began picking up the food she had dropped. I followed.

"Lexi told me about your parents," I said into the awkward silence. "They were good people."

"They were good to us," she said, staring off as if gazing out at a pleasant memory of them. "I do miss them from time to time. Mostly when I'm alone."

There was another stretch of silence between us. She did not even look over at me as she finished her work.

"Silence is unlike you," I said.

"Forgive me," she said, still looking away. "I do not know what to say. It's just, none of us thought . . ."

"That I would come?"

She shook her head. "That you still lived."

"Am I dead to you, then?"

She looked up. "I did not say that. Only . . ."

"Lexi brought me word a week ago . . ." I paused, trying to rein in my feelings and my tongue, but I couldn't. "On his way to Rome. *Rome*, Deborah. *Rome!* Have you taught them nothing?"

"I have taught them much," she said. "And without the support of a husband."

"Why has everyone forgotten that it was *you* that left *me?*"

"Why would I—"

"Stay? Hold the reprimand. Lexi already delivered it. He has already expressed the way all of you feel because you do not approve of my actions."

"The fight is still the same," Deborah said. "Nothing has changed. You are the same as the day we left."

"But you are not," I said. "A disturbing strength and boldness have crept into your words."

"I have had to be strong. The world is not an easy place for a mother and three children alone."

"You had your parents' house, and their money. It could not have been too difficult."

"Do you think it was easy to leave you?" she asked with considerable force. "You make it sound like I wanted to."

"But you did, didn't you?"

"No."

"I don't believe it," I said, and I didn't. "You were the one who first spoke of leaving. It was you who took the children away from their home."

"And should I have left them with you? You didn't love them, you couldn't care for them. You were too busy going out after dark with your friends. You were too busy trying to get yourself killed to provide for them. And you *know* it wasn't a hasty decision. You had been that way for years. I was upset and confused. I was scared to leave. Do you not think I wanted to come home many times? To return to you?"

"Then why didn't you?"

"The same reason you didn't follow us."

Deborah stepped outside and began tending to the chickens and other animals kept in the small barn in back. She kept talking as she worked.

"The way was hard," she said, "and the days and nights long. But as hard as the journey was, it was harder to face the questions when I returned. My parents tried to understand, but they couldn't. They couldn't know what it was like to be looked down upon in disgrace. I was a woman without her husband. Many thought I was widowed, and I had several proposals for marriage. Can you know the shame and embarrassment I had to face, trying to explain why I could not accept their love and concern, why you had not joined me?"

"And what did you tell them?" I asked. "I want to know. What reason could you give?"

Deborah paused. "I don't know."

"So I was dead to you," I said.

"Living under the same roof for ten years you were not there when we needed you," she fired back. "At least here there was an abundance of love. My father became Alexander and Rufus's father and taught them the things you should have taught them. They learned the scriptures from him. They learned a trade from him. They learned to be men from him. And the love and support I needed, I received from them. And why? Why did you choose your fight over us?"

"Because I refused to live as a slave!"

She thrust her wrists out. "Do you see us in chains?"

I did not answer right away, but stepped to the wall and pulled back the leaves of the trees. I pointed at the Roman flags atop Antonia slapping in the wind.

"Not around your hands," I said, "but around your necks—and your hearts. Rome leads you where they want you to go, and you do what they tell you to do. You buy food and pay tribute with money bearing the face of their Caesar and their gods. And they enforce their laws with the sword. Antonia, built by our ancestors to defend our great city, is now theirs—a mighty stronghold, looking down on us even as we pray. You worship God only because they permit it."

"They leave us alone, for the most part."

"They are Israel's masters."

"No one applauds them," Deborah said. "Least of all me, but they have done much to improve life in the city . . . and elsewhere."

"Rome is nothing but an imposter, and unoriginal in all but matters of war and destruction," I shot back. "Their knowledge they stole from the Greeks; even their gods are not their own. And what is the cost of their benevolent leadership? Working as slaves in their mines, building their roads and canals. And when you have outlived your productive years, you furnish sport in their arenas. *Life?* We cannot even die when we choose."

Deborah took a deep breath and closed her eyes for a moment.

"You used to be so strong," Deborah said, showing now a soft composure. "What happened to your hope? Your faith?"

"*Faith?* Was I to continue dedicating my life to a God that could let them kill my son? What faith I had, I traded in to fight the battle you are unwilling to fight."

"There are those of us who have not given up. There are great teachers in the land again, some say prophets, who teach that patience and hope are yet required of us if we would be free. They say that the kingdom of God is at hand."

"The kingdom of God?" I said. "There is only the kingdom of Rome."

"No, no," she said. There was a strange, imploring look in her eyes. "The Lord has promised, and I believe we shall see it. These rabbis, the Lord speaks through them. He is preparing a great work. Vengeance is the Lord's. We are to love our enemies and let God punish those who do wrong."

"You have changed much since I saw you last," I said. "I did not think you to be foolish enough to believe such words. Who speaks such nonsense?"

"It is the truth," Deborah said. "I feel it. We are not to agree with them, or condone what they do that is wrong, but it is our duty to forgive, to let go of the offense and let God judge in the end. He speaks in parables, and the stories he tells are truly marvelous. His words carry with them such power and love. Hannah believes him to be . . ."

"Who, Deborah?"

"He is a prophet, Simon. If you could hear his words, feel of his spirit, you would believe. The Lord will deliver us. We look and wait—"

"The Lord? The Lord has forgotten us. We are left to fend for ourselves. If we are ever to be free it must be because we are willing to fight for that freedom at all costs."

"But not at the price of shedding innocent blood."

"No Roman blood is innocent!"

Deborah sat down, sighed, and looked away, but I continued, unable to quench my vengeful words.

"Israel has too long been the sheep waiting for the arrival of our Good Shepherd. And while we stand idly by, we are easy conquest for wolves, for every empire or self-proclaimed king. The soil is tainted with the blood of our ancestors. How many times have we been assailed and conquered, and those who were not fortunate enough to die marched from their lands as slaves, our city left a wilderness of briars and thorns."

"But we returned," Deborah said. "And with God's help, we rebuilt it bigger and stronger."

"Only because a new ruler *allowed* us to return."

"You would have us be slaves still?"

"But we still are. Why can you not see it? And nowhere is our God. Where is this Messiah? He waits and our enemies grow stronger. Every Hebrew child who studies the Law knows the prophecies. He should have been here by now. Where is He?"

"Do not tempt God," Deborah said. "It is a sin."

"Do not speak to me of sin!" I said. "Is it not a greater sin to wait and do nothing? Why can you not see that no one is coming to save us?"

"But you saw the star," Deborah said. "We both did. These days there are many who refuse to believe it."

"Always this talk of the star, this 'sign' that deliverance is nigh. Then where is He? Why has He not come to free us and save us from our enemies? I will tell you why—because we are a weak and broken people. The days of action seem to be all but past. My father knew what was needed. Did I ever tell you? When I was a boy, I followed him the day they stormed the palace and stripped Rome's ensign, their giant eagle, from its place atop the Temple, where Herod had positioned it. They tore it down and attacked it with axes, cutting it to pieces. I was so proud."

I paced as I spoke. "The Lord did not take down the eagle; men like my father did. Men who knew when and how to act. What would they say if they were here, to all this talk of waiting and doing nothing? There is only one way—fight back! Strike fast and strike hard, and victory will be ours. We will be our own saviors. Freedom is not to be found in the waiting, but in the doing. Action, swift and strong. It is the only way Israel will ever be free!"

Deborah looked up, her face tired and distant. "You fight, and blood is shed, and for what? Nothing is changed, except Rome tightens its grip."

I exploded in rage. "What would you have me do? Am I to forget what happened? What they did? I cannot, and until the stars fall from the heavens, I will not!"

"Thirty years have passed," Deborah said softly. "Has the time done nothing to ease your pain?"

"Time has given me nothing more than a thousand nights to relive that night: the cries, the images, vivid and relentless. Time does nothing to heal a wound this grievous."

"And fighting does?"

"It is the only balm that relieves the pain."

"Our children were infants when you ransomed our freedom from Roman bondage, and still you are the one held captive."

"You were not forced to watch . . . your child was not ripped from your arms."

"Yes," she said, "he was."

"Why are you determined to take even my hatred from me?" I asked.

"Why do you hold onto it?" she asked.

"Because it is all I have left!" I said. "God took Joshua, you took the others. My feelings are all I have left."

"No," she said, resisting my attempts to drag her down into my fight. "You were the one who removed yourself from everyone you knew and loved, including God. They were not taken. It was you that left."

"But you were not held helpless while they took him, and . . ." I turned away. "What had Joshua done to them? To God? Why did God cause this to happen?"

"I have heard that God makes it to rain on both the wicked and the righteous."

"Rain?" I could not believe what I was hearing! "It was not rain God delivered on us or on Joshua. It was death."

"What is it you want?" she asked.

"What do I want?" I spun around to face her. "What do I want? I want every last Roman dead!"

"Lower your voice."

"I will *not* be quiet! Nor will I be questioned and spoken to in this manner by my own wife."

"Killing them will not bring Joshua back." Tears welled up in Deborah's strong eyes. "Do you believe that I do not think of him, of that night? When I set the table for meals, am I not reminded that I have lost a son? And not only a son, but a husband also."

She paused. "There is room in my home, and my heart, for sadness and grief," she said. "But not for anger and hatred."

I felt my chest constrict. In my anger, I had no sympathy for her lack of courage—not fifteen years ago when she left, and not today. Nothing had changed, and nothing ever would. She still chose not to understand. Jacob had been right to warn me. Jacob was always right about everything.

"It was a mistake to come," I said, and left.

CHAPTER 9

We had finished the afternoon meal hours ago, seated at an outside table amid the chaos of the city all around us, and still Jacob listened with a sympathetic ear.

"Why does she not understand?" I said. "How can she accept Israel's fate so easily? Does not the Lord require us to do our part? God didn't build the ark; God didn't offer up Abraham's son; God didn't lead us out of Egypt. In every case, men were compelled to do their part. Is today any different? Do we not have hands? Can we not think, and reason, and plan? She and all those like her are wrong. Freedom can only be attained by action. Faith *is* action."

Jacob leaned back and smiled as if remembering some pleasant thought.

"I was twelve when my brother left home," he said. "He wasn't much older at sixteen but thought he was a man. Maybe he was. I remember him being quick to anger, even before we lost our father. Our father's death hit him hardest. He was the oldest and closer to Father than I was. When he died, my brother began picking fights with everyone—me, my mother, the other children in the city. It didn't seem to matter who he hit. My mother was always apologizing for his actions, and despite her loving attempts to correct her wayward and angry son, he continued to fight and strike back at the world. In many ways, you have always reminded me of him."

Jacob paused in his story. I had never heard him speak of his family like this. For a moment at least, I forgot my own troubles and listened.

"Then," Jacob continued, "he left home at sixteen, though it was more like fleeing home. One afternoon he and one of his friends waited atop the city walls and threw rocks at a small troop of soldiers as they approached. The soldiers gave chase, but they were two boys in a city of thousands. They escaped, and from that day forth my brother was changed. He was different from having lashed out at what he thought was the cause of his pain. In the days and weeks that were to follow, my brother organized more attacks, recruiting others who felt as he did. The stones grew larger and more numerous. In the streets they struck, and in the hills outside the city. In the end, we all knew he couldn't stay. If the authorities could not catch him, they would settle for his family. He left a short while later, traveling to Jerusalem with one of his friends. I have not seen him since that day, though I think of him often. He knew at sixteen what I did not learn until much later: that freedom is had at the end of the road of struggle, that, as you say, faith is action."

"And you believe he still lives here?" I asked.

"I know so," he said. "Or so I did almost a year ago. We have sent a few letters to each other over the past six or seven years. By the largest of coincidences, a merchant traveling from Crete to Jerusalem stopped in Apollonia and noticed my pendant as I was working at the docks. He had seen another like it and asked me about it. As fate would have it, he knew my brother and offered to bring word to him. He has passed letters across the distance as often as his travels took him to the north of Africa. In my brother's last letter he mentioned a small meeting house, hidden and forgotten, deep in the tanner's quarter."

"That is quite a story," I said.

"I cannot stop thinking of it. I've said it before, and I know you feel differently about it, but I believe our lives were spared—and on the eve of news that would bring us to Jerusalem. There cannot be any coincidence. There is a great design that brings us here: you to your daughter, and me to my brother. But, then, you do not believe there is a higher plan at work, do you?"

Jacob's last words were of some levity, but they were a continuation of the talk we'd had on the mountainside two weeks ago.

"Again with the blind talk of interventions and plans and things meant to be," I said. "You speak of lessons learned when you were young. I have a story of my own. When I was a young man of twenty years, I was about to embark on one of life's most treacherous journeys without the support or guidance of either of my parents. I was going to be a father. I tried to tell myself that their passing was part of a plan, designed by deity and laid out with a higher purpose. But I could not understand it. My mother had wanted to be a grandmother more than anything else in the whole world. Even though she had only one child, she would tell me that she had enough love for ten or more."

"She never saw him born?"

"She died the winter before," I said, feeling the pain and loss weigh down my heart even further. "They both did. And still I wanted to believe there was a reason for being left alone as I began my new life as a father."

I felt my chest tighten as I prepared for the words that were to come next. "But when they . . . took Joshua, I questioned God. In the months that followed, I would doubt that God had a plan at all. How could His plan include the killing of innocent children? Maybe it was all chaotic chance. Maybe God wasn't in control. Maybe there was no grand design. Maybe there was no God."

"You don't really believe that," Jacob said.

"I wish I did."

Jacob shook his head slowly. "To believe that way stands in the face of all reason."

"But that was not the God I worshiped. I did not know this God. Maybe I never had known Him."

"It is the same God."

"Who is God?" I said. "Why does He keep His silence?" I waved my hands over the crowds of Jews come from every corner of the world to worship at the celebration. "Does He not hear our prayers? Where is He? Deborah waits for deliverance; Israel waits. We are running out of time. Day by day, year by year, century by century the powers of the world oppress and confine us, carving up our land like butchers, and destroying those who resist. If we wait much longer there will be no Israel to set free."

Jacob stood, stretched the long day from his back, and leaned upon a wall. "We have outlasted them all," he said with visible pride. "The Assyrians, the Babylonians, the Persians, the Greeks, and we will outlast the great Roman Empire."

"Then why fight? If all that is required is submission and patience, if we and our children's children will live to see Rome fall without any contribution made by us, why do we fight?"

Jacob became serious in his language and manner. "Because we are the chosen people of God, and with that privilage and blessing come great responsibilities equal to that call. We are not weak; we are a strong people. Because we are, we *have* to fight; we *have* to survive."

"I have never heard you speak this way before, Jacob," I said. "I did not know you believe God speaks or cares for us anymore."

"I fight not in spite of a silent God; I fight to petition His aid and prove my readiness and worthiness of being set free."

I sat there silent and confused. I had never heard Jacob speak with such passion and conviction before. But as his words settled on my mind, I thought I understood what he was saying. I had never heard him speak of scripture, of attending synagogue, or heard him utter a single prayer. But it was clear to me now that all along his fight *was* his prayer.

My appreciation for my longtime friend grew in that moment, but was replaced almost immediately with ill-feelings. It seemed so simple for Jacob. He had no doubts about his course of action or his faith, while I was beset with questions I could not yet put into words. And at the heart of the questions was an emptiness that frightened me to answer. It seemed as if I was aware of some great, distant pain, but as long as I didn't acknowledge it, it wouldn't hurt. But I knew that wasn't true, and all at once, I knew there was something I needed to do. A single task remained to be done while there was still light and before I left the city, though my most inward parts begged me not to do it.

Without explanation, I sprang to my feet and cut through the river of people to the lower city, pushing some out of my way. Jacob scrambled to gather his bag and follow. With more and more force and anger, I plunged myself into the old quarter. The sweet smells of food and wine, prepared for sale and profit in the marketplace, quickly gave way to the odor of the poor. The mixed smell of decaying garbage, livestock sweating in the sun, and dozens of Passover meals cooking for the week's celebration was a foul combination. These streets were a breeding ground for disease and violence.

Even in full daylight one did not feel entirely safe. Secretly I would have welcomed an attack by a street malefactor or drunken soldier— anything to serve as an outlet for my inflamed feelings. My breath came in short puffs and my hands began to shake. I balled them into fists to focus my strength.

The long years melted away as I wound my way through the streets. Another lifetime ago I had known them well, and I was surprised at how little the houses and courtyards had changed in thirty years. Everywhere there was the stench of poverty. Where was the land flowing with milk and honey? Did God's promise to the children of Israel only apply to those with riches to buy it? We passed a few children playing down deserted alleys, chasing each other and giggling, happy in their ignorance of life and the world around them. My heart felt heavy and without hope for them. They would grow up knowing only struggle and servitude. I could not bear the thought, and my quick pace became a run.

At a cold and dirty little house I stopped. I reached out and put my hand on the mud-bricked wall. Pieces flaked off. It was in obvious neglect, and not destined to remain standing for much longer. But it was not abandoned; there were sounds and smells coming from inside.

"What is this place?" Jacob asked.

"Joshua was born here," I said. I knelt there, sifting through the years, trying to remember my life before that night. "It is difficult to recall the sunshine that used to warm the sand, or the sounds of a younger life that used to fill the air." I was only half aware I was speaking aloud. "We were poor, but the streets used to be happy with life." I turned around and nodded my head toward a small cluster of houses. "There used to be a common area there. Deborah would spend the day there with him. The grass was hot, and the shade was scarce, but, oh, how they loved to play there."

I moved on, wandering through the streets, perhaps not entirely aimlessly. Down a quiet alley, I stopped. I knelt and began smoothing out a patch of sand. Like flashes of lightning against a black sky, the images of that night blinded my senses; and sounding loudly in my ears were the cries of my firstborn. For a moment I felt tears pushing from the back of my throat, but I would not let them out.

Jacob had followed but now stopped a few feet behind me. "Is this where it happened?" I did not need to answer. It was tangible. The bricks and stones still remembered. This was holy ground, sanctified by innocent blood.

"Thank you for bringing me here," Jacob said, after several long moments had passed.

"I didn't come here for you," I said, still smoothing. "As I said before, I need to be sure. I have seen what I have given up, what I have traded in for the fight. I need to know if what I am doing is right. I need to know if the life I am living is still worth the struggle."

As I said the words, I knew it was. Events had been set in motion thirty years earlier, on that very spot, that would not end until my last breath was spent. I took a small handful of sand and rubbed it through my hair and on my face, washed and anointed by the surety of what I was doing. Sacrifices had to be made for the greater good, and though Deborah would never understand me, I was fighting for her, and Hannah, and the grandchild now I knew I might never see. My commitment was renewed. There was no doubt, there would be no more hesitation, and there was no going back.

Jacob approached and reached out a hand. I could hear the concern in his voice. "You promised to show me the Temple this day," he said, sensing that there was no reason to remain at this hurtful place. "The day is waning."

"But we should visit your brother."

"Later," he said. "Besides, if he is half as popular with Rome as he reports in his letters, I think it would be best to seek him out after dark."

"You are a good friend," I said, standing to join him.

"I am your only friend," he teased, trying to lighten the mood. "Come."

* * *

Between the lower city and the Temple lay the famed Jerusalem marketplace. Open stalls and booths, filled with goods and services tailored to meet every need, solicited our attention and our money. From the first light of morning to the dimming twilight hours, the pounding of hammers and mallets belonging to wood and metal craftsmen rose only slightly above the din of raucous haggling as money, goods, and livestock exchanged hands. Down side alleys, hidden in shadow, painted women whispered promises of love at a fair price to the weary and lonely traveler.

"Has Jerusalem always been this way?" Jacob said, shouting to be heard over the noise.

I wanted desperately to blame this moral decline on Rome, but I couldn't, so I only nodded regretfully and we pushed on.

As we broke free of the merchants' paradise, a blast from the Temple trumpets filled the city, calling the crowds to the traditional prayer at the sixth hour. But no one paused; no one fell to their knees. A few religious pilgrims were startled briefly but quickly returned to their business.

Where was the religious zeal they pretended to have? Where was their faith in observance of the small and simple points of the Law? Was the burden too great to pause and remember the Lord their God they professed to believe in? I, too, was startled, not by the fanfare, but by the hour that it represented. I checked the position of the sun.

"What is it?" Jacob asked.

"I had imagined the events of this day would be vastly different than they have been," I mused. "Now the day is only a few hours from being over, and I have neither reconciled with my family nor seen the daughter whose call I answered."

"You may yet see them again," Jacob offered. "You have only just arrived. Tomorrow may dawn another opportunity. Only believe."

We rounded the corner, and there before us towered the fortress and the heart of Judaism: the mighty Temple of Herod. The nearly completed structure looked just as I had always imagined it.

"God be praised," Jacob said, his breath taken away at the sight. "I did not think I should ever see something as beautiful as the Temple even from afar, but to be this close to it, to feel its magnitude, its power. I have never seen anything so magnificent . . . so . . ." His words were swallowed up in wonder.

"But this is only the outer shell," I said. "We have yet to see the Temple itself."

We approached the south side of the Temple complex. Stretched out almost its entire length was the outer wall of the Temple meeting hall. Here, I suspected, was where the Jewish council—the Sanhedrin—met to discuss the Law and bring those accused of transgression to ecclesiastical justice. I pointed to either side of the hall at the two towers that stood at the corners of the wall.

"Those are the pinnacles of the Temple," I said.

"From up there one could see not only the Temple grounds but most of the city and surrounding country," Jacob marveled. "It must be a spectacular view."

"Very few are allowed to their roofs. The east pinnacle towers over the city and the Kidron Valley below. It's several hundred feet to the rocky floor below. One could fall and dash himself to pieces. But it is not for safety reasons they forbid it. To die so close to the Temple would require purification of the entire Temple Mount. The priests would not be pleased."

We joined the long lines that wound down the west stairs, over the viaduct, and around the base of the Temple. The lines contracted and relaxed as thousands pushed their way to the Temple Mount.

"Was the Temple completed when you were . . . when you left the city?"

"Parts of it," I said. "The Temple itself and some of the foundation, but not the colonnades and hall and porticoes all around it. It was functioning, but it looked nothing close to this."

"Then how is it you know so much about it?"

"My father," I said. "He loved the Temple. Construction began before I was born. From my earliest memories I can recall my father speaking of the Temple that was being built in Jerusalem. He was a priest by occupation, and news of this pleased him more than anything I can remember. When I was a child he would leave us for a week or two at a time and travel to Jerusalem to work on its construction. Later, we moved to be closer to the Temple. Some nights he would return to us dirty and smelling of dust and sweat, eager to tell my mother and me of its grandeur and beauty.

"The King, Herod, was liked only by those who had political power to gain from feigning an interest in him. Many doubted his intentions with the new Temple and were quick to criticize and monitor the progress. By some miracle, he decreed that over a thousand priests be trained in carpentry and masonry to assist in the work. My father believed himself blessed to be one of those thousand. His hands had never before known such hard work; when he came home at night, he would have to soak and bandage them. But never did I hear him complain. Just the opposite. He would thank God for his pain and pray for strength to carry on."

With a new eye I looked now at the walls and base foundation and wondered if I was looking at stones my father had helped shape and set.

"He must have been very proud to see its completion," Jacob said. "To behold this is to know that the Lord is God."

"When he closed his eyes for the final time, I knew he did," I said.

As we approached the gates, I could see what looked like heaps of old clothes and rags lining the Temple steps and outer wall. I was surprised that the priests would allow such filth to touch something so holy. As we neared and then passed by, I realized that the refuse was alive. The poor, the beggars, the sick and afflicted, all living in wretched poverty, took up their posts near the gates in hopes of alms and perhaps a miracle or two. My heart felt heavy as we passed by them. *Why is it that God is the last resort of the hopeless?* I thought.

The noise and chaos that assaulted us as we stepped through the gates rivaled that of the marketplace. Before us was a sea of people, filling the entire Temple square. And out of the middle of this sea rose the island which was the Temple. Jacob's questions were many at that instant, and I spent the next while discussing with him the purpose and history of the House of the Lord, filling in the gaps of what he did not already know.

We discussed the temple's role for our people; a vital element in the worship of the children of Israel, the first temple had been only a traveling tent during the times of Moses. It was here that sacred ceremonies and ordinances were performed for the benefit of man, regardless of the temple's permanence. It was here that God could visit and speak to his prophets and children. It was the most sacred place in all the earth. But once the children of Israel reached the promised land, it would take years to build a permanent structure. King David was the first to suggest construction of a house to the Lord, but it was his son, Solomon, who would make the dream a reality. We were proud of the fulfillment of that dream. Built of only the finest materials found in the world at that time, the Temple was a marvel, and an ensign to the world that the God of the Jews was not to be taken lightly. The Temple took only seven years to complete due to the efforts of thirty thousand Israelites, as well as the world's best craftsmen and metalsmiths. But the Temple of Solomon was not to stand forever, as it had been designed to.

Four hundred years later the Temple was destroyed by the Babylonian king, Nebuchadnezzar, before he conquered Israel and enslaved the nation.

"But the God of Israel would not be denied His House," I reminded Jacob. "The second temple was built after returning to Jerusalem under the rule of the Persian king Cyrus. It would remain a place of worship and sacrifice and even serve as a stronghold during the civil wars that would follow. About the time you and I were born, Herod had it destroyed and torn down to build this." I opened my arms to include all that he saw here that day.

Jacob looked around and was confused.

"But there are those of other cultures and faiths here," he said. "How can they, not being Jews, visit the Temple of our God?"

"We are standing in what is called the Court of the Gentiles. Anyone can stand on these stones and behold our architectural wonder and pay their respects with an offering or sacrifice. But it is the inner courts and beyond that are forbidden to outsiders."

I remembered an interesting component of the Temple structure, and now I led Jacob near the inner precincts. We stopped at the balustrade that surrounded the inner courts. The low, stone wall stood only about the height of a man and would not greatly deter those who wanted to pass through its many gates but for the inscriptions written on it. The statements were written in both Greek and Latin and Jacob had to push forward and lean in to read the words prohibiting foreigners from entering the sacred court grounds surrounding the Temple. With this warning was the promise that "anyone caught doing so will bear the responsibility for his own ensuing death." Jacob pulled back and looked at me with a look of surprise on his face. "Such a strong warning for the House of God."

"They are only words," I said, "but they seem to hold a great deal of power."

Jacob motioned to the wall. "What is on the other side?"

I pointed to where the wall opened up in a narrow archway. "That is the gate to the Court of Women, the farthest a woman may approach. Beyond their courtyard is the Court of the Israelites, and even beyond that is the Court of the Priests leading to the Temple. It is there that the sacrifices are prepared and offered. It is there that the prayers and faith of the people are sent heavenward in a thick cloud of smoke."

"May we see it?" Jacob asked.

I shook my head. "To enter even the Court of Women one must bathe in a mikveh."

"What is a mikveh?"

"A ritual cleansing bath," I explained. "We passed some below the steps to the Temple. It is not so much that the body must be clean to worship in the House of the Lord, but it is important that the spirit is. There is not time today to begin the ceremony. Perhaps another day."

Jacob nodded, but I doubted he had heard all of my words. He still looked to be drinking in the sights and sounds of this sacred destination for all Jews scattered throughout the world. His gaze rested on the golden ridges that lined the roof of the Temple. After a while he asked, "What is in the Holy of Holies?"

My lips thinned as I prepared to give my friend an answer he would not like.

"Nothing."

"It is empty?" Jacob asked in disbelief.

"What did you expect?" I said. "Did you think God would be in there?"

"I don't know what I expected to be in there," Jacob said. "I had heard that the Ark of the Covenant was housed there."

"The Ark hasn't been there for six hundred years or more."

"Then where is it?"

"Lost," I said. "Like our strength as a nation."

Jacob looked disappointed, and I regretted the manner in which I answered this last question. It was not my place to taint his experience with my doubts and cynicism. Though, I thought, nothing I had told him was untrue.

The ninth hour was approaching, and the Temple would soon shut down in observance of Passover. Long lines had formed at tables where temple officials weighed for exchange the only tender accepted by the priests for the temple tax and other sacred donations. A hundred merchants, shoulder to shoulder, manned crude and filthy stalls, bartering and selling sheep, rams, and goats to the wealthy for sacrifice at the temple altars. For the poorer pilgrims, those who could not afford the greater blessings, there were cages piled deep with doves. The air was scented heavily with incense to offset the smells of the sacrifices. It was a foul mix.

We left the inner courts and were walking toward the shaded colonnades when I spied them. My heart raced briefly in surprise. On the far side of the court, where the steps of Antonia spilled onto holy ground, stood a group of Roman soldiers, dressed in full armor and armed for battle. Through the masses of people, I saw others, over a dozen or more, spread throughout the Temple grounds, their very presence an ominous threat. *Our sanctuary,* I thought. *Our faith, our God—surrounded.* This was most unusual, even for Rome. Temple affairs were usually left to temple guards.

I slipped through one of the lines and bent the ear of a merchant to ask him the reason for such strong Roman numbers.

"For our protection," he said.

"Your protection?" I couldn't believe it. "Protection from who?"

"Madmen. Mad, I tell you," he said, continuing to conduct business as he spoke. "Last week a man came to the Temple claiming to be a prophet. He overturned all of our tables and set the animals free, mine included. I lost a week's worth of birds and lambs, and I never did recover all my money that was scattered. And when we tried to stop him, he took a whip from one of the stables and used it to drive us all back. It was madness. He was possessed of evil spirits. He called *us* thieves. Thieves—us—providing a sacred service. Do we not have the right to make a living? To provide food and a roof for our children? It was an outrage. And the temple guards did nothing." Every word was spoken with clear contempt. "They just stood by, and some even ran and shrank from the fight.

What are they good for? We have rights, you know. So we demanded that Rome keep the peace—"

Just then he was distracted and swore. Someone had knocked over one of his cages of doves and the latch had come undone. A few birds found their freedom and took flight to escape. Greedy hands, thrust from the crowds, tried to grab one or two, but obviously not with the intent to return them to their owner. I wondered, with more than a little disgust, if one could offer up a stolen sacrifice to the Lord. What had happened to our people?

"This is not a house of order," I said to Jacob as we walked away. "Money is traded here and swindled for. Money is the object of worship, not the Lord. But greed is not their only fault; it is merely an outward symptom of an inward disease."

"Perhaps you are too harsh with them," Jacob said.

"The Lord was right not to trust us to govern ourselves," I said. "At every turn, and for every circumstance, we need direction. These people live their lives performing rituals and ordinances but have forgotten the meaning and the reason for them. We were created and delivered by God as a people to be free, and even now His laws enslave us."

"But is not obedience better than disobedience?" Jacob asked.

"Are you a rabbi now?" I asked with sarcasm. "Perhaps you should take to a couch under the portcullis and lead a discussion with the other rabbis."

"I am just saying that if one does what one can, is that so bad?"

"But look at them. The Pharisees walk where they can be seen and profess their strict adherence to the Law and the oral traditions, yet they separate themselves from the common masses with their pride. And the Sadducees, with their claim to high office, have little compassion for the poor. And we must not forget the radical and militant Essenes. There are dozens more. And what have they brought Israel but contention, division, and hatred? Look at this . . . mess. There is much to say about obedience, but what can be said for unity? We are a divided people. That is why we are slaves. That is why we will always be slaves."

"You had best be careful," Jacob said, with a touch of levity. "Talk like that could free a nation."

"Perhaps," I said. "But what can one man do?"

Jacob looked longingly at the Temple towering over the wall of the court. "Sometimes one man can be the difference between victory and death."

A sudden cry for help, barely audible, rose over the irreverent babble, but it was loud enough for us to hear. Instinct and years of conditioning took over as I searched for the source. A second cry focused my attention on a far corner. Two Roman guards were having some difficulty containing a Hebrew man. The struggle was soon over, but then the cruel games began. One soldier held the man while the other began driving his fists into the victim's midsection. As I pushed through the crowd toward them, I saw that others had heard his cries for help too, but no one did anything except nervously turn their backs.

Jacob, who had followed, finally caught my arm as if to hold me back. "It is not our fight."

"Every fight is our fight!" I said, shaking off his grip.

"Against a dozen guards and soldiers, with a thousand more just a few feet away? That's not a fight, that's suicide," Jacob tried to reason with me.

The injustice of what I was watching triggered emotions that overcame me. "Is your cowardice stronger than your courage?" I did not mean those words to my friend, but I could not stop from speaking them.

"You're speaking foolishness," Jacob said. "You may be willing to die this day, but I am not. Listen to me, we can do nothing for him. You cannot save everyone."

"But we can save him!"

"Are you sure it's *him* you want to save?"

"What do you mean?"

"I have known you were in pain for years," Jacob said. "You fight because you hurt. And finally, I believe I understand why."

"You understand nothing! You do not know what it is like to lose a child."

"And you cannot know what it is like never to have had one," he said. "If I have ever been your friend, you will listen to what I have to say."

He always had been, and so I stayed.

"You see him everywhere, don't you?"

"See who?"

"The one you told me about. The soldier that killed your son. You see him in every uniform, you saw him in the face of that soldier in Apollonia, and you see him over there, beating on that man. You see him bearing every standard, and in the face of anyone owing allegiance to the Empire. Tell me that I am wrong. Tell me that you don't look for him in every company of soldiers we see."

His words gave me pause. "You're wrong," I said. "I stopped looking for him years ago."

"And what would you have done if you had found him?"

"Killed him."

"And then what? Would you have found healing with his death?"

"It is the only thing that matters."

"Killing him won't replace your son."

"Deborah said the same thing."

"Because it is true."

"I wish we had died on the *Vindicare!*" I spat. "At least I would not have to endure this preaching from a man I have known for twenty years. A man I thought to be like me enough to be my brother. You've lost your drive, you instinct to fight since then." The sounds of the man in pain continued to reach our ears, and I had heard enough from my friend. "You are either with me or against me. You have begun to sound like the others who speak of freedom but are not willing to fight for it."

"Do not do this," Jacob pleaded. "Not like this."

I looked over at the soldiers holding the man down. Every blow delivered with sadistic pleasure made my blood course, boiling, through my veins. Every hit he took felt like a strike against me, and I knew his pain and helplessness. But this time I was not helpless. "You may be willing to tolerate this abuse, but I cannot," I said, ripping my arm from his fingers and pushing my way through the crowds to rescue my Jewish brother.

Neither of the two guards noticed my approach until it was too late. My size and speed were to my advantage as I threw myself into the one inflicting the abuse. He couldn't brace himself in time, and my full weight knocked him into the wall. His head struck the stone wall, and he crumpled at its base.

The man I had saved scrambled to his feet and skittered away as a small crowd gathered around us to watch.

Behind me the sound of sharpened steel being unsheathed captivated my very being, and I spun around to face my armed attacker. Off in the distance, I heard an alarmed shout for more soldiers. Whatever I hoped to do, I knew I had to do it quickly.

But the Roman did nothing. There I stood, waiting for his strike, waiting for him to expose a flaw in his attack that I could prey upon, but he did nothing. He just stood there, sword ready.

Behind me the other soldier was coming to, and I understood the delay. In a few moments the fight would number two on one—a coward's fight. And then the others would arrive. But what did I expect? Rome knew nothing else. The dazed soldier struggled to his feet behind me, wiping the blood from his nose and mouth, slurring his curses through broken teeth. Something needed to happen, and it needed to happen soon. As trained as I was, I knew I was no match for two such men, armed as they were. I had to draw the soldier into the fight.

In my best Latin, I accused his mother of being the offspring of a desert dog and a baboon, but if he understood he did not react.

With all the speed my old body could generate, I turned quickly and drove my foot deep into the recovering soldier's solar plexis. His leather jerkin did nothing to protect him, and he again dropped to the ground.

Pockets of guarded cheers from the temple crowd sprung up all around, but I did not have the time to enjoy them or rally with them. The moment my back was turned, the second soldier made his move. I turned and sidestepped the cut I knew would be coming, but the blade was stopped. At my side appeared Jacob, who had used someone's walking stick as a staff to block the heavy sword. He smiled at me as if to apologize for taking so long, and then, with a skill all his own, beat back the surprised soldier.

From the crowd, a third soldier burst onto the scene. I reached down and took the sword from the soldier struggling for breath at my feet. I was trading blows with the newcomer when I noticed the crowd dispersing as a half dozen soldiers from the court pushed their way through to us.

"Jacob!" I yelled.

Jacob looked back and nodded. It was time to finish this.

At the soldier's next thrust I parried the blow down and stepped in close enough to see his jagged row of yellowed teeth and smell the years of rot on his putrid breath. My left fist connected squarely with the point of his nose, and I could see in his eyes the pain of shattering bone and cartilage. I hit him again, then, discarding my sword, reached around the back of his head with both hands, pulling his face down to meet my rising knee. He fell backward and landed, quite unconscious, atop his fallen friend.

Jacob was having similar success, and with a full swing of his makeshift quarterstaff, his Roman foe was felled to the ground. He stepped over the heaps of the mighty defenders of the Empire to join me. He was winded, as was I, but we were both proud of our little exhibition before the steps of the House of God.

"We must go," I said, and took him by the shoulder. Then, without warning, Jacob was shoved forward into the frightened crowds. I almost lost my balance with the jolt but immediately whipped around when I heard a woman scream. Jacob just stood there, his face etched with concern. Then he dropped to his knees before falling to his side, a spear buried deep in his back.

The crowds of people scattered away in all directions, leaving Jacob and me alone amid the bedlam of fear and panic. I collapsed beside him.

"Lie still," I told him, holding him from the ground as best I could.

"No . . ." Each word was a struggle. "You must go."

"I'll not leave you."

"Then Israel loses two men today," he said.

Jacob pulled from around his neck his stone pendant and pressed it to my palm, wet with his blood. I closed my hand around his.

"You must finish this. You have always been one to make a difference. Israel is already free." His words were a whisper now. "The Temple . . . it is beautiful, isn't it?"

He breathed his last, and his hand slipped from mine.

Seething with rage, I picked up the sword and attempted to run it through the first Roman to reach us. His breastplate deflected the mortal blow and left him instead with an enormous gash in his hip and side. I threw down the weapon, picked up Jacob's bag, and ducked into the mass of people, shedding my sheepskin coat to blend with the hundreds of others rushing toward the Temple gates. The courtyard resembled a stable even more as many of the sacrificial animals broke free of their corrals and cages, adding to the panic. By some chance, I made it to Solomon's Porch and was pushed through the east gate with many of the others.

Beyond the gate I quickly crossed over the Kidron Valley and found cover at the base of the Mount of Olives. At my back the sun was low in the sky, and I could feel the weight of the day heavy on my heart and my eyes. God was nothing if He wasn't cruel. What had I done to anger him? First Joshua, and now Jacob, and so many I could not even count in between. *Why does He let me live when those I care for, those I love, are needlessly killed?*

I unclenched my fist and looked closely at Jacob's family seal. Justice would be had. A life for a life. No, ten—a hundred Roman lives for his. From where I stood Antonia towered high above the city wall, its standards dancing in the wind. "I will fight," I pledged softly, draping Jacob's stone seal over my head, "until every soldier, every tribune, every citizen of the Empire comes to fear and honor the name of Israel."

At the Temple gate a few soldiers appeared. Their search was now expanding outside the city. People would be stopped and questions would be asked. There were many gardens at the base of the mount that provided countless places to hide. But they were popular refuges from the late afternoon heat. The fewer who saw me, the better.

Veering off the road, I found a perfectly secluded recess behind a large almond tree. I could not be seen from the road, the rocky valley, or the hills above me. Confident that I could remain there unseen as long as I needed, I leaned back and looked toward the heavens. Wisps of clouds were beginning to take color from the evening sun. Many chaotic thoughts sliced through my mind, and I made no attempt to control them. I knew that I could not. I was so confused. Our success at Apollonia, Lexi's visit, Hannah's news, and now Jacob's death.

None of it made any sense to me. Pieces of a puzzle that were scattered and their meaning lost to me. The only thing I was sure of was that Jacob's death would not go unanswered.

The grass was soft and the shade a welcome respite from the heat. A pain throbbed wildly behind my ears. I closed my eyes, intending to rest them for only a few moments, to rethink, to regroup.

Instead I slept for hours.

CHAPTER 10

I awoke abruptly to the sound of an approaching army. The stars were bright, and I was disoriented for a moment. My first thought was that I was dreaming again, forced to replay those unwanted memories in the recesses of my mind. But I quickly shook off the sleep and scrambled up the hill to glimpse the road. I watched in horror as at least a hundred Roman soldiers exited the city north of the Temple by the gate nearest Antonia and marched across the stone bridge toward me. I felt a surge of energy fill every recess of my body.

Somehow they have found me, I thought. However unlikely or impossible it seemed, a scout must have discovered me as I slept, and now an army was closing in for the kill. My chest could barely contain my pounding heart as they neared, but I did not panic. To run would only hasten my fate; instead, I began listing my possible courses of action, which were few indeed. Then I noticed Temple guards marching with them. Did the night deceive me? I looked more closely at the militia and saw a man dressed in the priestly robes of the Temple in front, leading them all. The way he carried himself, confident and proud, made me wonder if he could be the high priest. What would he be doing out so late at night? Spread across his face was a most unpleasant look. Wherever they were going, they were in a terrible hurry.

I lay still in the dark foliage at the edge of the road and held my breath as the company marched by. The ground trembled as they passed.

My heart was racing so fast I knew sleep would not visit me the rest of the night, nor did I want more of it, and for the first time I noticed how cold I was. High above, the evening stars had already passed overhead and were now falling toward the western mountains. That would put the time at the second or third watch. It was closer to morning, but first light was still hours away.

I leaned back and tried to relax, forcing myself to breathe easier and deeper. Below me the city was asleep.

What a strange city Jerusalem was. For a thousand years it had stood, and since its beginning it had been coveted by the nations of the world. But to look at it, the city had nothing to be desired by others. It had no rich soil to till and plant and raise crops that might fetch the money to make a little profit or even to support itself. It was not along any trade routes or coastal ports to exchange goods with the other far-reaching corners of the world. It could not even claim to be an oasis in the desert. It had no water to speak of. There were wells located here and there, but they were mostly found in the hills and mountains that surrounded it. Providing water to the city involved a complex system of tunnels and canals that were interrupted regularly. No, Jerusalem was a small city, founded and loved by a small group of people wanting to live apart and in peace. But for some reason, it had been the object of desire for Jew and Gentile alike for centuries.

Every Hebrew child was told the stories of the city's birth. With considerable flair, they were told of Moses' journey through the wilderness as God prepared His people to find and enter the land especially chosen for their inheritance. They would imagine the miracle that Joshua performed as the multitudes crossed the river Jordan and into the land that was promised to them.

Jerusalem was not yet a city of the Jews then. At the time, it was the home of the Jebusites and was called Jebus. It was not until King David, centuries later, conquered the hilltop fortress and claimed it as his own that it acquired any special importance other than strategic worth. It was here that the tribes of Israel would be united for a time, and it was here the Lord would instruct David, through His prophet, to build an altar to the Lord.

I turned my attention to the immense Temple courtyard below. It looked as if the entire city was built as an appendage to it. It was the center of the city. To Jews it was the center of the world. Many villages and cities were not as large as the complex laid out to support and enclose this House of the Lord. My father claimed that the height of the walls and double doors of the sanctuary were double or triple the size of any other building's in the city. Bathed in gold and silver, the Temple's beauty was matched only by its superior workmanship in stone and wood. It truly was without equal anywhere in the world. But the magnificence that had attracted the vermin of the world for many hundreds of years was not always so apparent, and every child was taught Jerusalem's more humble beginnings.

My own father had taught me that in the days of King David there was a plague on all of Israel. The Lord told him to rear an altar on the threshing floor of a Jebusite named Araunah. The Jebusite was quick to offer to donate the land and even the animal for sacrifice. But David would not accept the gift, and therein lies the lesson. David said, "Nay; but I will surely buy it of thee at a price: neither will I offer burnt offerings unto the Lord my God of that which doth cost me nothing." So for fifty shekels the land was purchased, the sacrifice offered, and the plague was lifted.

On that spot a permanent altar was erected, and later a sanctuary would be built to house the Ark of the Covenant. From that sanctuary, King David's son, Solomon, would raise the first temple. Two more would be constructed over time, but none would be as grand or spectacular as the temple that Herod built—a marvel to attract the curious and faithful the world over.

Jerusalem: the City of Righteousness, the City of Peace. But it had experienced anything but peace since its founding. *The Assyrians, the Babylonians, the Persians, the Ptolemies, the Seleucids, the Parthians, the Romans—why can't the world leave us alone?* I thought. But they did not, importing their cultures and beliefs, imposing their religions and their gods, all in the attempt to better the "primitive" and "docile" Jews. *Jacob is right,* I thought. *We will endure and outlast them all, but the fight is still required of us.*

I could feel the cold seeping deep into my chest. The spring night air was not a fit place for a man without bed or coat. My attention was suddenly drawn to the noise of a scuffle down in the dark valley. Whether it was made by Roman soldiers making their search up the mountain or thieves and robbers in search of their next victim, I knew I had to find safe shelter; out here, alone as I was and with no weapon, I was no match for either. I shouldered Jacob's bag along with mine and hurried across the Kidron Valley.

In celebration of the Passover, the city gates were left open, and I made haste to the safety they offered. I made the steep climb and entered at the west gate, spilling into a section of the city that touched the Temple steps and looked down on the lower city.

The streets were quiet, and without being aware of it for some time, I kept to the shadows as I walked. It was unlawful for me, or any Jew, to be out on the night of Passover. To be out was symbolically tempting God to punish you, as He did our enemies in Egypt. All Jews were to be safe behind door frames painted with lamb's blood as a sign to the destroying angel to pass over our households. This night, perhaps more than most, Jerusalem took on a different look and feel. It was a different city this night. There was no longer the excitement that accompanied the flood of pilgrims earlier. There was no anticipation; no energy in the streets—merely an expectant stillness that amazed me for a city of Jerusalem's size. Tonight there were no Jews to be seen out, only the unbelievers, the outcasts, and the injured.

Tonight the city belonged to the Gentiles.

Soldiers drunk on cheap wine were the streets' most common company. Most had found some quiet corner to pass out in, while the stronger ones still found the means to stand and walk as they moved throughout the sleeping city with painted women on their arms. Such behavior was disgraceful by Jewish standards, but for a Roman the accomplishment of such debauchery was an admirable feat. But soldiers were not the only ones out tonight. Greeks, Egyptians, Syrians, and others whose origins I could only guess, had all been left behind and were fast becoming friends as the Jews of the city withdrew to their homes at sundown to honor tradition. Many of them, I suspected, had nothing in common except for the fact that none of them were Jews. Here they were, though, drinking well into the early morning hours as if they had been the closest of friends for years.

I hadn't noticed it when Jacob and I entered the city, but now I could see that much of the city was changing its look. The upper city had always been a place where different cultures and their styles of architecture were plainly manifest to the city around it. But even here, in the common parts of the city, the homes and businesses that lined the streets were losing the feel of old Jerusalem. Everywhere I went there were Grecian columns and porches, with domes atop many of them. The city did not look much like I remembered it. Why did we have to relate to the rest of the world? Why couldn't we be left alone?

The streets were still as I wandered through them with no particular place to go, and I found myself missing Jacob. But not Jacob only; I felt an empty place for my family as well. Why was it that God punished me by taking my family away? *What evil have I done to deserve this?* And *if* it was part of a larger plan, why did God keep its details so closely guarded? At times like these, rare as they were, when the calm surrounded me completely, I wondered where I could turn for help. If not to God, then whom? Were we all, in fact, lost?

At that moment the street ended, and I chanced upon a clear view of the Temple's meeting hall. There was a light coming from one of the windows and, like a beacon, it seemed to call to me. It was strange, a lamp lit at this hour and on this night when everyone should be home, but with nowhere else to go, I accepted its invitation to approach and enter. Across the wide courtyard and up the steps I walked, more than once looking over my shoulder, afraid of being seen and stopped for questioning. By Jewish authorities or Roman, it wouldn't matter. I was in violation with both that night. As I passed through the double archways and into the meeting hall, I breathed a little easier. But only for a moment.

Something did not feel right as I entered and saw the many lamps giving light to the spacious hall. Though many side rooms and smaller halls were dark, the great hall, the court of the Jewish council, looked ready to convene its high court. But that was impossible; it was illegal to hold court at night. I suddenly wondered if I was not alone. Looking around and keeping a keen ear to the air, I knew that I was the only one there and ventured in farther.

I thought of the rise of the council. Originally a gathering of the city's aristocracy, this early Jewish senate evolved into the Sanhedrin, becoming the body of seventy-one religious, political, and community leaders who wielded supreme power when it came to matters of interpretation and enforcement of the Law and its practices. My father had spoken of this group of wealthy and learned men often, usually with a tone of misgiving. He had, if I remembered right, been asked to sit on its council for a time, but refused, choosing to teach in the synagogue and uplift and instruct instead of condemn and bring down. It was a position of power and influence to be counted among its members, but my father was always one to stand by his ideals regardless of the consequences. *He was a righteous man,* I thought, with wistful pride in the father I remembered with a child's eyes. Israel would benefit from more men like him.

The meeting hall itself was large and rectangular in shape. On one end, stone benches lined the walls and then met, forming a crude semicircle. It was there, at the top of the curve, that the leader of the Sanhedrin, the Temple high priest, would sit and pass judgement. The other end was left open for the accused to stand and be arraigned, intimidated by his many judges. On either side of the man or woman brought before them stood the clerks of this court. It was their job to poll the council and record their final judgment of innocence or guilt.

On the other end of the room were rows of benches. These seats were reserved for students of the Law and those studying to be lawyers. I'd had many opportunities to sit on these hard seats and watch as the Law was explained, and men and women were either set free or found at fault by it. It had been a different time for me back then, a time I could scarcely remember even now, sitting in this once-familiar hall. Most of my memories were overwhelmed by the pain and emptiness left by Joshua's death.

Behind the benches, just in front of the back wall, there stood a stone half-wall that I did not remember being there thirty years ago. I may just have never noticed it before, or it may have been built since then, but it spurred a curiosity that I felt compelled to satisfy. It provided a barrier between the court and a small flight of stairs. Taking one of the lamps from the wall sconce, I shone the light down and stepped carefully. The stairwell opened up into a large hall with scrolls and parchments stacked on shelves higher than a man. It was a cache; an archive storing temple records of some sort.

I pulled one of the many scrolls out and opened it, holding it up to the light. This one was a financial accounting of donations made to the

Temple treasury from almost five years ago. The lists and columns of numbers were impressive testaments of the faithful who sacrificed what was of value to them and turned it over to the priests for dedication to the Lord. I carefully rolled it up and put it back.

From another shelf I removed a rolled parchment made of some animal's hide and written on with a thick, brittle ink. Pieces of the letters fell off as I opened it and read a few lines. Here were the teachings of the high priest from seven years ago upon his return from a visit to the southern synagogues of the Diaspora—the many settlements of "dispersed" Jews that had been driven from Jerusalem over the centuries required the guidance of those closer to the center of our faith. There were many, I knew, and they were spread throughout the world. Life for a Jew in these cities was especially difficult because of the lack of strength and unity from being so far from the Temple. Priests would travel by assignment to visit these cities and offer the love and support of the priesthood in Jerusalem. It must have been an exceptional reason for the high priest himself to visit these outlying areas, but I did not have the time or desire to search out his reasons.

There were hundreds of other scrolls and records, maybe a thousand or more. I looked at several of them, pulling them out at random and searching the first few lines for anything of interest or importance. In a dusty scroll pulled from the back shelf one word caught my eye. A name. The name of a rabbi: Eleazer. I hadn't spoken that name for what seemed like forever. *Could it be my old teacher and friend?* I read on. The extensive work he'd done in the city was recorded, as was an account of his ministry to Galilee. The scribe who had recorded this had taken great care to chronicle Eleazer's teachings as he traveled, and I could feel from the written praise that Rabbi Eleazer had been well loved by more men than just me. I suddenly felt ashamed. What would he think of the man I had become? Would he approve of my actions over the years? Would his smile still shine on me?

My eyes read the parchment, but my thoughts were elsewhere until another name written on the scroll caused my hands to start shaking. It was my name. Here, amid the thousands of entries, was my name, recorded for all to see. It was here that Rabbi Eleazer had presented my name to the council of elders for bestowal of the title of Rabbi. Like falling into a deep sleep, the room around me faded away and was replaced with a picture of myself, reclining under the shade of the Temple walls, surrounded by a dozen young boys, eagerly looking to me for wisdom and truth to guide them as they moved toward adulthood. Was this the life I had been meant to live? I looked much like I do now, but something was different about me. As I looked on, I could not place it. Maybe it was the priestly clothes I was wearing, or the fresh faces that were trained on me with eager ears that listened to every word I spoke, but I did not think that was it. It was something else. I could sense some inner strength, some peace emanating from deep inside me. It saddened me, for a moment, to glimpse what could have been.

Then as quickly as it appeared, the vision was gone, and I continued reading. The next words, though, sent daggers through my heart. Under my name was this note: *Arrested for striking an emissary on errand of the king. Punishment: slavery under the watch of Rome.*

"Errand of the king?" I said aloud softly. Is that how that night was being remembered? No mention of my loss. No mention of the blood or the screams for mercy. No mention of the blades and the soldiers.

I scanned the remainder of the scroll and, finding nothing more about that night, threw it down and began frantically looking through the others. What *errand* had the soldiers been on that night? Why couldn't I find this out? In all my years, the question I most wanted answered was "why?" What secret is being held? Why did my son die?

In my haste, many of the scrolls were damaged. The brittle ones crumbled, but I didn't care. I had to find out. I had never been so close to having my burning question answered. But nowhere could I find anything that would provide any more insight. It was like it had never happened.

But it *had* happened, and I would find out.

One scroll almost dropped from my hand as my eyes recognized what was written on it, and I rested from my search, if only for a moment. It was yellowed with age, and parts of it had already begun to break off. Many of the words were faded, but I could read plainly what it was. I was holding the Temple registry of twenty years earlier.

On its pages were written the names of the male children presented to the priests of the Temple for blessing and circumcision according to the Law. The names of both the children and parents were listed here as a testimony to their faithfulness.

I began searching the rolled scrolls nearby, reading the dates carefully until I found the one I was looking for. I took it to the stairs to study it more carefully and in better light. I opened it gently and softly ran my fingers down the list of names. My chest felt tight, and my eyes began to water. It was the name of my son. Joshua.

I sat there and tried to remember that day. It took some doing, so deeply was it buried, but I was able to draw out the memory of the day we presented Joshua at the Temple. Deborah was so pleased when he was born. We had both felt that the child growing within her was male, and when the midwife brought forth a son to my arms, God was praised with shouts of joy. We were young then, and ardent in our devotion to God, looking forward to the day when Joshua was to be presented and sacrifice offered in thanks for the answer to our prayers. I could recall that the day was bright and the air fragrant with the scent of wildflowers from the surrounding mountainsides. In my mind's eye, I watched as a proud, young father held his child high and handed him to the priests, declaring his name for all to hear. The day could only have been made more special if my own parents had been alive to share in that joy.

A noise in the meeting hall startled me, and I was ripped back from that distant memory to my present situation. Footfalls were approaching, and they were not single. I was not supposed to be there. If I were caught, I would be taken, questioned, and punished according to the Law. I put down the registry and quickly blew out the small flame in my lamp. At first I remained motionless, fearing I would be found, but as the men entered the room, I crept up to the wall and peered around it.

I could see the backs of four men. Three of them were dressed as temple officials. The other was bound and dressed in common clothes. Had this man been arrested at night? But that was not permitted under the Law. Then one of the officials stepped out and faced the man in custody. I couldn't see the official's face, only that he was an older man with white hair and a dirty gray beard.

"You have caused enough trouble for us," this man said. "But no more. We have evidence now against you that will seal your fate. Those who follow you will be hunted down and tried as well."

The bearded old man carried himself with an air of power and authority as he paced. He was clearly a priest of the Temple, but in his words was the unmistakable sound of fear.

"Without your disciples, you are nothing," he continued. "What have you to say about them now? Will you not plead for their lives? Would you not save theirs, and renounce this foolishness you teach? You can save them. Just admit that you were wrong, that you are not who they say you are. Just a few simple words and all can be forgiven." He stepped close in a threatening move. "Say it! Quit this blasphemous talk, and you can save them all! Would you kill them because of your madness? Say the words. Say them!"

The priest's railing was cut short by a tapping sound on the stone floor that approached and filled the giant hall. An old man, bent over a staff and crippled with age, walked toward them and took a seat on the bench.

"This had better be of the utmost importance," the old man said.

"I wanted you to see him before he is tried and killed," the priest said.

"Who is he?"

The priest paced back and forth in front of the accused man. "Tell him. Tell him who you are. No, no, tell him who your disciples say you are. Tell him what new doctrine you teach and spread throughout the land. Tell him."

The bound man looked up to meet their eyes.

"I spake openly to the world," he said. "I ever taught in the synagogue, and in the Temple, whither the Jews always resort; and in secret I have said nothing. Why do you ask me? Ask them which heard me, and what I have said unto them: behold, they know what I said."

One of the temple officials holding him bound stepped in front of him and slapped him across the face. It was with such force that the sound echoed throughout the hall and caused me to recoil at it. "Do you answer the high priest so?"

The high priest? Was one of these men the Temple high priest? There was a time that I wouldn't believe that such an example to the people would violate the Law, even to convict a criminal. But for all I had seen since arriving in the city, I did not doubt it now.

The accused man recovered from his pain and insult and turned to speak to his abuser with a remarkable display of calm and self-control.

"If I have spoken evil, bear witness of the evil; but if well, why do you smite me?"

The official was rebuked and looked to the ground as if shamed as he stepped back in line and took his place next to the accused.

The hall was beginning to fill with noise as more men were coming. Could the remainder of the Sanhedrin be coming to conduct this man's trial this night?

"You brought me here for this?" the old man asked finally. "You are the high priest now. Take him and do as you will. Though I do not think you need my permission. You never needed anyone's permission to do what you want." And with these last cutting words, the old man rose and left, leaning heavily on his cane.

The high priest recovered quickly from the rebuke, moving through the room and greeting his brothers on the council. His words were filled with thanks and gratitude for their coming at night, and he apologized for the unusual circumstances for their emergency convening. Many of the places were empty, and I could see that not every member of the council was present. Those that were there took their seats, and the meeting was brought to order.

"My brethren in the priesthood, revered elders of the communities, and those men of wisdom and influence in our great land," the high priest began. "The matter that brings us together is a grave threat to our position; to our authority to rule as is our calling and our right. Many of you know, or least know the sight of, this man standing before you. I present to you the Galilean."

There was a rumble of voices as all acknowledged that they did know him. Still, I could not see the accused man's face, nor had I seen clearly the face of the high priest.

"Amazing," one member of the Sanhedrin said. "I did not think it possible. He has eluded our efforts to apprehend him in the past. How was it done?"

"He was hiding in the hills just outside the city," the high priest answered. "One of his disciples, Judas, led us to him."

"Betrayed by one of his own?" the council member asked, almost in disbelief.

The high priest returned to his place conducting the trial of this man. "And now he stands before you, charged with rebellion against the Temple and accused of blasphemy of the most severe kind. He defies the Law, incites the people to insurrection, teaches of a new, 'higher' law, is a breaker of the Sabbath, and he claims to be the Messiah."

The rumble of voices grew louder and the council seemed appalled at the news. The high priest had to shout now to be heard as he finished the list of charges. "Others even say that he is the Son of God himself!"

This last charge sent the room into a fit. "Blasphemy!" they cried, and their words were hard, without compassion or mercy. The Law said that a man was innocent until evidence of guilt could be presented, but with this council, the burden of attaining evidence seemed to be cast in the other direction. One member of the council spoke up when the voices subsided.

"These are strong accusations," he said. "We assume you have witnesses to support your claim?"

The high priest looked around and smiled. "Yes. To the charge of threatening harm to the House of the Lord, even our own holy Temple. What more than that is needed to condemn him to death? Bring in the first witness."

The high priest took his seat at the head of the council, while one of the officials that had come in with him disappeared into an adjoining room. Whispered words were shared, filling the time they spent waiting. When the official returned he brought with him a young man, dressed in the poorest of clothes, and looking like he hadn't bathed in a some time. This "witness" looked around the room and cowered back. The temple official had to prod him forward, pushing him to the center square. He looked not only scared, but terrified.

"Speak to us your name," the high priest called from his judgment seat.

"D-David," he said timidly.

"Louder," one of the priests demanded.

"David," the witness repeated with fright, "son of—"

"Thank you," the high priest interrupted. "Do you know this man?"

The witness turned, looked at the accused, and nodded.

"You must speak up!" another member of the Sanhedrin called out. "Gestures alone cannot convict this man. Now, do you know him? Yes or no?"

"Yes."

"And how do you know him?" the high priest continued.

"I have seen him around the city," the witness said. "He has performed many mir—" he looked sharply toward the official, "tricks among the people."

"And did you not hear him speak concerning the Temple?"

Again the witness nodded, then corrected himself and said, "Yes."

"Would you tell us what you heard him say?"

The witness started to fidget with the hem of his shabby old cloak. "Th—this man said, 'I am able to destroy the Temple of God, and to build it in three days.'"

Again the room filled with angry words, and judgment seemed imminent. The high priest looked pleased, and from the back of the room I realized I had seen his face before. It did not take long for me to place him. He was the priest I had seen marching with the army of Roman soldiers earlier that night. I looked again at the man bound and standing accused in all meekness. So this was the man an army was sent to apprehend?

"Thank you," the high priest said. "Your service has been to a greater good this night. You may have a seat there," he said, and he pointed to the rows of benches allowed for students and other observers. "Bring in the other witness."

The Temple official left and returned with another witness. This second witness I could not see clearly. He was standing on the other side of the room. The same routine was followed, his name taken for their records, and then he was asked about what he had heard the accused man say.

"We heard him say, 'I will destroy this temple that is made with hands, and within three days I will build another made without hands,'" the second witness said. "But that's not possible. No one can do that."

"That will be quite enough," the high priest said. "Your testimony of his words is sufficient."

"But look at him," the second witness said. "You don't really believe that he—"

"You will refrain from speaking to this council unless a question is put to you!" the high priest barked. "You may join your companion over there."

The high priest leaned forward, staring with cold hatred into the eyes of the accused. "You have heard the witnesses against you. What have you to say for yourself?"

The accused man replied nothing. The high priest was not satisfied with the mocking silence returned to his questions. He stood from his chair. "Do you answer nothing?" Still the man held his peace.

One elderly member of the council motioned for an opportunity to address the other members. "Do not think that I stand to defend him—we all feel justice is required for his insurrections and hard words toward us—but saying 'I will destroy the Temple' and 'I am able to destroy the Temple' are inconsistent and different in their meaning and charge. We must proceed correctly. It would seem that the Law demands another voice before we may pass judgment."

"What?" the high priest cried. "It is semantics. 'I will' or 'I am able.' What matters the exact words that were used? But if your conscience now requires it, I will ask them again." He pointed to the first witness. "You are certain he said that he was only *able* to destroy the Temple?"

The first witness, David, stood on shaky knees and nodded.

"Is it that difficult to form the words yes or no?" The high priest was losing his temper. He seemed enraged that he needed to press the witnesses for a clearer testimony to convict the accused. "Say it! 'Yes' or 'No'?"

"Yes," the witness said. "He said 'able.'"

The members of the Sanhedrin began whispering among themselves. The doubt in their minds was evident now among them. At the discrepancy, the conviction could not be passed.

The high priest then jumped out of his seat. "Are you the Christ? Tell us!" he yelled.

For the first time did the accused speak. "If I tell you, you will not believe. And if I also ask you, you will not answer me, nor let me go."

The high priest screamed out in frustration at his near-crumbling plan, then strode to the front of the room. "I adjure you by the living God that you tell us whether you be the Christ, the Son of God!"

The two men stood face to face. One was calm, full of composure and restraint. The other was shaking with anger and breathing heavily, spittle trailing over his lips and onto his beard. The question was twofold. Claiming to be the Christ was not the same as claiming to be the Son of God. One was to be a king, or deliverer of the people sent by God to free His people; the other was to be God. The first was not a crime; the other was blasphemy, punishable by death.

"Thou hast said," the accused answered. "Nevertheless, I say unto you, hereafter shall ye see the Son of Man sitting on the right hand of the power of God."

"Are you then the Son of God?" the high priest railed.

"Ye say that I am."

The high priest clenched his fists and raised them over his head. For a moment I thought he might strike the man as the Temple official had. But he did not, and instead screamed in his face, *"Are you the Christ?!"*

The man standing there, hands bound in tight leather straps, paused and looked at the high priest with a calmness I thought noble. Though I had not been able to see his face during the trial, I could see the way in which the others looked at him, and imagined, for a moment, what he must have looked like. Then he spoke for the room to hear.

"I am."

The high priest cried out and took his own shirt, rending it in two. "He hath spoken blasphemy! What further need have we of witnesses?"

He was barely heard over the outrage of the other members of the Sanhedrin. Cries of "Blasphemy!" and shouts of disgust were repeated in abundance. It was as if the words of this man came as a surprise to them. But I could see that it was not so. They had hoped for those words. Their displays of shock and abhorrence seemed more for show than from any real offense.

"Behold," the high priest said over the din of the meeting hall, "now ye have heard this blasphemy. What think ye?"

"Death!" came the voices. Cheers and applause accompanied the declaration of the sentence. Many came down from their seats to look upon this man they had condemned to death, the man they had designed to convict.

"They say he is a prophet," one member said.

"We shall see," said another, removing his sash. He approached the man and tied the strip over his eyes.

"They say you are a prophet," he mocked, and then he struck him hard across the face. "Prophesy! Who is it that strikes you?"

They all laughed, and others joined in, taking turns striking the man, spinning him around to meet the palms of their hands. It was a loathsome display of abuse and disrespect, not only for this man, but for the Law they claimed to have upheld.

I had seen enough. I had to escape this place, but how? From where I was sitting on the stairs, the only exit to the city outside was past the crowd of men. There was nothing to hide behind or use as a shield between where I stood and the door. I thought I might be able to reach the doors before they could catch me, but at their alarm, the temple guards would be awakened and a search would ensue. If I stayed and waited much longer, they would find me when the official acting as clerk came to record the trial and sentence.

Careful to step lightly on the stone floor, I went back to the stairs to plan my escape. In the darkness, though, I felt something at my foot, and before I could recoil from it I heard the sharp sound of wooden dowel on stone, tumbling end over end down the stairs. I froze and listened as some of the noise from the hall hushed.

"Did you hear that?" someone asked.

"I heard it," another answered.

"Over there! Behind the wall. It came from the archive."

"You said we were alone!" one of the council members accused the high priest. "What trickery is this?"

"Find him," the high priest ordered.

I did not wait to be discovered and arrested. Before *this* council I would be found guilty of a crime deserving of death and would never see the light of morning. Without another thought, I sprinted for the doors.

"Stop him!" the high priest shouted. "He must not escape!"

My action must have taken them by surprise, because I reached the doorway well ahead of them. Of course, they were the rich of the city, and most of them had filled out with the gluttonous life of power and luxury they made for themselves and could not even run a few steps to catch me. My fit condition benefitted me as I passed the outer doors and broke free into the night.

Atop the stairs, a small group of men and women had set up camp. The only conclusion I could reach was that they were there to witness the trial from a distance. I had no choice but to run through, kicking up their fire as I ran out then down to the dark, empty courtyard below.

As I reached the first street, I turned and looked for any sign that I was followed, resting briefly while leaning on a shop wall. I could not see any temple guards out, and at the top of the stairs the priests had stopped, pointing off in my general direction. They clearly did not have the ability or the drive to follow me. Maybe they thought their threatening words as I fled would be enough to inspire my silence. They were right. What I had just witnessed was wrong, but who was I to make it right? If I tried, it would be my word against theirs. Had Israel become so corrupt that its leaders would try a man contrary to all points of the Law?

Somewhere a cock crowed to forewarn of the approaching morning, though the sky had not yet begun to hint at the approaching dawn. I knew I needed to find some place to rest until I could determine what to do next. Yesterday I had passed through the city gates with hope and a best friend; in less than one day I had managed to lose both.

Down one of the side streets I saw movement in the shadows. I looked around and thought I saw something behind me dart around a corner. I began to feel that I was no safer inside the city walls than I was outside them. More than for rest only, I needed to find a safe place to spend the remainder of the night. And this night, there was only one place left I knew I could go.

* * *

Jacob's brother lived behind the tanner's market, a place foul to sight and smell. His last letter to Jacob, giving directions to find him, had been tucked securely into Jacob's bag. Where the street leveled off for a stretch, and to the east, was a narrow alley hidden by skins hung there to dry. Even at night, I did not think that I would have any trouble finding it.

The streets were filthy and cramped, and were quite literally a maze through that densely populated quarter of the city. With a thousand side streets and alleys, it was the perfect place to shroud a patriot and a rebel.

As I passed the covered windows and still houses, I became aware of the distinct feeling that my every step was being watched. I had felt eyes take notice of me for some time, but not until now did I feel that I was in any danger. Then I saw it; I was sure of it. The windows were covered with planks of wood, and the place appeared to be devoid of life, but as my eyes adjusted more fully, I caught a dim glow inside and heard an almost inaudible rumble of voices. I strained to pick out words, or even the language that was being spoken, but the noises were so faint I wondered whether I was hearing them at all.

To my left a shadow moved. Before I could react, I saw another. From behind I was grabbed around the chest, strong hands clasping like a vice. I took hold of them and leaned forward, dropping to one knee. My assailant fell over my shoulder and let go to brace for his own fall. I moved to stand, but before I could take up a defensive position, two more hit me from each side and grabbed my arms.

"Let me explain!" I shouted, but they were not inclined to talk, and before the words left my lips, three more jumped from dark recesses and I was dragged to the ground. There was a nervous rustle from within, and then a door opened slightly and a dark set of eyes peered out.

No one spoke, but I knew they were waiting for the answer to a question they had not yet asked.

"I am a friend," I said. "I am looking for the brother of Jacob, the one called Barabbas."

CHAPTER 11

Those hard eyes did not move, or leave mine. Suddenly the door was thrown open wide, and I was pushed into waiting hands. I was forced to the floor, and I heard several swords loosed from their sheaths. The light was poor, and I could not distinguish the walls from the darkness. I could see, however, that the room had been cleared of furniture to make room for the thirty or forty men that filled it. A few oil lamps illuminated the faces of those who were not masked with desert kaffiyehs. All of them looked as if they would as soon slay a man as spit. No one spoke above a whisper, and many of them looked at me as if I had been tried and found guilty of some monstrous act. Friend of Jacob's or not, the grave reality of my situation was sinking in.

But something was not right with them. No one acted. There was a sense of confusion in the room, like soldiers without a captain.

They lifted me to my feet, and before they could act out of that fear and confusion, I took the offense and spoke.

"Where is Barabbas?" I demanded. "You know him; this is his house, but he is not here."

A few of them looked nervously at each other, but most just stood there as if made of stone, their stares fixed on me. A tall man finally stepped from the back shadows. His every move was smooth and fluid, and as he neared, the dim light from one of the lamps reflected in his cool and cunning eyes. Was he there to help me or to see that my sentence was carried out? I couldn't tell. Some of his facial features reminded me vaguely of Jacob, but from his age, I knew he could not be Barabbas. This man was young, in his thirties or early forties, but not the brother to my old friend. But whatever his name or relation, he was clearly what passed for their leader.

I jerked my arms free of the two men that held me. They reached toward me again, but the tall one raised his hand and stopped them.

"I was told by Jacob, brother to Barabbas, that I would find brothers-in-arms here, sympathetic to the cause against Rome—men that I could call friends."

The tall man reached out to the pendant hanging from my neck. He inspected the stone-cut star and then, satisfied, let it fall to my chest. His countenance softened as he clapped his hand on my back.

"Welcome, brother!" he said. His deep voice matched his strong appearance. "My name is Gideon."

"Peace be with you," I responded, more out of tradition and habit than any real wish for peace.

"Peace?" Gideon smiled and looked around at the men. "Yes, peace. Perhaps one day."

A few in the room chuckled as if it were a joke.

"Come," Gideon said. "You must be tired and hungry."

With Gideon's welcome, the others lost interest in me and broke into smaller groups dispersed throughout the room. Gideon led me to the center of the room and offered me of their food and wine, which I ate heartily. I couldn't explain it, but I felt an instant kinship with this man. As we talked, I sensed his intelligence and was taken with his charismatic nature. Though I was nearly old enough to have been his father, he had the air of a fine leader, and I would have wagered that he had seen as much action against Rome as I had at his age. I spoke of my trip across the sea with Jacob, and our journeying through the desert, and he found great humor in my setting of the horses free in the storm. In the end, I told him of Jacob's death on the Temple grounds the day before.

"We know," Gideon said. "Some of us were there."

"He was as brave a man, as loyal to his country and his God as there ever lived," I said.

"Barabbas has spoken of him, and of your fight on the northern coast. We hear great things."

"It is difficult to find the devotion, the spirit, the yearning to be free among the people. Much of that has been lost. Most weakly accept Rome's rule."

"It is as if they have forgotten," Gideon said.

"Or never learned." *Like my own sons,* I thought. "The younger generation is not taught freedom or independence. They learn our nation's history, but do not learn the lessons from our mistakes."

"They live as if there is no other way," Gideon agreed, "and will never be."

For some time Gideon was silent. Then he asked, "What brings you in from the country?"

I didn't answer right away, but finally said, "A mistake."

Gideon smiled as if my words were amusing to him.

"Ah, yes. Many a mistake has turned out to be a wise decision in disguise. Is it a mistake you are now here with us? Is it a mistake that our list of friends has grown today by one? No, my new friend, there are no mistakes, only opportunities."

I did not agree. "But for my mistake, Jacob would still be alive," I said. "Mistake or opportunity, you may call it whatever you wish. In the end, it killed my friend."

Gideon shook his head. "It was not you that threw the spear that caught Jacob in the back, nor was it you that put him in harm's way, fighting at the Temple. Jacob was not your slave; he did not have to come with you. In all things, Jacob chose his own fate, a fate that would have kept him alive if not for the Roman who reached for his spear, took aim, and of his own action, threw it into Jacob's back. Neither you, nor your actions, had anything to do with his death," he said with some force. "You would have saved him if you'd had the chance, would you not?"

"I would have taken the spear in my back if I could have."

"Then why do you carry this guilt?" Gideon asked. "To spend time finding ways to blame another's fate on yourself is foolish and destructive. We all do what we can, and in the end it is up to God."

Everywhere I went there was this foolish notion that everything in life, even death, was tied to God's design. I did not believe it. I never would. And as for his talk of not being responsible for another in your care, I doubted he had ever lost a friend . . . or a son. I wanted to speak to this point, but had the presence of mind to bind my tongue and shift the subject of the conversation.

"Tell me," I said. "I have been long absent from Jerusalem and her politics. News travels slowly or not at all over such distances.

Everywhere I see Roman soldiers, but tell me, what king rules over Judea?"

Gideon looked to some of his men, and a few smiles were exchanged over my question.

"A king?" one of them said. "Israel has been without a king for . . . twenty or thirty years now."

"The Jerusalem you once knew is all but gone," another said.

"The last king was Herod the Great."

"You mean, Herod the Terrible," yet another said. Many of them laughed and agreed with the title.

"I did hear of his death," I said. "It was a great day for me and my family."

"You did not like the king?" one asked.

"Like?" I spat on the floor. "His death was an answer to a prayer. He was an evil man—on that we can all agree. A beast unfit to bear the title of Jew."

"But did you hear of *how* he died?" asked one of the men, older than most of the others. I had heard his name was Asher. "I was living here at the time," he continued. "I was a child then, but not so young as to let news of our wretched king pass by unheard. In his last years he became deranged, seeing conspiracies all around him. Most, I believe, were true—"

"Or if they weren't, they ought to have been," one interrupted. Again, they all laughed.

"Yes, true," Asher said. "All around him were suspicions and threats of death and murder. Everyone around him was an enemy, everyone wanted his crown and throne. And at the center of most of these plots was his own family. One by one, sometimes in groups, Herod had them killed or banished, most without benefit of proof or trial."

"Do you know what I heard?" a young man said. "I heard that it was better to be a swine in Herod's court than to be his own son." Many joined him in his laughter.

"How, then, did he die?" I asked, eager for the ending.

"Stricken with a multitude of plagues, the like of which no man has ever experienced. I have heard physicians still speak of it. They are confounded to this day."

"A just punishment for the ills he placed on Jerusalem and her people," the young man said.

"But it was still not enough," I said. "His crimes exceeded those generally known and reported. It was he who covenanted with Rome, scheming for aid to help him regain his throne from the invading Parthians. And then the killings began. The stories my father told when he didn't know I was listening were almost too horrible for a boy to hear. By Herod's word, most of the Jewish senate was put to death. My father knew many of those killed. The same fate awaited the Jewish nobility and the wealthy and influential leaders of the city. His long reign was filled with such countless deaths. I am glad to hear that his own was fitting."

"And so ended the reign of Herod the Great."

Gideon then spoke up, having let the stories come from whomever they may. "Herod's sin, as you say, was in his loyalty to Rome and her wealth and power. Barabbas has spoken of him on occasion. He tells a story of when he was young, before I and most here were born. He and a small group of priests and students of the Law tore down an effigy of the Roman eagle from the Temple gates. When Herod heard of it, he had the leaders caught and burned at the stake. And their crime according to Herod? Defacing the Temple! When it was Herod who had desecrated the holy house by putting such symbols there."

"Herod was a dog who wagged his tail in the presence of his Roman masters," Asher added quickly.

"My father was with those men at the Temple," I said. Many of the men, including Gideon, looked at me in awe and surprise. "I followed them that afternoon. The images are still clear and the feelings I had then, even as a boy, are just as strong today."

"You come from a proud heritage," Gideon said.

I nodded a silent thanks. "So then, if Herod was the last king of Judea, what happened at his death? He had many wives, I know, and a dozen sons; surely all of them were not killed?"

Gideon took lead of the storytelling. "No. By Herod's last decree, his son Archelaus was to reign in his stead over most of his kingdom. Two other sons, Herod Philip and Herod Antipas, divided out the eastern and northern lands. But to be king took the approval and appointment of

Caesar himself, and Augustus was unwilling to have another Herod rule as king. Instead, he made the boy the ethnarch, a governor of sorts."

"There were riots in the streets," Asher remembered. "Archelaus called in an army; Rome sent another. Thousands were killed. The uprising spread throughout Judea until the governor in Syria sent his own army to restore order."

"When it was over," Gideon continued, "much of the city was destroyed, and part of the Temple burned, its treasury stolen. Barabbas speaks of those dark days with reverence and respect. So many of our brothers died in that revolution. Those days brought change to Jerusalem. Caesar had Archelaus exiled and declared his lands—Judea, Idumea, and Samaria—forever an official province of Rome, to be ruled and governed by military prefects."

A spell of silence came over the room for a moment, a reflection on the land and times in which they had lived and fought. Then someone shouted, "Death to Rome and the Romans!" Others joined in, swords were raised, and the crowd was roused back to life.

"So tell me," I said to Gideon. "Where is Barabbas? When will I meet him? There is much I wish to speak to him about. The news of his brother's death should not wait."

The renewed energy in the room vanished, and everyone waited for Gideon's answer.

"News of his brother, though important, will have to wait."

"If he is away, I will go to him," I said. "If you will only tell me where he is, I will—"

"Imprisoned," Gideon said. "He sits in the dungeons beneath Antonia, guarded by a dozen men." I could see him struggling with an intense sadness. "He is condemned to die in the morning."

Though I was sitting, I suddenly felt thrown off balance and reached out to steady myself. My heart started to beat in a panic, and I felt the weight of a stone grow in my chest. Could this all be happening? It couldn't be possible. For forty years two brothers had been fighting the enemies of Israel a thousand miles away from each other, and now they were to die two days apart.

"I . . . I can't believe it," I stuttered to say. "How can this be?"

"He was taken over a week ago, during a raid on a Roman caravan from Joppa," said a young man. "Somehow they knew we'd attack and were waiting for us. We rode right into a trap. Our way for escape was blocked by a company of soldiers, and we were forced to fight. We are strong men," he said, waving his arms over the men in the room, "and we are not defenseless when swords are drawn, but the numbers with which they met us were too great."

"But then he saved us," said this same young man, standing taller with pride. "None of us would have escaped if not for him. I owe him my life. He is a savior."

I looked to Gideon for further explanation.

"Barabbas launched himself at a mounted soldier and killed him, taking his horse. With the new advantage, he slew the other two on horseback and told us to take their horses. He pushed into the heart of their attack and drew their attention away sufficiently to allow our escape. When it was over, he alone was taken captive. That was nearly ten days ago."

"God be thanked that he still lives," I said.

Gideon shook his head. "Pilate tortures him and keeps him just this side of death, hoping to discover our whereabouts. It would seem that the provincial governor, Vitellius—as far away as Syria—has taken notice of our little band and has ordered us found at all costs. The city has many places to hide, as you have seen, and Barabbas is his only hope of finding us. But Pilate grows weary. Barabbas is stronger than he imagined."

"The weakest Jew is stronger than the mightiest Roman," I said with a firm conviction.

Words of agreement filled the room.

"But you cannot let his sentence be carried out," I said.

They all looked at one another, and I then understood what I had stumbled into. "You're planning another raid," I said. "A rescue."

Gideon nodded cautiously.

"You must let me help. I am older than anyone here, I know, but I am not unskilled in this fight. I owe too much to Jacob to sit by while others fight for his brother's freedom." Then I added, "I owe too much to Israel."

With eyes that seemed to pierce my very soul, Gideon nodded again, this time in approval, and I was taken into their confidences. I learned that Barabbas was to be part of a triple execution. In the morning, the condemned men would be marched from the Roman courts of Antonia, through the western part of the city, and up to Golgotha. There, all three would be crucified and left to die. Security would be tight both at Antonia and at the place of execution.

"The only chance we have to free him," Gideon continued, "is along the route out of the city. The streets are narrow, and at one point only one or two guards will be able to march alongside the procession."

"A strait," I said, understanding precisely what had to be done. "Controlled and confined. They will be marching along three or four deep. But where the street narrows, they will have to walk through in single file. They will be at their weakest at that point."

"Weak as they may be, they will still be formidable, even for the best of us. They will be the Praetorian Guard of Antonia, and centurions, each one an expert in warfare and close combat."

"My hands and my heart are yours to command."

Gideon raised his hands and shook his head. "Before you commit yourself, you must understand that many of us will not survive this. Those of us who do will be hunted down. No means will be thought too cruel to apprehend us. Leaving the city will be our only hope for survival. Mounting an attack in this way will invoke their wrath at all levels. We will never be able to return. You must be sure."

I knew he spoke the truth. The city would be unsafe for any of us. It is one thing to lay siege to an outlying post or caravan; it is quite another to steal an enemy of the state right from under the shadow of their mighty fortress. Since night the question had beset my mind: What was I going to do next? I couldn't stay here in the city, so close to a family I could not see. Even if I could raise the money for passage back, I didn't want to return home. What was left for me to return to? Without Jacob's friendship and company, I had little to look forward to. Perhaps here, with his brother, I would find new meaning for life and new direction to follow.

No, I thought, giving myself to Gideon was the best, the only choice I could make.

"It is the only thing I am sure of," I said. "I have no reason to return. None whatsoever."

Gideon did not smile as I thought he might. Instead, his every presence expressed the grave decision we had all made to save this one man. "Then eat and rest well, my brother," he said, loud enough to inspire everyone there. "The events of tomorrow will be written about for centuries and live forever. Tomorrow, Israel shall be set free."

* * *

I spent the next few hours fielding questions about the world at large and the fight in far-off corners of it. It seemed that Gideon's acceptance of my loyalties had cleared the way for the others to speak with me freely and admit me into their confidences. But for all of their questions, none were so readily asked, or more eagerly answered, than of the greater fight against the Empire. Most of Gideon's men were natives to Judea, a few were from the northern countries of Galilee and Gaulanitis, and one was from the southern tip of Idumea, near the hilltop fortress of Masada. As a whole, they knew very little of the men and women who struggled, as they did in Apollonia, for independence from Caesar. They were part of a larger brotherhood, I assured them, and their part was crucial to the freedom of Israel.

In a short time, and without telling them of my direct involvement, I told them of the *Vindicare* and its fate. I found that I told the story with great pleasure. They were amazed, and many suggested the culprits were fools for attempting such a feat. They took delight in the descriptions of the fire on the water, and especially of Phillip's part, causing it to rain down fire. By the look in some of their eyes, I wondered how many raids from then on would include an archer's skill with similar fires. They were all incensed when I told them about the small company of soldiers along the caravan route, and laughed when I told them what I did later that night to their horses. For the first time in years I felt at home, surrounded by men who shared with me a common aim.

My age, however, did raise several concerns about my commitment and ability to fight the kind of battle they were preparing to wage. But I had become accustomed to sidelong looks and doubts when it came to my physical condition; even though I looked strong enough, the younger generation still questioned me. This group was no exception. For the next hour or so, I spent time instructing them in some of the close fighting techniques I had found particularly effective over the years, especially the use of knees and elbows. These strikes, I told them, could deliver crushing blows with little movement or practice. I demonstrated what I meant on many of those there. They were grateful students, and I was honored to teach them. They were a willing army, and I thought that Israel should be proud to call them her sons.

CHAPTER 12

No one slept the rest of the night.

It did not take long for preparations to be made. Everyone knew his role in the morning's raid. Six men would rush Barabbas and the soldiers attending to him, striking without mercy. A dozen others, some in front and some behind, would keep the other soldiers at bay while the rescue ensued. The rest would patrol the streets and provide for a seamless escape. Each man was armed with a sword or club, and beneath our clothes we were all fitted with wide strips of leather across our chests for protection from Rome's sharpened steel.

As the hours passed, stories and words of encouragement became nervous chatter, as would be expected before men embark into the dangerous unknown. But the anxiety was tempered with confidence in our cause, for we were not only men, but soldiers—an army of God—marching as to war. As the hours passed, a meditative calm settled in the room as many of the men mentally and emotionally readied themselves for the fight, choosing not to trade what they all knew might be their last hours alive for mere words. I wondered how many of them had families and children, and which ones would never see them again; I couldn't help but think of my Hannah. Would she understand why I had to leave? Would she ever know that though I could not stay, I continued to fight for her and her young family?

I was not surprised to learn that many there were of the Essene faith; the dark morning hours were filled with their rhythmic prayers professing their trust in the Lord God of Israel, petitioning His ear to hear and His mighty hand to protect them and save them, declaring that He, alone, was their rock and their fortress. Though my faith lay only in my skills with the sword, and not in my God, their prayers were somewhat of a comfort.

Gideon had been noticeably absent from the early morning preparations for an hour or two. I found Asher and asked him where Gideon was.

"Up top. He always spends time alone before we go into action. Says it calms him down—helps him think. I'd want to do the same if I were leading this band."

"Would you?" I asked.

"Would I what?"

"Lead this band—if you had the chance."

He shook his head. "Barabbas is like no other I've ever fought with, and I've known the best and strongest of them. His kind is a lost breed. He is a man who cares for freedom—mine, yours, all of ours. A man strong enough to stand up to all Rome can throw at us; a man that can save you from the point of a dagger one moment and sacrifice you for a greater good the next. Men like him are all but gone." He paused to reflect on his estimation of the man. "Me, lead? No. I don't have it in me. I can fight as good as, or maybe even better than, the next man, but I don't have what it takes to lead. Don't want it, to tell you the truth."

"Gideon seems a fine substitute."

"He should be," he said. "Gideon and Barabbas are—"

"Brothers-in-arms." It was Gideon. He was standing at the back door. "We have been fighting at each other's side for many years. What Barabbas has taught I have been there to learn. He is my best friend."

Asher slipped away at a look from Gideon and left us alone.

"Join me on the roof," Gideon said.

The air was crisp, bordering closely on cold, as we sat on woven mats and reclined on coarse pillows. The dark city had not yet made the slightest distinction between day and night, light and shadow, but already the sounds of a city at work were springing up all around. Hammers pounding nails and saws crosscutting timber were the first to fill the air.

"You have a fine group of men downstairs," I said. "They are devoted and love Barabbas with a zealous loyalty. You are fortunate to have them. Where I live, one can search a lifetime and find only a fraction of their numbers."

"Barabbas is the kind of leader who is there on the front lines and is not afraid to shed the first blood. These men sense that, and would follow him into hell if he commanded them to."

"Tell me about him," I said. "Jacob had little time to speak of him."

"What would you know?"

"Tell me of his enemies," I said. "I have always said the measure of a heroic man is the measure of his enemies. Tell me about this prefect, Pilate."

Gideon looked to the gray sky. "Barabbas and Pilate have long been enemies. Their struggle began even before Pilate arrived in the city. The two of them have been opponents since."

"I knew this when you said that Pilate has been torturing him for a week. It seemed personal."

"I'm sure it is. Pilate only needed the opportunity. Now he can exact his own sadistic pleasure on one of the greatest champions Israel has ever known."

"Jacob was such a man also," I said.

Gideon nodded. "With the appointment of Pontius Pilate, Jerusalem has been beset with troubles and open strife. The prefects before him all ruled with marked indifference to what we did in our own city. Rome's presence was light and we were left, largely, to govern ourselves. There was still the struggle against the heavy taxes and decrees from Rome, but things were manageable then.

"About seven years ago, word was noised that a new prefect was coming to Judea by special appointment of Caesar himself. Nothing was known about him for a long while, except his name. Rumors were started and fears fanned, but in a short time we learned all we needed to know about him."

Gideon offered me a basket of honeyed figs and took a handful for himself. He continued talking as he ate.

"It was in the month of Kislev, during the celebration of Hanukkah, I remember, when the soldiers arrived, marching through the dark streets with a great deal of sound and fanfare. A show of force such as this would have been sign enough that things in our great city were about to change for the worse. Then we noticed something else. For the first time since anyone could remember, the silver Roman ensigns were engraved with effigies of Caesar. The graven images were paraded for all to see, mocking our law. We learned that Pilate's first command in his new position was to order the soldiers at Caesarea to take winter quarters here. He meant his troops to abolish our laws and replace them with Rome's."

"What did you do?" I asked.

"What could we do? The army was enormous, and, I am sad to admit, we had grown soft and spoiled by our years of relative peace with the Empire. But it was decided by the priests and rabbis that a delegation should be sent to Pilate, still on the coast, to persuade him that the effigies be removed. Pilate, of course, refused, claiming loyalty to his emperor and saying that removing them would be a great offense to him. But the priests would not give up. For days they sent word and would not leave him be. Finally Pilate could take no more. At one gathering of court, soldiers were secreted throughout the large crowds, and at a signal from Pilate they surrounded the delegates, demanding that they leave and never speak of the effigies again."

"Were they . . . ?"

"Killed? No. But they well could have been. When swords were drawn and the plot against them discovered, they threw themselves on their knees and bared their necks and chests, declaring that they would rather die than have their laws transgressed."

"And Pilate refused?"

"No. To the contrary. He gave in and declared that Jewish laws were to remain in full force and effect. A week later the effigies were gone and headed back to Caesarea."

"The priests, no doubt, called it a miracle," I said.

"They declared that God had touched the heart of the new prefect. Judea was to be blessed with peace, then and forever. It seemed, though, that Pilate's tolerance and God's blessing of peace lasted only as long as it took Pilate to travel to Jerusalem."

Gideon looked away and out over the city now emerging with the approaching dawn.

"The effigies may have gone," Gideon continued, "but the armies stayed, and not just for the winter. Pilate was consumed with his own power and did whatever he wanted, fearing neither Rome's law nor God's. And at every turn was Barabbas. Only a few years ago, Pilate ordered that the temple treasury be opened to him. He used the sacred money to build a waterway nearly two hundred furlongs to bring water from his favorite well into the city. The citizens were outraged. Barabbas and I led a series of attacks on the construction sites, but they were too heavily guarded for us to cause any real damage. And while we acted on the crime against our people, another delegation was organized to protest the misuse of the temple funds. If God intervened once to support His people, surely He would do it again. But this time Pilate did not concede. Soldiers fell on the crowd. Not everyone there at court was protesting Pilate's actions, but their daggers didn't care. The soldiers attacked everyone there—old, young . . . it didn't matter. A great number were killed, and more fled wounded.

"From that day a line was drawn. Pilate is forever an enemy of the people, and of none more so than Barabbas." Gideon lifted his shirt, revealing a scar about the length of a man's hand, and straight, as one would get from a blade. "Or me."

"You were there?"

He nodded. "I wanted to see Pilate up close. That was as good an opportunity as I'd get. Since that day, he has lived like a mountain hermit, hiding in his palace behind gates of iron and ruling from afar."

"He is a coward," I said.

"Perhaps, but the power of the office is great, and his armies live to serve only him."

The sky was now the shade of blue that reminded me of a shallow bay or lagoon. The high clouds were bright yellow streaks, stretching from horizon to horizon. The smell of baking breads drifted on the slight breeze as more of the city awakened to meet the day. Gideon took the quiet opportunity to stand.

"If you will excuse me for a moment," Gideon said. "I will return shortly."

Gideon climbed down and was inside the house for only a moment, then joined me again.

"Forgive my interruption," he said, resuming his reclined position. "A small matter of business needed to be directed."

In the streets below, two of Gideon's men hurried from the house and disappeared from sight at the first corner.

"Abram and Judah," Gideon explained. "They are to wait near the courtyards at Antonia and await the first signs of the trial and sentencing. There can be no room for mistakes today. There is no telling what Pilate may attempt. He is wily and not to be trusted, even to conduct court according to his own laws."

"Your plans cannot do anything but succeed," I said. "The details and the dedication of those below are without flaw. Barabbas will be free this day, I know it."

Gideon just looked at me and smiled.

"What?" I asked. "Did something I say amuse you?"

"No," he said. "It is just I have not told the stories, or shown my scar, to many men before. You now know more about Barabbas and me than many of our men. Perhaps it is your age, or the convictions we share, but you have a presence that allows men to speak freely when they are with you."

"I don't know about any presence," I said, "but I do listen— something younger men are slow to do."

"Perhaps, perhaps," he said. "But you have impressed many of them with your stories and instruction in close fighting," he said. "They like you and you have won their confidence—no small task, I assure you. They do not generally accept new recruits so quickly. So, you see, there is something special about you, whether you see it or not. But there is something else about you that is not right, and that concerns me." Gideon's tone became more serious. "When you speak, I can hear it in the way you breathe."

"Jacob's death affects me still," I said. "And will, I suppose, forever."

Gideon shook his head. "No. Death is something you are used to. I can feel that with you. There is something more."

"You question my pain?" I said. "Jacob was like a brother to me. We could have been closer only if we had shared blood."

"Barabbas and I know these men," he gestured to the full house. "Everyone a brother, a friend. We know their strengths, but more importantly, we know their weaknesses. They trust us with their lives, and their lives depend on us knowing who is suited for one task and who for another. Jacob is dead, I mourn his passing with you. He was killed by an agent of Rome; for this, and for other reasons, I join with you in your anger. But there is more depth to your hatred."

"How much deeper can my desire be to see Israel set free from Rome's oppression?"

"Injustice can be found everywhere," Gideon said. "There are many causes that men fight for. But there is always a *reason* one fights before a cause is found and taken up. I do not doubt your cause. You have shared much with us tonight, but you have yet to mention the reason you fight. Why did you pick up the sword?"

"Is it not enough that I do? Why is everyone interested in why I do?" I asked, my heart racing as fast as my tongue. "First Jacob, then my wife, and now you? Why do you care? Why do any of you? But I'll give an answer: to kill every Roman if it were possible. Is that good enough? Is that what you wanted to hear?"

Gideon did not answer right away, contemplating my remarks, but finally said, "You are lying."

My hand went to the hilt of the sword at my hip. As quick as I was, Gideon's hand was on top of mine.

"Your lie is not to me, but to yourself," Gideon said. "You told me last night that you have been fighting Rome since you were a young man. I mean no offense, but you are an old man now. There must be a great deal of fuel to feed that fire for so long." He released my hand. "Tell me."

"Rome has taken all that I loved, and to me they must be made to repay with their blood."

"I do not understand. What did they take?"

"They took my infant son. They killed him. In the night. Searching every house, killing all young boys."

Gideon's eyes widened with recognition at my words. "I know of what you speak," he said. "But there are not many who remember, or even know the evils of that night. But you fought back. You would not stand by and let this happen."

"There were too many of them. I lashed out and cut one with a stone . . . " I traced a line from my lip to my ear, " . . . but it wasn't enough. They still took him. And then they . . . then he . . ."

Gideon leaned back as if a great discovery had been made. "Then it is not Rome you want to kill," he said with wisdom reserved for men twice his age. "Though they are connected, they are not the same. With every Roman you strike down, you are trying to kill the pain caused by that night. It is this pain that drives you and consumes your every thought, eating away at your very soul. You will never be whole while it affects you like this. In whatever you do, you must look for an end—a cure—to this pain."

Without a word I stood and started walking away. Was it possible? Was this true? I was confused, and I needed some time to think. I wanted to scream that he was wrong, that I *did* want to kill every Roman for what they had done, but something in his words struck true. *Was* I trying only to dismiss the pain, the anger? But if not by cutting down the military might that caused the pain, then how? Wasn't one destroyed by destroying the other?

"This Roman you cut," Gideon called out, "is it possible that he lives still?"

"He was young then," I said. "We both were."

There was a glint in Gideon's eye, but before he could say more, there was a sudden commotion below on the streets. The alarm had been sounded. Men were coming. Gideon sprang to his feet and went inside. I followed on his heels. Every man was on his feet and two dozen swords were held ready as Gideon stepped to the door and peered out before throwing open the door.

Abram, one of the two men sent to the palace earlier that morning, hurried in, but he was not alone. With him was another, bound with cords and a canvas sack over his head. I noticed that the captive was well dressed, and was wearing fine, pleated robes usually associated with serving in the Temple. For a moment, I thought I recognized the clothing.

The door was quickly bolted behind them, and everyone gathered around.

"What is the meaning of this?" Gideon was not amused. "Has the trial begun?"

Abram shook his head. "He asked for you."

"And so you did as you were told?" Gideon struck Abram with the back of his hand, sending him into the men standing behind him. "There are many who would find us. If one of Pilate's men inquired of you, I only hope you would show better judgment."

Abram was crushed, and melted through the crowd to the back of the room.

"Do not be hard on him, Gideon," the captive said beneath the sack. I knew that voice.

Gideon drew the Temple priest close and ripped the hood from his head. Immediately I recognized him. It was the same priest I had seen the night before on the Mount of Olives, and again in the meeting hall of the Temple, and now, so close to him and in this weak light, he looked vaguely familiar, like I had once known him.

"I saw this man last night," I said, moving to Gideon's side. "He was leading a small army of Roman soldiers and temple guards outside the city wall. He is working for Rome."

The priest shot a look at me as venomous as a cobra's bite. "That is a lie!" he spat.

"He may be many things," Gideon said, putting his hand on my chest to calm me, "but one thing the high priest is not is a traitor to Israel. True, Caiaphas?"

Caiaphas? Joseph Caiaphas? In an instant I recognized him as the young, hungry student of the Law who could not understand my lack of ambition for power. So this was what path he had taken. I remembered his words from the trial in the night, and he repulsed me even more. If ever there was a mistake made, it was in advancing a man of such pride to the rank of rabbi. And as to not being a traitor to Israel, perhaps he wasn't, but he surely was a traitor to the Law.

In the time it takes one to blink, Gideon reached out and took the priest by the jaw, forcing their eyes to meet. He was in no way intimidated by or fearful of the office the priest held. "In different circles, we may tolerate each other, but I do not need you today, not now! So speak old man, priest or traitor," he said coldly, releasing his grip. "What is it you have to say?"

"You . . . you . . ." Caiaphas stuttered, unable to form the words. Last night I had seen a very different man. Among his peers he was an impressive figure, strong, forceful, and commanding respect. Last night he had held the power of life and death in his hands. But here, now, he was a scared old man. "You are friends of the condemned called Barabbas?"

"You were not brought here to ask us questions you already know the answers to." Gideon's anger was boiling.

"I can help free your friend."

"The Temple has long been opposed to what we do. You, yourself, have spoken against us. Why would you help us now? Do not ask me to believe that you have secretly supported us and now, at this hour, wish to join us." Gideon's tone became very much a threat. "My patience is wearing thin with your presence."

The priest called Caiaphas swallowed hard before speaking. "Pilate has announced that he will present one condemned prisoner to the people for release for the Day of Indulgence—it is a Passover tradition. We know that Barabbas is to die today." He looked around at our armed militia. "There is a way to free him."

"Again I find it difficult, nay, impossible, to believe that you would seek us out, risking your very life, to help us free a man your council has condemned, and whose life you have sought in the past."

"His name has already been suggested for release, and now Pilate asks the people."

"Abram?" he called. Abram quickly answered the summons, not wanting to displease Gideon twice in one morning. "Is what he says true?"

Abram nodded. "I heard it with my own ears. Pilate offers to set our brother free."

A ripple of excitement circulated throughout the room. But what appeared to be a miracle, sent at our final hour, did not sit well with me.

"Why him?" Gideon asked. "Why Barabbas?"

"Though we cannot officially condone your means, Barabbas is popular among the people. To some he is a legend, a champion of Israel. There are many that desire to see him set free."

Gideon raised a brow. There was more to the priest's story, something he was holding back. Gideon and I shared a concerned look; then he spoke again.

"Why?"

"Because all of Israel—"

"Finish your lie," Gideon said, interrupting, "and I will kill you where you stand. Man of God or not, I do not care, and neither will my blade."

The room quieted and the high priest looked around, undoubtedly realizing that he had made a mistake.

"You were seen last night in command of an army," Gideon reminded him. "The truth." There was an edge of finality to his words, and he gripped the pommel of his sword for emphasis. "Or the blade."

"There is another who must die in his place."

"The one you tried last night?" I asked. It was time to reveal the deed done in secret.

The high priest looked at me in a new way as he realized that it must have been me they had chased from the temple steps only a few hours ago. His eyes communicated his clear contempt and anger for having to speak of such things here and now.

"And what would you know of such things?" he said, looking long and hard at me.

"I know you tried a man at night," I said, listing off the errors in their action. "I know you convicted him solely on his own testimony, prohibited by the Law."

"Do I know you?" he asked. "Have we met before?"

"You have not answered my question."

"I recall no question being asked."

"Is this man's guilt worth trampling underfoot the Law with lies and deceit?"

"Are you a rabbi?" Caiaphas asked.

Did he recognize me? I did not think so, but his simple words cut me down inside and pained me. I should have been—and would have been if not for the corrupt ambitions of kings and caesars.

"You do not have to be a scholar to know the points of the Law," I answered.

The high priest must have known he had hurt me, for he gave away the hint of a smile before returning to his front of power and authority.

"You are in no position to lecture me on ethics or the Law," he said. "You, and those like you, who raise arms and shed blood—it is you that should be condemned for what you are doing."

My conscience was pricked, for I had shed blood in years past. But for those deaths I was justified.

"This is war," I said.

Caiaphas smiled contemptuously again. "It is war we wage as well. Only we fight on a different battlefield and use words instead of swords."

"And last night?"

"A victory."

"But blasphemy is not a capital offense under Roman law," I said, stating the obvious. I wasn't finished with this man who called himself the high priest. "What crime did you present him guilty of when you handed him over to the Roman authorities?"

"What he has done is between us and Pilate!" The priest lost all semblance of being either a holy or a wise man. "But he must surely die today, and we need your voices to join with ours. It is your choice."

Gideon considered this for a moment.

"And Barabbas goes free?"

"There are many who secretly sympathize with your struggle against Rome."

"The desperate lie of a desperate man," I said to Gideon. "There is still something else, I am sure of it. Perhaps it is a trap, offering Barabbas to lure you and your men to the very steps of the garrison. Pilate has done it before. We would be taken, or killed, every one of us."

"I swear to you, it is not!" Caiaphas said. "It was we who asked that Barabbas be released. I swear to you, we mean to free your brother."

"No," I said. "You plan to condemn another."

Gideon considered the choice now before him. "If this is a trap," he promised the high priest, "whether by your design or Rome's, neither you nor your loved ones will be safe from our reach."

Caiaphas tried to show his confidence but could not. "You must hurry," he said.

CHAPTER 13

The crowd was of considerable size, given the early hour, and was made up of the sort of people one would expect to attend such public displays of Rome's might and supposed mercy. There were political activists—both for and against Rome's authority—lawyers there to watch and learn, and visitors to the city, eager to see for themselves a Roman trial and execution. But mostly, the square was filled with the poor, those unwanted and unloved who had nowhere else to go and nothing else to do.

Gideon led a dozen of us through to the front gates of the courtyard. The rest stayed behind to warn of an ambush. Everyone was on high alert. The stories of Pilate's cowardice in years past had been told and retold earlier to underscore the danger we were all going into.

As we pushed through, I noticed the presence of many priests, and others dressed in the clothes of the aristocracy, and recognized many of the men I had seen in the night at the meeting of the great Jewish council. But most surprising was the cooperation of the Sadducees and Pharisees. These two leading sects of Judaism had been at odds with each other, even enemies, for years. I was surprised to see them agreeing on any point. And if their coming together for the condemnation of this other man was not strange enough, what I saw many of them doing gave me serious pause.

The priests were positioned throughout the crowd, paired up almost strategically, speaking in hushed voices to groups of the most undesirable men and handing out coins. Were these men here with Caiaphas? I could not think of any other explanation. It was clear there was a considerable effort being made to ensure the conviction of one man. The thought crossed my mind that if the evidence was not sufficient to convict him—without the support of our band and the paid poor—then perhaps he did not deserve to die. Were the crowds here to support Barabbas, or condemn the other man? But was it not the same thing? I shook off my uneasiness.

I had never been so close to a Roman military court without having plans to start a riot or inflict upon it some damage; now I had to push such thoughts away and remind myself that we were here to do a much greater thing. Barabbas's freedom would mean a hundred more strikes and a thousand more raids. Rome would be weaker for his life and leadership. But still, I could not shake the feeling that I shouldn't be there, that it was a mistake of some kind, that somewhere there was laid a trap.

"Are you sure we are safe?" I asked Gideon quietly.

"We have men at every gate, and down every street connecting to the garrison. We will know at the first move if this is a trap. Stay with me and you'll remain safe."

"So you do think maybe Caiaphas—"

"The high priest is a fool," Gideon said, the time to guard his words over. "He hungers for power and is concerned only for himself. We all know him. If it wasn't for his father-in-law, Annas, he would be nothing in the world he now commands."

"Annas, you say?" I said. "There was a time, long ago, that I knew a Temple priest of that name. A teacher I once had."

"As bad as Annas ever was, he was nothing like his successor. The priestly power corrupted Annas long ago, and it came as no surprise when he chose Caiaphas to wed his daughter."

It was all making sense—young Caiaphas's thirst for power knew no bounds. Marrying the daughter of the high priest was a sure way to make the sort of connections that would catapult him to the top. And now he was the high priest himself.

Gideon continued. "Caiaphas's hypocrisy is only bested by his lust for power. He thinks himself better than all of us because he is the high priest; because he can read and write volumes where most of us cannot spell our own names, he places himself above us. What he cannot see is that his sort of power is fragile. What is a high priest without those who believe and offer sacrifice? What is a king without subjects? What he doesn't know, and never will, is that he needs us. On the other hand, we need no one but ourselves—and our God."

Gideon was telling me things I already knew, but I was amazed to hear them being spoken from one so young. His insight into the workings of power and the nature of men was nothing short of rabbinical. I suddenly thought of my own sons and was embarrassed that they refused to see the battle being waged all around them; but I was also comforted to know that men like Gideon existed. Men who were being taught at an early age the truth—that freedom had a price. Jacob's words from the mountains outside of Apollonia returned to me. He had asked if I ever saw the time that we could entrust the fight to the younger generation. With men like Gideon, and Levi back home, leading the fight, the war would never be lost.

Military trumpets suddenly cut through the noise and all eyes went to the balcony overlooking the court. From the shaded interior stepped a short man wearing the toga praetexts, the official outer garment signifying his invested authority over the Roman province. The white robe was bordered with purple in the royal fashion, and was draped over his stocky body.

"This little man is the powerful Roman governor, Pontius Pilate?" I asked. "He doesn't look the part of the Roman fist sent to control and subdue the will and heart of Israel."

He was short, even for a Roman, and had fine, delicate—almost effeminate—features. He was younger than I had expected the governor to be and did not carry himself with the power that was his. He also did not look well.

He stepped to the rail and held up his hands to quiet the crowds. "Whom will ye that I release unto you?" he called out. "Barabbas . . . ?"

He paused as two soldiers dragged a bruised and beaten man into the courtyard below him. Though he was weak and his head hung low, I could tell that under different circumstances he was a tall and formidable man. When he looked up against the bright morning sun, I could see the strong family resemblance to Jacob. Barabbas looked around and then up to the balcony, and I could see in his intense stare how any man who crossed his path might end up dead, or worse. Rome had good reason to fear this man.

Pilate continued.

" . . . Or Jesus . . ."

Jesus? Where had I heard that name? Then I remembered. Yesterday, the leper who had been healed said the man who had cured him was named Jesus. Was this the same man?

Two more soldiers led another man out into the light. Like Barabbas, he too was tall and had a strong frame. His face was cut and bruised from recent abuse. He was arrayed in the poorest of clothes, tattered and dirty, but even so, there was something charismatic about him, a gentle strength and quiet power. He did not have the look of one to incite the people, nor did he have the look of a criminal.

" . . . which is called the Christ?" Pilate finished.

The Christ? In an instant I recognized him, though I had never before seen his face. This was the same man brought before the Sanhedrin in the night. So this was the man an army was sent to capture. For the sake of condemning this man, a generation of Jewish and Temple leadership would violate and profane the law they swore to uphold and protect. I remembered his few words from the night before and could picture them being spoken by this serene man. But what was he doing in a Roman court and in front of a Roman judge? His crime, as I heard it pronounced, was that of blasphemy. That was not a Roman crime. But here he stood. I had many questions, but knew not where to ask them.

Gideon leaned in close, but his eyes never left the courtyard. "I have seen this man, this Jesus. He has caused quite a stir among the rabbis and chief priests. Some claim he is a prophet, others say he is The One. But he produces only words, and a miracle or two. Freedom never came from words," he said, returning his full attention to the trial before him.

Pilate listened as the timid crowd began to stir, afraid to ask for what they wanted. Again he asked, annoyed at the lack of response from the crowd. "Whether of the twain will ye that I release unto you?"

Gideon looked to the crowd and then took the lead. "Barabbas!" he yelled. It was the spark that ignited the flames of other cries for his release. The name Barabbas quickly became a unified chant.

No one cheered for the man called Jesus.

I watched Pilate closely.

"What will he do?" I asked. "Will he really release one responsible for the death of three soldiers of Rome?" As much as I wanted to hope he would, the logic of it just wasn't sound.

Pilate looked to the advisors and soldiers who stood at his side. He sought help, but found none. He watched us for a long moment, then he leaned over the stone rail and pointed to the other one standing there accused.

"What shall I do then with Jesus, which is called Christ?"

Off to my left I noticed a young priest nervously stroking the hem of his outer garments. His eyes darted from the pavement to the crowds, and all around him. I followed his gaze as he searched the crowds until he stopped at Caiaphas standing along the back wall. The high priest then nodded. The young priest returned the sign and with a voice that shook with timid fear, called out, "Crucify him!"

So Caiaphas did not even have the courage himself to pronounce sentence on this accused man?

"Why?" Pilate called back. "What evil hath he done?"

But the governor's words were drowned out in the clamor. As before, the crowd was quickly ignited and took up the chant, "Crucify him!" Their voices grew until they reached a frenzy, wild and wicked. It was difficult not to get caught up in the energy and excitement. I had never before seen such emotion, such hatred.

Or had I?

With every chant, Pilate became visibly more angry. He gripped the stone rail until his knuckles turned white. As he was about to speak again, a woman, dressed in similar robes of Roman royalty, stole to his side and whispered in his ear.

"Who is that?" I asked.

"His wife," Gideon said.

Pilate pulled back and looked at her suddenly, startling her. Though from my distance I will never be sure, it looked as if his face turned a pale, ashen color. His smooth face became creased, deep with worry. He looked down at us, then to his wife, and finally to his advisors standing behind him, who again did him no good. What did she say? What words could she have spoken to her husband, the governor, to produce such dread and fear?

Pilate then called to someone behind him, and a moment later a servant appeared at his side with a wash basin. He dipped his hands in the water for all to see.

"I am innocent of the blood of this just person," Pilate said. "See ye to it."

Was the governor mad? Had the hot Judean sun boiled away all logic and rational thinking from this man? Pilate seemed not concerned in the least with the release of Barabbas, but instead showed only concern and remorse for the condemnation of the other man on trial.

The crowd cheered their approval, but were they cheering for the release of Barabbas, or that Jesus was to be crucified instead? Again I wondered, was there a difference?

Over the rapturous applause, someone called out, "His blood be upon us!" followed closely by another, "And on our children!" If the words were stones they could not have had a more real effect on me.

"Do they know what they're saying?" I asked. "Taking responsibility for a man's death where the Law did not provide for it was a serious oath. And not only on them, but on their posterity as well. Pilate is not the only mad one here today."

On the pavement, the soldiers holding Barabbas looked to their governor for instruction. Pilate looked over the cheering crowds, then motioned for his release. Many of the soldiers exchanged looks of disbelief and anger as Barabbas was taken to the gate, unshackled, and pushed out into the waiting embraces of his brothers-in-arms. He was whisked away at Gideon's instruction, in the likely event that Rome might suddenly change its mind.

"God be praised this day!" Gideon leaned over and said.

"Indeed," I had to admit, "it is a miracle. No weapons were drawn, no blood was spilt, and no one had to die to free our brother."

But I knew that wasn't true. One man would.

Caiaphas was smiling from the back wall, and I felt a burning hatred for the man. He had played us all to his end. A few more priests joined him and they began speaking to each other with smiles and congratulating each other. But as he stood there, admiring the work of his corrupt hands, thoughts entered my mind that would steal away his victory.

I looked back to Jesus, still standing there and facing the violent crowds still chanting his name and his sentence. I had seen enough of him since last night to know that he did not deserve being unjustly condemned by both Jew and Gentile alike. He must be set free. I leaned over to Gideon.

"You cannot let Caiaphas do this," I said.

"Do what?" Gideon asked. "He has helped us free our brother."

"We cannot let this other man die," I said.

"What can we do?" he said. "We can't risk it. Is this Jesus' life worth more than what we have just received?"

I didn't like it. Jacob had given his life to set a peasant free. Was I now going to let this man die at the hands of conspiring men?

Gideon must have seen the dilemma on my face. "Let it go. You can't save everyone."

"What did you say?" Jacob had spoken those words before I charged in at the Temple, and now they came to haunt me. I had thought I could, and instead had killed my best and only friend. Maybe they were right. But to honor Jacob's memory, I knew I wanted to try. Not so much to save the man's life, but to spite the high priest. Yet they were right. What could I do?

I gave one final look to Pilate, defeated this day by a crowd of commoners and priests. Victories like this were rare. I was sure that what I had just witnessed would be talked about for years to come.

I turned to follow Gideon but stopped suddenly.

"What is it?" Gideon asked.

I didn't know. Something inside my head and my heart was screaming to be heard. What had I missed? What was it? I turned back around and looked one more time at the consortium of people on the balcony. Advisors and servants, two Praetorian guards, and, closer to Pilate, another soldier, wearing the insignia of a centurion. In all of Judea there were maybe three thousand soldiers of Rome, mercenaries most of them, led by a handful of centurions. It was a position of power. But it was not his rank that held my attention.

It was his scar.

All currents of my blood stopped and a cold river raced through my center and spilled into my stomach. *It is him!*

His face was older, weathered by the sun and time, but there was no mistaking it. Images from thirty years of nightmares assaulted my every sense. Though no man touched me, I felt the grip of the two soldiers who held me fast while I was forced to watch, helpless, as this devil took my son in his hands. My head inexplicably hurt, and all at once a single tear trailed down my face. It seemed scarce an hour since he had ripped Joshua from my arms. And there, no more than a javelin's throw away, stood the demon, the monster who had stolen my life. He had become a ghost, a shadow, an invisible presence with me, haunting my every hour. Yet there he was in reality, standing at the right hand of the governor.

This centurion leaned close to Pilate, speaking passionately, but Pilate raised his hand and dismissed him.

Gideon shook me to get my attention. "What is wrong?"

I knocked his hands away. "When were you going to tell me?"

"What?" Gideon asked.

"That *he* lives!" I pointed to the balcony. "Who is he?"

Gideon paused and breathed deep. "The centurion?" At my nod he continued. "He arrived from Capernaum in the winter and is known to many of us in the city, but I had heard of him before then. The man has done many good things for our people scattered throughout the country. He is a friend to Israel and her God, and is the only fair and decent man to be born of Rome."

"He murdered my son!" I cried out. *Fair and decent?* These words were an outrage! How could Gideon speak them

"His name is Quintus," Gideon said. "He is a follower of this Jesus."

My hand shot to the sword at my side, but Gideon ripped it from my fingers and replaced it with a small, sheathed knife. It was a slick blade, long, and good for stabbing.

"Though I would persuade you not to do this, I understand your anger and thirst for justice. I know you must settle this," Gideon said. "But hear me now, friend. If you are the victor, you can no longer return to us. Your crime would put us all in danger. I cannot allow your actions to put us at risk. So I will bid you farewell. I hope with his death you find an end to your pain."

Movement in the courtyard attracted my attention, and I watched, teeth clenched, as the soldiers took the condemned away, leading him back into Antonia's inner court. Above, the centurion left as commanded.

Gideon was busy directing his men to clear a safe path for their released brother to travel, not only away from the garrison, but also through the streets and to a safe place. Before he left with them he turned and clasped my hand as a friend would.

"A wise rabbi once explained to me," Gideon said, "that with the things of God there is no coincidence. There can be no other way."

"I understand," I said, believing that I did. God had brought me here to punish one guilty of violating His laws, and the Law demanded punishment in this wise: a life for a life. The soldier's life for my son's. Although this soldier was a heathen and not held to the Law by lineage, he had killed one who was, and that made him punishable under the Law. Our Law. God's Law. Perhaps I had been mistaken. Perhaps God did have a plan for each of us. I gripped the knife tightly. It felt good in my hand. "My coming to Jerusalem was not a mistake after all," I said in farewell.

Gideon touched my shoulder. "Then go with God." He turned and was gone.

CHAPTER 14

Jesus was taken from the outer pavement and led to the inner court, called the praetorium. Once his guard and he stepped through the arch they rounded a corner, and I lost sight of them. This prisoner, I knew, was my link to the centurion. If the centurion was present at the public trial, he might also show himself at the punishments and execution. If I followed this Jesus, I would find him.

I scrambled and pushed my way back out through the crowd. I looked down the many streets and alleys that touched the Roman fortress Antonia. The streets were filling up quickly as the sun freed itself from the hills on the horizon, but I found what I was searching for. Halfway up the wall along a dead-end street, I spotted a group of children crowded around a small, barred window. They stood on steps they had engineered themselves. Curiosity and ingenuity, a cause of so much trouble with young boys, was also a source for creative and simple solutions to problems. That morning they had solved mine.

They scattered as I approached, and I climbed their homemade steps to the port that overlooked the inner court. Cautiously I peered into the hall. The soldiers had already begun.

Across the Empire, scourging was a favorite recreation for Roman soldiers, a sick and cruel entertainment. A prisoner, already condemned to die, would be stripped of his clothes and tied to a stake where he would be whipped thirty-nine times. Their law demands forty, but one is abated—for mercy—in honor of their pagan gods. If a man was to be later crucified, the scourging would be lighter to preserve his strength; if not, it was severe. Were the whip only braided leather, the punishment would be terrible enough, but these whips, I knew, were far worse. Barbed with jagged bits of sheep bone and metal, each lash tore the flesh of the back. Many a prisoner was spared the cross by dying under the whip.

The prisoner must have been of some fame because dozens of soldiers had come to the inner court to watch. I searched their faces, but none had the mark. My eyes finally rested on the prisoner held fast under the whip. For a moment I forgot about the centurion; for, though grunts acknowledged the pain with every strike, there were no screams for mercy, and no curses for his captors. Not a word escaped his lips, and a thought struck me as hard as any physical blow. *What manner of man is this?*

Half a dozen soldiers looked on, but the one I so desperately needed to see was not there. The trip from the balcony to the inner court was a short one. Where had he gone?

They cut the prisoner loose and threw him, barely conscious, to his knees. One of them produced a brightly colored robe and draped it over his bleeding back and shoulders. Then another, clearly enjoying the sport of the day, forced a wreath of plaited thorns he had been weaving down over the prisoner's head. One of the barbs pricked his finger, and he swore and struck this Jesus as if it were his fault.

Another guard found a dry reed and placed it in the Jew's right hand. I could not imagine what they were doing until they all took to one knee in mock reverence, bowing, and each called out, "Hail, King of the Jews!"

Then they all laughed and took turns striking him.

Suddenly the centurion burst into the hall. He was winded, and I could see that fresh blood trailed down his forehead. There was an angry fire ablaze in his eyes. The soldiers were startled to their feet. Two of them, a small one in particular, looked frightened and backed into the farthest wall. But the centurion did not pursue him. Instead, he pushed the other soldiers away and helped the beaten prisoner to his feet. He tossed the reed away and was about to remove the crown of thorns when a voice boomed from the shadows just beyond my view.

"Leave it!" It was Pilate. "Bring him here." Had the governor witnessed the savage beating?

The centurion put his arms around the prisoner and lifted him to his feet. Together the three of them walked back to the outer court.

I jumped from the wall and sprinted back to the gate. With Gideon's men gone, the crowd had thinned a little. At the sight of Pilate—or of this Jesus, I do not know which—their voices rose to an almost deafening roar. This time Pilate, standing now beside the prisoner, made no attempt to quiet the people. Instead he took Jesus' bound hands and raised them with his own.

"Behold the man!" Pilate declared, shouting to be heard over them. This announcement fueled the crowd, and with foul words and screams they demanded his crucifixion. It was a riot on the edge of tumult. More guards were called in to strengthen the court's gate. Could one man's life be worth all this? Pilate searched one more time for mercy, but finding none, released Jesus' arms.

"Take ye him and crucify him," he said, sounding defeated. "I find no fault in him."

Innocent in the eyes of Rome? Yet condemned to die? I had the anxious sensation that I was witness to a play in the final act. What had happened to lead up to this moment? Had Pilate spoken to this Jesus before? It seemed that he knew him, or at least of him, and was already convinced of his innocence. What deal had been struck to condemn this man and set an enemy of Rome free? What did Caiaphas have hanging over the head of the Roman governor to force the release of one who had stolen from the Empire and killed three of her own? The crowd was great, but surely there were soldiers enough to quash any uprising, soldiers who would only be satisfied with the blood of Barabbas shed.

And still the questions came. Why did Pilate care whether this man died or not? Was he not the Roman governor, the most powerful man in Palestine? Why would he so adamantly declare the innocence of this one convicted Hebrew? Later I would wonder why, with all of this power, he did not simply free the man if he so believed in his innocence.

"We have a law, and by that law he ought to die!" someone shouted. This time it was Caiaphas, his voice somehow carried over the shouts and applause. "Because he made himself the Son of God!"

Some of the color drained again from Pilate's face. Was this charge new to him? But with his pantheon of gods, why should this statement so affect him and strike fear in his heart? And it *was* fear. He looked to the prisoner at his side and then up to the balcony where his wife still watched. She acknowledged his look and then lowered her eyes to the ground and retreated into the palace shadows.

Pilate withdrew to the large judgment seat still shaded beneath the balcony, and with a quick word, the centurion followed, Jesus in tow. They were too far away, and the crowds were too noisy to hear what they were saying, but I could see that Pilate was asking questions of Jesus which he answered in turn. Pilate then stood and pulled the dagger from the centurion's belt and cut the ropes that held Jesus bound. In an instant Caiaphas was at the gate.

"If you let this man go," he called out to Pilate, "you are not Caesar's friend. Whosoever makes himself a king, speaks against Caesar!"

I could not understand the high priest's hatred of the prisoner. Jesus was clearly no king; if so, where was his following? Where was his army? His soldiers? Where was his rescue from the hands of his accusers? Still the crowd called out the sentence, "Crucify him!"

Pilate no longer tried to hide his anger toward the high priest as he erupted from the great wooden seat, grabbing Jesus by the wrist and pulling him out into the open. He thrust him forward for all to see, but this was a personal battle between himself and Caiaphas.

"Behold your king!" Pilate offered. "Shall I crucify your king?"

The Roman governor was shrewd, and had the skill and wit usually reserved for lawyers and those who argue the points of the law. Neither the high priest nor the governor believed this man was a king, yet this is what he stood accused of. An answer either way would affect the sentence and this man's fate. If they answered yes, acknowledging him as their king, he would be entitled to a new trial as a person of status; if no, then his sentence would be commuted and, given the new charge of blasphemy, he would be turned over to the high priest for sentence. Either way, Jesus would not die that day by his hand.

But what Caiaphas answered back would haunt me forever.

"We have no king but Caesar!"

The crowds of Jews cheered all the more, caught up in the frenzy and repeating the blasphemy. Did they know what they were saying? Did any of them understand? Israel has only one King, and He is

God. We'd had many taskmasters, Caesar and his Empire at that moment, but we had never voluntarily bowed to another king. It would be better for us to die. And yet this priest, this servant of the God of Abraham, Isaac, and Jacob, of our Lord and our King, would blaspheme his holy office and calling, guilty now of the same offense of which this Jesus stood condemned. Why?

But then, it did not matter why. He had. They all had. They were all guilty. If God had indeed abandoned Israel, it was only because Israel abandoned Him first.

One last time Pilate scanned the crowd in search of mercy, but he found none. In clear disgust he turned his back to Jesus and the crowds and, with a flick of his royal hand, the sentence was passed. Final and forever.

The centurion touched Jesus on the shoulder, and together they walked back to the inner court where the last preparations would be made for the trek to Golgotha.

People screamed their hysterical approval and turned abruptly, pushing and shoving their way to the execution route. I stayed behind and watched until the centurion and Jesus were gone from my sight. Caiaphas stayed too. He seemed proud of what he had done; it was, to me, a sickening display of deceit and blasphemy. And we had been part of it.

I felt for the knife, hidden now in the folds of my shirt, to make sure it was in place, then followed the crowd out. As I reached the streets a man was forcing his way back through the people with a look of frightened desperation in his eyes. His shoulder struck mine as we passed, and a small purse fell from his clutches. Several pieces of silver fell out, which he quickly gathered up. I stopped and watched as this latecomer rushed to Caiaphas at the gate, holding out the small purse.

"What is it you want with us now?" Caiaphas asked him.

"I fear there has been a mistake," the man said.

"There is no mistake. Your price is not up for renegotiation. It is as we agreed."

"No," the man pleaded, "you don't understand. I fear I have sinned. I have betrayed an innocent man."

"What's this? A change of heart?" Caiaphas asked shrewdly. "Last night you were so sure even that you betrayed him with a kiss."

These words were familiar to me. I had heard them speak of a disciple of Jesus betraying him in the night. They said his name was Judas.

"You must stop this!" Judas said.

"Have you forgotten that it was *you* who came to *us?*" Caiaphas said. "Without your help we never would have been able to find him. Again, let me offer you our thanks."

"No! No . . . no . . . You must understand, the night I came to you—"

Caiaphas interrupted him. "Your reasons are your own and no concern of ours."

The disciple who had betrayed his master looked to be in physical pain as he faced the high priest. He winced and took sharp breaths as he spoke. I had never before seen guilt exhibit itself on the body such as I was seeing here. I did not think I could begin to understand the anguish and remorse he was going through.

"But . . . but why have him killed?" Judas asked. "Because he heals on the Sabbath? Because he teaches of forgiveness instead of retribution? What has he done deserving of death at your hands?"

"*Our* hands?" The high priest shook his head. "Rome punishes him, not us."

"Pilate speaks the words you script. Everyone in Jerusalem knows this. You have the power to save him. You could save him."

Caiaphas chuckled softly to himself. "I do not know what power you think I have—"

"You lie! You have the power to stop this! It is still not too late!"

"Do not forget who I am," Caiaphas argued, his calm pretense dissolving with these questions and accusations. "I could have you tried and stoned for speaking to me with such contempt."

"*Why are you doing this?*" Judas shouted.

With an eruption of dark emotion, Caiaphas pushed Judas to the ground and stood over him. "I am the high priest!" he cried. "All my life I have served God. The duty is mine to protect and defend the purity and integrity of Israel. If God was to choose a Messiah He would not choose a carpenter's son, a Nazarene, a Galilean. It cannot be him. Israel's sheep have been deceived. I am simply correcting their mistake. It is God's will that Jesus die."

"I have betrayed my Lord," the man said. "I must stop it."

"What can you do?" Caiaphas said.

"He will die!" Judas was wild in his remorse.

"Yes," Caiaphas said. There was pleasure in his words. "He will."

"May God forgive me."

"You have your money—a slave's price," Caiaphas said. "Now be gone!"

The man burst into terrified tears, leapt to his feet, and ran past me and out to the streets toward the Temple. His wailing could be heard for some time. When I turned back around, Caiaphas was grinning in satisfaction. He then noticed me and bowed slightly at the waist in mock gratitude for my unwitting help in condemning Jesus. I felt unclean. But whatever feelings of disgust and disdain I felt for him and what I had just witnessed, I left them there. Executions were swift, I knew. When murder was in order, Rome made no delay.

CHAPTER 15

The narrow streets leading from Antonia out of the city were lined with men, women, and even children, all eager to view the morning's savage event. I knew from making plans the night before what route the soldiers would take, and found the stretch of road where the street narrowed. I forced my way through to the front of the crowd. It was perfect. The walls were high and the crowds thick; across the street was an alley narrow enough to allow only one man at a time. It was well suited for the rescue attempt, just as Gideon had planned. But now it would serve me just as well. The plan had formed in perfect detail as I made my way through the streets. Here I would exact revenge, and then save this one, condemned man—a ransom for Jacob's life. I gripped the knife's hilt as the procession made its way toward me. I waited.

Calls and curses announced the arrival of the cruel Roman justice, marching the offenders through the streets for all to see. From where I was, I noted just over a dozen guards and soldiers, each busy pushing back the crowds to make way for the three condemned that were to die that day.

Then I saw him.

The centurion too was pushing back the angry mobs, but he was also shielding Jesus from the rocks and insults. He even steadied the prisoner as Jesus stumbled under the weight of the wood strapped to his shoulders. Such a show of compassion for a Hebrew puzzled me. Where was that compassion when he took my son? When he drew his polished blade?

The murderous centurion was now only twenty paces away. I could see more clearly the scar that disfigured his face. It connected his lip to his ear. I had cut him deep that night. But not deeply enough, for he still lived. With every step he took, my heart beat with more force, and my breathing became rapid.

Fifteen paces.

Here they had to proceed in single file.

The first of the prisoners passed by, cursing and swearing by heaven that he was innocent of any wrongdoing. He found no mercy or compassion from any within the sound of his cries. The second walked closely behind, sobbing like a frightened child, accepting the fate that awaited him on Golgotha's crest. He trudged along, seemingly oblivious to the jeers and stones that pummeled his wasted body.

Ten paces.

I believed my chest would burst. The anger. The rage. The fear. My tongue felt swollen and my fingers and toes were cold.

Jesus had fallen behind the others, undoubtedly weak from the terrible scourging he had recently endured, and by his side walked the thief of my life. But they were moving too slow. Unable to wait a moment longer for him to come to me, I slipped through the masses and stalked toward the centurion, my prey. My palm was sweaty on the leather hilt of the blade that would finally silence my nightmares and give me back my life.

Jesus fell to one knee on the uneven ground. The centurion moved to his side and reached down to help him up. Now was my chance! *Today you are avenged, my son! An eye for an eye! Your life for mine!*

I charged into the street.

His back was laid open and unprotected from my attack. I had drawn the knife from the folds of my clothes, my every sense heightened and focused on what I had to do next, when a powerful hand from behind took my shoulder and spun me around. The knife caught on my sleeve and fell from my fingers to the street. It was one of the other soldiers; in his hand he held his sword ready. My heart screamed in protest! Was this how it was to end? After thirty years of agony and pain, to die only an arm's length from the monster who had murdered my son and destroyed my life. He could not be allowed to live. Would I forever be denied my right to blood?

The fatal stroke of the soldier's long blade did not come as I expected. Instead, his fingers dug into my shoulder.

"What is your name?" he demanded.

In thirty years I had never given into any demand or request of any Roman at any time, so I was surprised to hear my name escape my lips.

"Simon."

Still holding me tight with one hand, the giant soldier stepped over to Jesus, raised his sword high, and cut the ropes that kept the large beam on his cut and bleeding shoulders.

"You will bear his cross."

I was forced to my knees to await this man's burden. As the wood was hefted from his shoulders and placed on my back, our eyes briefly met. With a power stronger than my hatred and thirst for blood, he commanded my every thought and feeling, and I was unaware of anything or anyone but him. In a city thronged with people, it was as if we two were all alone. Though no guard was left on me, I did not flee or scramble for the knife that was still within my reach. I had no thought to resist. How could I?

His eyes were strong and majestic, and in that beautiful, striking gaze I felt the presence of a king. Nowhere in them was the smallest inkling of fear—no anger for the crowds, for their spit or their stones or their foul words. There was, though, welled up in those glorious eyes, a sadness, deep and profound. Not for him and his fate, I sensed, but for those persecuting and reviling against him. Yet, amid all that was happening to him, there seemed to be gratitude in his look for what I was being compelled to do.

The single moment that I shared with him seemed suspended above the events that surrounded us. I was aware of nothing else as he looked upon me. But if I am never sure of anything else as long as I live, I am sure that he knew me. Not just at that moment, but knew of everything—the death of my son, the loss of my family, my actions against Rome, and my dark intentions that day. In his darkest hour, he knew my pain, my hurt, and . . . he shared it with me . . . the suffering, the anger, the guilt I carried. This was no mere attempt to sympathize with my pain. I somehow felt it in my bosom—and it overcame me. This was boundless empathy, a sharing of my experience, every detail fully and completely known. He was looking upon the thoughts and intents of my wounded heart, and he, alone, understood my loss. But how could he? *Who is this man?* I wondered. What power did he possess to calm, if only for a moment, the raging sea of my soul with a mere gaze from his beautiful eyes?

And then the moment passed. His eyes left mine, and his attention was drawn to a gathering of women who had pushed their way to the street, weeping and attending to him with water and wine. He spoke to them, but I could not hear his words.

The wood was tied securely to my back, and we were both lifted to our feet and prodded forward. Jesus led, with the continued support of the centurion, and I followed in their footsteps. Then a thing quite unexpected happened. Compelled to carry his cross, I joined with Jesus as the object of so much vile and unexplained hatred. Every step was filled with evil speaking and obscene curses. *But for what?* I wanted to cry. Then with immense force, the words of the governor returned to my ears, *What evil hath he done?* At the moment I glimpsed, perhaps, Pilate's desperate confusion at the trial. His question was now mine: *What has he done to deserve this punishment?*

The weight of the wood was enormous, but I found strength enough in my neck to look up and into the faces of the accusers, their faces ugly and hideous as only anger and hatred can be. As I glanced over them, I saw my own reflection in their faces. For the first time I realized how others must have seen me these many years—my wife, my family, my friends—and if them, then surely God. I could not bear to look at the mob any further, and walked behind them, unable to raise my eyes from the dust.

Powerful thoughts run through a man's mind when his world is altered by some catastrophe or wonderful event. I was no different from other men. I remembered distinctly the day Joshua was born. My world changed then, as did my place in it. I was no longer Simon, student of the Law, future scribe and rabbi, or even husband to a beautiful wife. I was now a father. And with that most important title, I would begin a new life, with new priorities and dreams. My life would be even further from being my own. It was a blessing to be a father; but with that blessing came obligations, a stewardship over love and life, a duty to provide for and protect. I had prayed for it for such a long time, and God, in His wisdom, granted my petition. I was now partner with Him to care for and raise my new son.

A partnership I had failed Him in.

I was unworthy to bear the title of father. God was right to deny me a son for so long. This was my greatest fear. I had failed in my duties. I would never be forgiven for letting it happen. How could I be? Joshua was counting on me to protect him, and I failed. The sin was mine to bear. I had never before faced this thought; the pain of it was too immense. Anger, hatred, humiliation—they were all rooted in this one fear: I would be forever punished for my sin.

But *was* it my sin to bear? My mind and heart were filled with questions as I walked the streets behind the marvelous and surpassing man before me.

Beyond the city wall the crowds were forced back to a safe distance, and we could see the hill Golgotha—"the place of the skull." I had heard that its name came from the play of late afternoon shadows on the rocks as they took the vague shape of a skull. But as we marched to the top a different explanation became clear. To one side of the worn path there was a wide, shallow depression. The wind and rain had washed away much of the dirt, revealing the bones of a mass prisoners' grave. A few exposed skulls in niche-style graves looked out at us, and the sight made me shudder. Still we climbed.

Atop the hill, a dozen more soldiers, executioners by trade, went about their business of death in an impersonal manner. It was their duty; they showed no remorse or compassion. The two other criminals had already been raised, forming a pair of horrible crosses on display for the busy road below. Between them was an empty space that would soon be filled.

The beam was cut from my shoulders and taken from me, and a great sadness took my knees away. Sinking to the ground, I saw that my shirt had been stained with his blood. I watched as Jesus was stripped of the robe the soldiers had dressed him in and unceremoniously thrown over the cross piece. Again, he offered no resistance as his arms were stretched out and the crucifiers readied the enormous, bloodstained nails. The centurion I had intended to kill only a short while earlier approached Jesus with a bucket. The centurion dipped in a sponge and put a dark liquid to Jesus' lips.

"Drink," he begged. "Please."

I could see that Jesus knew what the centurion was trying to do. The liquid was a narcotic to dull the pain, offered in mercy. But for some reason, Jesus gently refused. Tears broke and trailed down the centurion's face.

My whole body folded in on itself, and an involuntary gasp forced its way out as the first nail was struck deep through his hand. Although I had seen from a distance many a condemned man hanging from the crossed beams over the years, I had never before been present when they were secured to it. I turned away. I could not endure to watch. But though my eyes were averted, my ears heard, and I bear record of his pain as he was nailed, hands and feet, to the cross—lifted up for all to see.

The wind began to rise and thick clouds filled the sky. The sun seemed to withhold its light. A storm was coming.

Helpless to do anything but watch, I knelt a short distance from the middle cross. I was in shock, stunned. Not by the cruel acts I was being witness to, but by the dignity with which Jesus bore it; for the moment, I had forgotten about the centurion.

Spectators and those there to mourn the condemned were forced to keep their distance along a perimeter around the hill site. No one but the rank of Rome were allowed within, yet no one seemed to take much notice of me. Off to one side, four or five soldiers knelt in a circle throwing dice and gambling for the robe that had belonged to Jesus. Was the robe of more importance to these men than the man who wore it? Another soldier climbed a ladder to the top of the cross and hung a piece of wood carved with words large enough for the crowd and passersby on the road below to see: Jesus of Nazareth, King of the Jews.

Then Jesus spoke, and for the first time that terrible day I heard his voice. It was deep and clear. I can hear it even now, and remember how it resounded through my entire body.

"Father, forgive them, for they know not what they do."

As those words were uttered, I felt as if some place deep in my chest had been cut open, and my pain, anger, and despair flowed from me in a flood of peace. Indeed, it was as if all hate was let from my veins. It started to rain, and as the water struck my face and rolled off, I felt suddenly clean. But it was more than a feeling. It was as if a physical transformation was taking place. My limbs were light, and my whole being felt lifted up. I was free for the first time in thirty years of the heavy burden which weighed down my heart. I was not at fault for failing to save my son. I would not be punished. I had done what I could, and with great release I let go of that guilt. For all the wisdom Gideon possessed, he had been wrong about one thing: freedom *was* to be found in words. These words, from this man.

From the crowd behind us I heard someone say, "He can save others, but not himself." I looked behind me and saw Caiaphas at the perimeter, standing in a row with others from the Temple, smiling in satisfaction. He called out, "Save yourself if thou be the Son of God!" and they all laughed.

One of the criminals suffering the same fate as Jesus must have heard the priests, and he voiced the same question with words that conveyed the excruciating pain racking his body.

"If thou be Christ, save thyself and us."

His words echoed and rang a familiar sound. Then a realization struck me. I had heard only a few men address Jesus since I first learned of his name the day before. Included in almost all their words was the word *If.* Always was this demand for proof. There seemed to be so much concern with this question. It almost seemed as if there was a united effort to make Jesus doubt who he was and what he was doing.

The other condemned man spoke up in the defense of Jesus and rebuked his fellow criminal.

"Do you not fear God, seeing you are in the same condemnation? And we justly, for we receive the due reward of our deeds; but this man has done nothing amiss." He let his head fall forward suddenly, and I thought that he might have died in the effort required to voice the harsh words. He then took as deep a breath as the tight ropes around his body would let him as he looked to Jesus instead with new tears in his eyes.

"Lord, remember me when Thou comest into Thy kingdom."

Everywhere also, it seemed, were men and women who believed this man's words and followed his teachings and miracles. Had this criminal been a follower of Jesus as well? Did he know of Jesus' innocence, too, and of his teachings and prophecies?

Then Jesus lifted his head and caught the gaze of the criminal suffering beside him. Though it was a private moment, I could not help but watch as something transpired between them, similar to mine a short while ago in the streets of the city. The criminal began weeping like a child.

"Today," Jesus said, "thou shalt be with me in paradise."

The words were sublime, and the peace that fell upon the hill was genuine, and in abundance. I wish I had been given—or had taken—time to learn of this man and hear his words.

I did not know how long I was there. In one respect it seemed like only an instant, but then it seemed as if another thirty years had passed. I took little notice as soldiers and guards busied themselves around me. My thoughts were of my son, my life, my actions, and the suffering I had inflicted upon my dear wife and our beautiful family. Every detail of thirty years played over in my mind as I recalled, in full recognition, my deeds and selfish intentions. Even as Hannah and my other sons were born to us, I had forsaken them through no fault of theirs. I had given them no love. Instead of helping Deborah and comforting her, acknowledging her pain and loss, I had only attended to my own grief. Could she forgive me after all I had done? Would she even want to?

A thunderclap directly overhead jolted me from my thoughts. Thick black clouds formed a low canopy over our heads, blotting out all traces of the sun. What hour was it? How much time had passed? For a moment I was disoriented. Jesus was looking at someone beyond the perimeter. I turned and looked behind me to see who it was and saw a young man holding and comforting an older woman given over to uncontrollable tears. What sadness, what love was in her expression. What devotion they must have possessed to remain despite the terrible storm.

"Woman!" Jesus suddenly cried out, loud enough to be heard over the wind and rain, but with a gentle compassion, "behold thy son!"

Could this be his mother? What love she must have for her son, I thought, to endure not only the winds and the rain, but the sight and sounds of her own flesh and blood being killed slowly, and for a crime he was innocent of. There was nothing she could do for him but look on and support him in his final hours as she, no doubt, had looked upon him for the first hours after his birth. *A great circle is life and death,* I thought.

She was sobbing still when Jesus spoke again, this time with an air of command to the young man standing beside her.

"Behold thy mother!"

I understood immediately what I had just witnessed. In his last moments alive, Jesus was entrusting his mother to the care of this man with her. No longer able to care for and support her, his last thoughts were for his mother's well-being. What depth must be this man's compassion for others. What strength he must have to expend it to the end for those around him: to his mother and friends, to the centurion, to the thief at his side, to the soldiers that inflicted the pain upon him.

To me.

A sudden gust of wind swept over the hill and would have knocked me down had I not already been on my knees. The wind seemed to tear at the rocks, and would have uprooted the Roman tree on which Jesus hung if it were possible. Then, in agony I cannot begin to comprehend, he suddenly cried out, "My God, my God, why hast thou forsaken me?"

For a time he appeared to be in such torment that I believed death would take him. What did he mean? How could God forsake a man such as this at his most crucial hour? Was this agony, this torment meant to be endured alone, even without the support of God for a time? Was his love and compassion for others only? Could he not bestow some of it on himself? In the true character of humility, I knew with inexplicable insight that he couldn't. He loved others more than he loved himself; he healed and saved others with no thought for his own being. A prophet such as he was, Israel had never before seen.

As quickly as the pain of separation took him it also left him, and he became silent and still. Scarcely more than a whisper, and barely audible over the howling wind, Jesus spoke.

"I thirst."

At his words the centurion jumped to his feet. I had not taken notice of him for some time nor given any thought to him. He dipped a rag into fresh water and tied it quickly to the end of a pole, then presented it to Jesus' lips. He drank and I could see new tears in the eyes of the centurion, grateful for the chance to serve this, the greatest of men.

"It is finished," Jesus said. He then cried with an air of triumphal strength. "Father, into thy hands I commend my spirit."

Then his body relaxed, free at last from the pain it bore.

Sharp streaks of lightning cut through the darkness and sizzled the air. Concussions from enormous thunderclaps pierced the whole earth and the heavens opened up, flooding the countryside, as if God Himself were weeping at the death of . . .

His Son. The Messiah. The words and accusations of the council hit me with full force.

At this revelation to my heart of who He was, I began to see my connection to Him even since my youth. I saw all of my training at the synagogue and in the Temple in light of who we were actually studying and preparing for. I remembered the star Deborah and I had seen—it was the sign proclaiming his birth. And the night the soldiers had moved through the city—they had been looking for *Him.* And then, quite suddenly, my heart was flooded by the thought that my son, indeed, all of the sons taken that night, had died so that this man might live.

The ground shook with one great convulsion, forcing everyone to their knees—mourners and soldiers alike. All were equal and made to kneel. One soldier crawled over to the centurion, in obvious fear for his life, and said, "This was a righteous man."

"No," the centurion said, speaking for the first time where I could hear his voice. "Truly this was the Son of God."

The simple testimony of one who believed. He had endured with Him to the end. This Roman, a heathen and a Gentile, had recognized Israel's God, the Great Jehovah, where so many Jews had not. This centurion had known Him, believed in Him, even loved Him. And that love was reciprocated. I could only stare in awe.

It was as if the centurion knew my gaze had fallen on him, for in that moment he turned his attention from the crucified Lord to me. The wind and rain stung our eyes, and though it seemed as if the whole earth was being destroyed around us, neither of us could look away.

All at once his expression turned to one of recognition, his eyes grew wide, and he crawled through the mud and buried his face before me, crying. I was confused. Offering himself before me was the man who, only a few hours ago, I wanted nothing more to do with than to bury a blade deep within his chest as he had done to my son. But now, with the opportunity so perfectly presented to me, I could not even think of it. What was happening to me? As unfamiliar thoughts collided with my old obsessions, a new insight emerged and was born that instant in my heart. Could it be that he had been plagued by that same night all these years, just as I had been? Did my pleas for mercy haunt his dreams, as his actions did mine? What burden of unsurmountable guilt he must have carried to recall my face so quickly after all these years.

No longer trapped beneath the oppressing weight that had suffocated my spirit for so long, a peculiar sensation entered me. It felt as if the furthest recesses of my soul were being warmed by the heat of the noonday sun. The frost that had encrusted my soul for so long started to melt, and its runoff welled up in my eyes. In that moment I understood what Deborah and Gideon, each in their own way, had been trying to tell me. There was freedom in forgiveness—a powerful release that allows healing to take place. In my desperate chase to kill the snake, the poison from his strike sped its way to my heart, killing my spirit and my faith. My growth had been stunted. I had been damned. But I would be denied life no longer.

I knew what the centurion was begging of me. His actions spoke a language I was only beginning to understand, and as we knelt there a quiet tremor filled my soul that shook me more than the earth that rumbled around us. Could I say those words to myself? Could I say them to him? This tremor grew in strength until I believed the words needed release and they leapt from my lips.

"I forgive you," I said.

The centurion looked up, his tears mixing with the rain on his face, a joyous look in his eyes as if we had been brothers reunited. In a sense we were brothers, I thought suddenly, fathered by that dark night so long ago.

I could see in his expression that there was much he wanted to tell me, when lightning suddenly cracked open the skies. We both recoiled from the fierce power, and my thoughts returned quickly to my family and their safety. Was it too late to beg their forgiveness?

Had too much time passed to make amends? Was it too late to repent? I did not know, but I knew I had to try. While I lived there was hope. Perhaps there would be time later to speak further with the centurion. For now, I had more important relationships to save. I stood, left the centurion, and ran down the rocky hill.

CHAPTER 16

The earth quaked until I believed the mountains would crumble. The great city of Jerusalem was aflame in a thousand places, and the smell of ash added to the picture of panic and debris. Houses split open and walls fell into ruin. The wind concentrated and magnified its mighty power as it was channeled through the streets, carrying away anything not fastened down. The rain fell with such increasing force that many of the narrow alleys had become swift rivers, sweeping away rubble; twice I was swept off my feet in their currents. The frightened screams of men, women, and children filled the air and reached into every house. *God is destroying this city and its people for what they have done,* I thought. I had to reach my family before His wrath did.

I had just passed the gates to the upper city when I suddenly felt a cold sensation, like ice, on my back and shoulders. It was accompanied by a strong force, and I fell forward, hitting my head on the hard ground. I thought I would drown in the water that rushed over and around me. I coughed to expel the fluid from my lungs. As I did, the feel of ice was replaced by a sharp pain in my head and neck and I realized that I couldn't move. Had I been struck by falling debris from the city that was crumbling all around me? It was possible, though I didn't remember being under a high wall. I slowly found some strength and managed to get to my hands and knees. I saw movement off to my side but was unable to react quickly enough to it, and I was kicked with considerable force. My breath was taken away. Stunned, and unable to move to defend myself, I was vulnerable for another attack. Again a swift foot connected squarely with the curve of my ribs, and I was knocked to my side.

Tears of pain mixed with the rain and blurred my vision even more. There, standing over me, was the shape of a man. I pushed myself away with feet kicking and slipping on the flagstone street. Behind him I could see blurs that were people running past, but no one stopped to help. I wondered if any of them could even see me through the veil of rain that was falling.

"Get up!" the figure shouted. "I have not watched you for weeks to have you fall down and stay down after the first hit. Now get up!" He kicked me again.

I wiped the water from my eyes. I had seen this man somewhere before, but I did not know him. *Where have I . . . ?* Then I remembered—the ship! And then with the caravan. It was the Bedouin who had traveled with us.

"What do you want?" I gasped out.

"To be rich!" he said.

"Rich?" I said weakly. "I have no money, and if you're—"

I stopped. The meaning of his words struck terror in my heart. He was no thief; he did not mean to rob me. He had followed us from Apollonia, and I was sure he was the same man we had chased in Alexandria. He had come to collect the bounty on our heads. "You . . . you're the one who tried to poison us."

He only nodded.

"But how did you . . . ?"

"Follow you?" he asked, finishing my question. "A child could have done it."

Lightning ignited the dark sky, and in the flash I saw the knife Gideon had given me earlier.

"You dropped this back there," he said. "Now get up I said!"

My strength had not the time to return, but I had to do something before the dagger could find its mark. I tried to spring past him, but he easily grabbed me and threw me to the ground.

"Running away?" he shouted. "They were right about you. You *are* soft, old man!"

Images of Cleophas speaking those exact words came to my mind. How did he know them?

"Who are you?" I asked.

"I've heard if you kill a man's brother you forever see him in the face of your enemies."

"You are Cleophas's brother?" My mind was racing to connect the points of what I was hearing. "When did you . . . how did you know we left the city?"

"When I saw Cleophas wasn't with you after you set fire to the ship, I knew you had left him there to die. Cleophas told me you would if you had the chance. He said you never liked him or his ideas."

"That's not true," I said. "Cleophas was killed—"

"By you!" he said. "You were the so-called leader of the group. It was your responsibility to see that everyone survived the attack. You let him die! *You* are to blame for his death!"

How could I tell him that his brother would have made it out alive if his stubborn will and pride had not consumed him and clouded his sight? But I knew I would not heal his brother's wounds to tell him that, nor did I think he would believe me.

"I don't want to fight you," I said. It was true. The desire that used to burn within me so strongly was gone. The peace I had experienced not one hour ago as I knelt at the foot of the cross still resonated throughout my entire frame. Even as I lay there, being threatened and stricken by my assailant's strong blows, my only thought for him was compassion. *If he only knew,* I thought to myself over and over. If he only knew the truth about his brother. If he only knew what had happened this day. If he only knew where I was going, and why. If only he could taste the change that was wrought in me this day, he would not be my enemy.

But he didn't know, and right now he *was* my enemy. He laughed.

"You don't want to fight? You don't have that choice," he said. "My fight is with you until the price of my brother's life is extracted from your old, miserable soul."

He paced back and forth, waiting for me to get to my feet and play into his deadly game. When I didn't move, he raised his arms and yelled out in frustration.

"Is it the blade?" he asked. "I'll throw it away. There. Now it's just you and me. Now, get up!"

He reached down and pulled me up. There wasn't time to duck his fist, but I was able to turn my cheek and move with the force of the first blow. The second and third connected with my face as they were intended to. When it was clear I would not strike him back, or even offer him the slightest resistance, he tired of me and pushed me away in disgust. I found the nearest wall to stand and rest against.

"Your friend gave me more of a fight as I loaded him on my cart," he said. "And he was dead."

"Jacob?"

"Do not look surprised. It was nothing to buy his body from the authorities. Of course, if they had known the value of it, they would have killed me for having tried to deceive them. I'm taking the two of you back with me. You can come dead or alive, it matters not. The money is paid either way."

The brother of Cleophas paused, taking pleasure in his taunting words.

"You would desecrate the dead for a little money?" I said.

"A little money? No. For the money they will pay for you two, I'd desecrate a thousand. And when we return, I'll collect on the child and the old tanner. Yes, I know about them too. I followed you home that night, and I haven't let you out of my sight since. The money won't bring Cleophas back; it *will* make for a comfortable living in his honor. So the only choice left to you is whether you want to reach Cyrenaica with your eyes open or with them shut."

As we talked, I could feel the numbing effects of his first strikes slip from my chest and arms and felt a warmth enter my hands and feet. The feeling worked inward toward my heart and chest as I began to feel alive again. This time, the fight would not be fueled by anger or hatred, for I still had none for him, but with a concern for the lives of my family and friends.

"I choose not to go back at all," I said, throwing myself at him. I must have caught him unaware, because I was able to take him around the neck and wrestle him down to the ground. The next few hits were mine, but there was no malice in them. I needed to disable him and prevent him from returning to my friends. I did not wish to kill him. In fact, it was an option I would not even consider.

My control of the fight was short-lived, and after a brief moment, it reverted back to the brother of Cleophas. He returned the pain I had just delivered with double the force. His fists were as hard as hammers, and he unleashed his fury without restraint.

For a moment I forgot about the pain and wondered if this was a punishment for all the hurt and anguish I had caused to so many people in my life—not only my family, but the countless Romans who were the focus of my anger and the recipients of my hateful acts. I was wrong to have blamed them for my stubborn refusal to heal. *Perhaps I am going to die tonight,* I thought, *and perhaps I am deserving of it.* But my concern was not for my life at that moment. All I could think about was my sweet family and how much I wanted to see them again, ask their forgiveness, and offer myself upon the altar of their mercy. Then I did something I hadn't done in thirty years—I prayed.

Please, God, let me see them again. The words were simple but captured my deepest desire. As if by a miracle, the beating stopped, and I was alone staring up at only the rain. My attacker was gone. I rolled to my stomach and then propped myself up on my elbow and looked for the reason for my reprieve.

Standing in the rain were two men. One of them was hitting Cleophas's brother over and over until he ceased to resist, then he forced my attacker down to his knees and held him there. I struggled to get to my feet again and clear my eyes of the water and tears. The man closest to me reached out and helped me up. I was pleased to recognize him at once.

"Gideon," I said, with what I hoped was a smile on my face.

Gideon's companion pulled back his fist and hit Cleophas's brother with enough force to render him unconscious. He too stepped to where I could see him. It was Barabbas.

As they stood next to each other, I could instantly see the resemblance of one in the face of the other. They were father and son. A great deal was explained by this revelation. Gideon's clear love and respect for Barabbas, as well as my quick acceptance into their fold. Jacob had been his uncle, and I, an unknowing friend of the family.

"This is him," Gideon said. "This is the friend of your brother."

Lightning struck so close I felt my chest quiver even before the deafening clap shook the city.

"What is happening here?" Barabbas asked, speaking to me for the first time. His voice sounded like Jacob's, and I was momentarily touched by the memory of his brother. But the weight of the question demanded an answer, and I gave him the only one I had.

"They have crucified the Lord," I said. "The man called Jesus."

I watched as my words sank deep into his understanding, and he began to comprehend their meaning. His life had been spared at the cost of the life of the Savior. Gideon looked to me, and then to his father in disbelief. The wind continued to gust from all directions, carrying the frightened screams of a city being destroyed. I would have stayed but for my pressing need to return to my family.

"That man has taken Jacob's body," I said, motioning to the brother of Cleophas. "See that it is found and buried properly. He cannot be allowed to leave Jerusalem, but do not kill him. There has been enough killing—today and forever."

I turned to go but stopped. I took the second bag from my shoulder and gave it to Barabbas. "This was Jacob's. He spent his last days writing his thoughts and feelings. I am sure he would want you to have it. He was a good man and a good friend. He died with dignity and in the service of his fellow men. I loved your brother. Take good care of his memory for me."

I reached under my shirt and pulled out Jacob's family pendant, taking it from around my neck. I handed it to Barabbas.

Without speaking, Barabbas took it gently from my fingers and stared at it. Then he gave it back to me. "You were his family for all these years. He spoke of you in his letters once. He loved you and considered you family. This is rightfully yours."

I replaced it around my neck and clasped his arm in mine, then nodded my thanks to Gideon.

When I turned to leave again I did not look back. Nothing would delay me further.

* * *

By the time I finally reached Deborah's house I feared that I was too late. The trees in the courtyard had been snapped in two by the gale winds and lay scattered like children's toys. Shielding my eyes from the wind, I briefly checked the house. It looked undamaged from what I could see, but the front door had been blown open. The window shutters banged and slammed into the walls, and the wood had begun to splinter off. There was no light from within.

"Deborah!" I called, bursting inside.

Rain was flooding in from the open skylight, and shards of broken pottery littered the wet floor. For an instant I believed that they were gone, but a sound from the roof captured my attention. I stepped to the open skylight and saw Matthias outside on the roof in a futile struggle with the wind. The opening's tent cover had long since blown away, and Matthias was trying to secure the permanent, wooden planks.

"Where are they?" I yelled up, but my words could not carry over the fury of the storm.

Matthias looked desperate as he fit one plank in place only to have two more blow off in the wind. Even under favorable conditions it was a job for two people. Given the extreme weather, Matthias didn't stand a chance. I ran to the back of the house, quickly righted the ladder that had been blown down, and joined him on the roof.

"Where are they?" I yelled as we worked. "Are they all right?"

Matthias didn't answer but nodded; all his strength was being expended tying down the wooden cover. In a matter of moments the planks were fitted, then nailed into place. Hurrying inside, we both set to work on the door and windows, and soon the storm was barricaded outside where it belonged.

I believed Matthias would collapse with exhaustion, but he sat down before his legs gave out.

"Thank you," he said, when he had caught his breath.

"Where is my family?" I asked.

I followed his look to the door of the back room where Hannah had been the day before. It was shut tight. Now, with most of the noise of the storm shut behind closed windows, I could hear noises coming from within.

"Is she . . . ?"

Before he could answer, the door was opened, and Deborah hurried out to a dry corner near the kitchen to grab a handful of towels.

"We need more hot water," she ordered. "See if you can—"

She stopped moving as suddenly as she had stopped speaking. She inhaled deeply, no doubt calling on her strength reserves to deal with me a second time.

She handed the towels to Matthias. "Take these."

"In there?" Matthias asked.

"And where else would you take them?"

"But it is not right for me to see her so soon after—"

"And who will attend to my daughter and your wife?" Deborah said. "Now do as I say!"

He wordlessly accepted the towels and did as he was told.

Deborah wiped her hands on the towel over her shoulder and stepped to the center of the room to meet me. With every deliberate step her strong, stern eyes sought to determine my intentions for coming back. I was terrified, standing face to face with her. A long moment passed between us.

"I did not expect you to ever return." Her words were as sharp and fierce as the cutting winds outside. "You are either mad or a fool to step foot in here again."

"I'm sorry," was all I could say.

"You're sorry?" she asked in anger. "Is there no one you can shift blame of your actions to this time? No excuse that Rome is at fault? Hannah heard your words when you left. Do you know what that did to her? She would not be comforted for hours. Can you understand her heartbreak?" She paused to make sure that I did. "How it is that one man can cause so much pain and misery, I will never know. We will never agree with what you do. So if you have come back to . . ."

But then she stopped. Maybe it was the rain still dripping from my clothes, or the tears in my red eyes, but her countenance softened. I took her hand, knelt at her feet, and for the first time since that terrible night, I began to cry, releasing the pain that I had only just been able to acknowledge and accept.

"Forgive me," I said when I had enough breath. "I beg you. Let me make it right, to be a worthy husband and father to your family. I have never been deserving of you. I have been dead without you. Now I want to live again. I want to love."

My words surprised me. I had not given thought to what I might say, and I realized that the words that had come out were the strongest desires of my heart. But it didn't feel like *my* heart; it was a new heart.

Deborah's only response was to kneel and raise my head with a finger under my chin. Behind her rough exterior, her eyes betrayed a gentle soul filled with compassion. But I did not want her to speak until I had said everything I knew I needed to.

"There is nothing I can say or do to make amends or replace what I have taken from you," I said. "But with time, perhaps I can correct the mistakes I have made . . . to ease the pain you have suffered . . ."

She noticed my shirt had been ripped, and touched the blood that had stained it. His blood, I remembered. From the cross.

"Are you hurt?" she asked. "What has happened?"

What has happened? Could I explain it, then or ever? Would she believe me? I scarcely believed it myself. The events of the last few hours seemed incomprehensible, but at the same time I longed to tell her everything.

"Simon," she spoke more forcefully now to get my attention. I had been lost in my thoughts. "What happened?"

"I watched a man die today," I said. "If it be lawful to call Him a man. I witnessed His sentencing at the palace this morning. I saw Him executed."

"Die?" Deborah was shocked. "Crucified?"

"I bore His cross."

She took her towel and began drying my face and neck.

"When my eyes first beheld Him at the courts of Pilate, He had already been tried and condemned."

"What were you doing there?"

I reflected a moment, choosing my words carefully. "Trying to find peace."

"What had he done, this man?"

"I never did hear the charges."

"Then who was he?"

"The Lamb of God."

She stopped and looked at her towel. It had touched my shirt and now carried some of the blood of the Lamb. Deborah's legs swiftly gave way but I reached out fast enough to catch her and gently lowered her to the floor. There we knelt as we spoke.

"He's dead?" She could not believe what she was hearing. "The Lamb, the Messiah, killed? Are you sure? Are you sure it was Him? There have been many who . . . Tell me . . . tell me His name. Was it . . ."

"Jesus," I said. "His name was Jesus."

At the sound of His name, Deborah burst into tears, though I did not know how she would have known His name. Unless—

"This prophet you spoke of," I said. "Is He this Jesus?"

"To wait our whole lives to see the Redeemer of Israel, the Messiah," Deborah said, still crying, "only to hear now of His death." She pulled the stained towel to her breast and sobbed.

When she could, she spoke her thoughts aloud.

"But Hannah said it would happen," Deborah spoke as if she were playing out scenes in her mind. "She said He spoke of His death, that He knew He would die to give us life. But I did not want to think that we . . . that Israel would . . ."

"You must tell me what you know," I said. "There is a hunger I feel inside, a thirst that would be quenched with words of Him."

"They said He was the Messiah, the Christ, but I wasn't sure. How could I be? I saw Him only once. Hannah begged me to come with her and listen to a prophet's voice. I could not resist her wide eyes and excitement. I had never seen her taken with a rabbi like this before and went with her. She took me to the Temple, to the Court of Women. His words were strong, yet soothing in every way. I was taken with Him, as Hannah was, and listened intently to every word."

Deborah looked around as if she were there at the Temple again. Finding herself at home instead, she continued.

"Then . . . then a party of scribes and Pharisees disturbed the sermon and presented a woman to Him, throwing her to the ground at His feet. They said she had been caught in the act of adultery, and they wanted to know what Jesus thought they should do. But I could tell that they were not seeking an answer. We all could. It seemed like they were trying to trap Him, to trick Him, to discredit Him. But do you know what He said? He said, 'He who is without sin among you, let him first cast a stone at her.' More wise than Solomon was this man, and one by one they all left with their heads bowed and their steps slow."

Deborah became excited. "But what He did next I will never forget. With a level of compassion I thought only possible for God to possess, He told her to go and sin no more. It felt as if He was forgiving her. I knew that God alone could forgive, but still, I knew in my heart that is what He did. I had so many questions, but I kept them locked inside." Deborah's voice quivered, and I thought she might cry again.

From the back room a voice weakly called out.

"Mother? Is it Father? Has he returned?"

"Yes, child," Deborah called gently, clearing the tears from her eyes. "Rest, my love. I will be there in a moment."

"How is she?" I asked.

"The labor was long, but she held up well." Pride beamed from her face.

"She is strong, like her mother," I said.

I stood and took Deborah by the hand to lift her up as well.

"And the baby?"

"Beautiful and strong," she answered.

A silence passed between us.

"Hannah loved Jesus and followed Him whenever He visited the city," Deborah said finally.

"We mustn't tell her, then. Not today. Not now."

Deborah nodded. "She will need her strength to recover. We will tell her, but later."

I nodded too.

Matthias cleared his throat from the back door. "There is someone who would like to see you."

Again, it seemed as if my heart would not get a rest from its incessant pounding. My feet felt rooted to the floor. I had traveled a thousand miles, crossed an ocean and deserts to respond to my daughter's invitation, and now, not ten paces away, I was unable to move. The realization of my past actions assailed my conscience and hurt my new heart. I had another to beg forgiveness of. I had hurt her in her love and her innocence not once, but twice. She was the reason I had come; hers was the voice I had answered. Were it not for Hannah's faith and love, I would not have thought to return. I would not have seen what I had seen, done what I had done, and changed to become who I was now. Deborah took my hand and led me.

The room was lit by two oil lamps on either side of the bed that nearly filled the room. The light was soft and warm, and cast an angelic glow on the beautiful face that greeted my entrance. My daughter. She was the very image of Deborah when I had been smitten with her at first sight. My beautiful little girl. But more than a girl; she was a woman now, a mother. A partner with God in His creation. More beautiful now than I remembered. So strong, so much like her mother.

"Abba," she said, her voice scarcely above a whisper but bearing a compassionate smile. Her eyes were heavy with the exhaustion of having braved the pains of giving life, but even then, the light in her eyes could not be dimmed as she looked upon her father for the first time after all these years. "Thank you for coming back."

I rushed to her bedside and knelt, taking her hand in mine. Tears again fell freely and without restraint. I had come back, not just from across the sea, or even from the day before, but from the dark and cold place my heart had been imprisoned in these many years. Far too many. "Can you ever forgive me?" I asked.

"I already have," she said.

From my bag I produced her lucky stone.

"I found this before I left," I said, handing it gently to her. "You were right; it does bring good luck."

Hannah took the stone and looked at it closely, then she began to cry softly.

"Thank you," she said again.

From the layers and folds of the blankets and furs covering the bed and keeping her warm against the storm outside, Matthias picked up a small bundle and stepped to my side of the bed. With every ginger step, he handled the wrapping like it was glass. I rose and reached out to receive the gift Matthias stood ready to offer. He gently placed it in the crook of my arm, both of us awkward with the transition; but in the end, Hannah's new life, a child and grandchild so tiny, was sound and resting in my arms.

The babe was the most beautiful thing I had ever beheld. It had been a long time since an infant had found rest in my old arms, and I was reminded vividly of another child I had held so many years past. I was astonished to find that the pain I usually associated with such memories had left me, gone with the lifting of the awful burden I had carried instead of the child for so many years. I was experiencing something I had not felt for so long, it now felt new: love, pure and unrestrained. It did not seem I had ever known such peace.

I looked to Deborah, who seemed to know my thoughts.

"A son," she said.

"A son," I whispered. He was so peaceful in my arms. "A blessing of life on this, of all days. God has not forgotten us, nor forsaken us. Thou art His proof, little one."

I looked up. "Has he a name yet?"

Deborah looked to Matthias, who nodded his approval.

"Jonas Simon," Deborah said. "Named for his two grandfathers."

I could not take my eyes from this beautiful miracle that now bore my name. My thanks went to God that he was not permitted to see the man who for so many years had been filled with ugliness.

"Thank you for thinking of me and sending for me," I said.

"I was just doing what I was told," Hannah said.

I looked to Deborah in confusion.

"Someone told you to send for me?"

"Why didn't you tell me this?" Deborah asked.

Hannah would have laughed if she'd had the strength. The best she could do was smile. "Not to me only, but to all of us listening to Him teach. Jesus said that if any of you have been offended by your brother—or father—go to him and speak with him, and make peace with him. I knew I couldn't go to you, being with child, but you could come to me, and I hoped and prayed you would."

Once again I repented of my belief that God did not care for us or watch over us with a grand design. He did. He always had. From the beginning He was watching over me and preparing a way for me to return.

A pounding on the door startled our repose.

I handed little Jonas Simon to his father. "Stay and watch over them," I told Deborah. "Close the bedroom door, and do not open it until I say everything is all right." The storm had compounded in force outside, and I was worried that the desperate weather would have spawned desperate men in search of shelter. I was the husband and father again; the duty to protect my family was once again mine.

The knock sounded again as I reached the door. The moment I unlatched it the wind forced it open, and there, filling its frame, was the scarred centurion. Over his uniform he wore a simple coat; his entire appearance was rain-soaked and windblown. The storm blew in around him, but I could not move to prevent it. He looked as afraid as I felt, and my tongue was unresponsive to my desire to speak.

Deborah approached and stood at my side. Though I had told her to stay, I was grateful now for her presence. "What is it, Simon? Who is this man?"

The centurion found the ability to speak before I did.

"It's you." His voice was strong yet gentle, filled with power tempered by compassion.

His words, not quite a question, seemed spoken in disbelief; he appeared pleased that he had found me. As he stood there, I still felt no ill will toward him. Though my thoughts argued that nothing had changed, that he was still the man I had blamed for so much pain in my life over the years, my heart, my *new* heart, welcomed him.

"Please," my words were eager, "enter."

He breathed in relief and bowed his respect.

"Simon, who is this man?" Deborah asked again, this time with a strain of concern in her voice.

"This is . . ." Was there a proper introduction for the man who had impacted our lives in such great and profound ways? If there was, I was at a loss to find it. "He is . . ."

"Quintus," he said, addressing Deborah with kindness and respect. "My name is Quintus."

Deborah gripped my arm tighter. "What is he doing here?"

Quintus returned his full attention to me. "I followed you here," he said. "But I had to return to my home first." He spoke over his shoulder. "Son, I have found him."

A tall, handsome man joined him. "Who?" the younger man asked.

"Your father."

The rages of the storm were drowned out by the most profound silence. A quiet gasp escaped my lips as I recognized Deborah's features in this stranger. Deborah must have seen the resemblance to Alexander and Rufus; she backed up until she found the wall to steady her. Was this our . . . ?

"Joshua?" Deborah asked in a whisper.

A look of complete surprise filled this young man's face at the sound of his name being spoken, and he, too, was struck dumb by the news revealed by this centurion of Rome. He reached out for Quintus and supported himself on his shoulder. He looked to Deborah, then to me, then to Quintus.

"Is it possible?" Joshua said, his voice quivering.

Quintus only nodded. I looked to Deborah, then to the centurion. A thousand unanswered questions ran through my mind.

"I could not do it," he said, answering the most pressing question that must have shown on my face. "That night . . . I could not."

Was it possible? I reached back for Deborah, and together we sat on one of the benches set up for the Passover feast. Quintus and Joshua did the same.

"I . . . don't understand," I said. Was this miracle a gift for my small service this day to my Lord and my God?

"I was young," the Roman centurion said. "It was my first assignment as a soldier, but I could not do as I was commanded."

"But I saw you. I watched you . . ."

Quintus shook his old, tired head. "For a moment I believed I would," he said. I could tell that his words brought both pain and relief as he spoke them. "You were struck, and when a call for help from another soldier sounded nearby, I was told to finish the deed and follow them, but the moment I was alone I dropped the knife to the ground and fell to my knees. Herod was mad, and I vowed to my gods and yours never to commit such horrible acts in the mere name of duty, even at the cost of my own life. So I hid until dawn, with your son safe and protected."

Quintus looked over at Joshua with the loving look of a father.

"Later, I looked for you, but you had already been taken away—a criminal for having tried to protect yourself and your family. I had no way to find you, and I feared to ask too many questions. If Herod learned that your child had lived, he would have killed us both. So I kept him, hid him, and later declared him as my servant."

"A slave?"

Quintus again shook his head. "To us, a son, though my wife and I could not produce children. Many knew this, and would become suspicious if we were suddenly with child. But Hebrew servants were common, and so we kept him hidden and we waited. When Herod died we announced Joshua. All our days my wife and I loved him as if her womb had carried and borne him. Until the hour of her death, my wife cared for him and loved him as her own."

"You told him?"

"When he was old enough." His voice quivered on the edge of tears. "I told him everything and begged his forgiveness, and promised him, one day . . ." Joshua reached out and took his hand to comfort him. "He was raised in the faith of his people. He was schooled in the language of your people and instructed in the laws of your God. Though he was like a son to me, I never once forgot what I had done."

Deborah stood and stepped slowly to Joshua, taking his big strong hand in hers, and sat down beside him. She rested her head on his shoulder and began to recite a prayer of thanksgiving. Outside the storm raged, but peace reigned beneath our roof.

"I became a friend to your faith, contributing where I could to the building up of your synagogues. Perhaps, I believed, I could make right my actions of that night. For so long I begged your God's forgiveness," he said, "and prayed that I would have this chance to confess myself to you. I am ashamed to say I had almost given up."

His words carried a sincerity I had never before felt. With all my being I believed him, and wanted to learn from this man who was fast becoming my brother, my friend.

I noticed the cut over his eye. It had opened up in the rain. "What happened?" I asked, pointing to it.

He touched it gently. "Though Roman citizens are free to worship any god we choose," he said, "faith in your God does not come without a price within the ranks of Caesar. I have become unpopular for my choices. It seems that some will never understand."

My life was taking on a new shape faster than I could manage; though I had so many questions about Joshua's life, my heart needed to know of other things. I thirsted still for what I could learn of Jesus.

Who was this extraordinary man whose life and death I had played a small part in? How had Quintus come to know Him?

"Tell me more of this Jesus," I said. "You were at His trial and at His side in His final moments. I would know what you would share."

"You were at the trial?" Quintus asked.

"The mockery it was."

"If I am to keep it inside a moment longer I fear I may burst. I have not even told Joshua. There has been no time."

"Then tell, we are eager to listen."

"Pilate would not listen to reason. He would not be persuaded otherwise. The high priest, and many others, brought Jesus in before morning's first light, claiming He was guilty of some great crime deserving of death. In desperation, the high priest said that Jesus had made himself to be a king of the people, and an inciter of the people. It was a lie, and no one believed it, including Pilate. Then he learned that Jesus was from Galilee. Herod Antipas, the ethnarch of that region, was in town for the celebration, and Pilate sent Jesus to him for examination, hoping to be rid of the Jewish accused and His fool accusers. I insisted on going with Him."

Quintus stopped and gathered his thoughts before continuing. "Herod could find nothing worthy of punishment and sent Him back. Pilate was satisfied for a while and refused to try and sentence Him, but your high priest persisted."

"Caiaphas is not *my* high priest," I said.

Quintus nodded in apology and went on. "I was fearful of what would happen next. Claims of sedition and revolution are serious crimes under Roman law. I was afraid Pilate would concede for appearances' sake. My mind was tortured, trying to think of some way I could save the man who had taught only love and peace, and was in no way deserving of death. I had to think as the lawyers might. Then I remembered a Jewish tradition and counseled with the governor. The law allowed him to pardon and set free one condemned man to the people. Jesus had done nothing wrong, but the charges were serious to Pilate's position and his standing with Tiberius. Pilate was quick to see my reasoning. He could release an innocent man, but at the same time be free of blame if news of the man or the charges reached Syria or even Rome. Pilate was grateful to have found a solution to the morning's dilemma and thus ordered it.

"The high priest quickly conferred with the other priests and advisors with him and came back demanding that Pilate present Him and another man named Barabbas to the people for a vote. Pilate was tired of this business and agreed, and a short time later the two were presented to the crowds gathered to watch the trials."

"That is why I was there," I said. "To support the release of the other." All eyes were suddenly on me in surprise. I raised a hand to calm them. "I will tell of that story another day. Please, Quintus." I motioned for him to continue.

"You were there; you saw what happened," Quintus said. "They chose Barabbas rather than Jesus to be released. From the ground, the high priest smiled up at us in clear, prideful victory. Pilate was infuriated.

"I begged him to stop the proceedings, reminding him that Jesus was guilty of no crime. The trial, though, had moved beyond guilt or innocence and become a personal struggle with the high priest below. Pilate ordered that Jesus be taken away and scourged, and muttered to himself about showing the people who was the master of Judea. When I protested I was dismissed out of hand. My plan was not unfolding as I had hoped. Jesus was meant to be a free man by then, but instead He was led away to meet with the whip. I thought I could stop it, and I hurried to the inner court.

"Many of my enemies knew that I followed Jesus and had a great love for Him. When they learned that Pilate had Him in custody and was considering a sentence of death, they made their own plans to hurt me and the man I loved and followed. On the way from the balcony, I was struck from behind. As I said before, worshiping the God of a captured people did not make me any friends among the ranks. There were many eager to replace me as centurion. Today an attempt was made, but I would not be delayed and escaped their plot with only this cut over my eye." He paused, feeling again the sadness the next part of his story evoked.

"I reached the inner court but was too late. They had already stripped Him . . . and . . ."

"I know," I said. "I watched on."

Quintus looked relieved he did not have to continue his narrative of the horrible violence that followed.

"I rushed to His aid and was about to free Him of his pain and humiliation when Pilate stopped me and commanded I bring Him back out as He was, bleeding and with a crown of thorns atop His head. Pilate tried once more to convince the people to set Jesus free, but they would hear nothing of it. Their thirst for blood was unlike anything I have ever seen. Defeated, Pilate left and ordered that Jesus be taken and crucified."

Quintus stood and began to pace the room. There was too much emotion in him to contain it while sitting.

"I spoke to Jesus," he said, "and begged Him to let me free Him. A word, a nod, a look and I would have given my life to spirit Him away, and used my last breath to set Him free that He might live."

When Quintus said these last words, a passage from Isaiah was forcefully brought to mind. Many years had passed, but still the words I learned as a child were recalled with perfect clarity.

"'But he was wounded for our transgressions,'" I began. "'He was bruised for our iniquities: the chastisement of our peace was upon him; and with his stripes we are healed. All we like sheep have gone astray; we have turned every one to his own way; and the Lord hath laid on him the iniquity of us all. He was oppressed, and he was afflicted, yet he opened not his mouth.'"

I was stunned to see for the first time the clarity with which the prophets had seen this very day. What inspiration, what perfect vision they'd had, and for a time we could not speak as we pondered the ancient words. Outside, the storm still beat down on the city.

"He spoke softly and reassured me that all was well," Quintus finally said, then he broke down in tears of his own. "In His darkest hour, His concern was for me."

"'Surely he hath borne our griefs, and carried our sorrows,'" I whispered, surprised to hear myself quoting again.

"Always has He showed compassion for me and for Joshua," Quintus said with awe and thanksgiving.

"Tell me," Deborah said, tearing her eyes from the beautiful face of the child she had believed lost to her. "Tell me of my son."

Quintus inhaled deeply and seemed to settle into a peace that had a calming effect on me too. "If he were my own flesh and blood I could not have loved him any more. He was a good child and easy to love. Though he was stubborn at times, he was quick to make amends and could be reasoned with at an early age."

Deborah looked up, meeting Joshua's eyes, and smiled as she pictured the man at her side as a little boy, with traits easily recognizable as her own.

Quintus continued. "My rank opened many doors to us, including access to the brightest teachers the country had to offer. Though my wife and I had him schooled in Hebrew and the Law by the best rabbis known to the local priests, we also had tutors from around the world visit us, teaching him to read and write Latin, Greek, and some Egyptian. The world, and its history, was opened up to him, and I could not have been more proud of his intelligence, wisdom, and love."

Quintus looked over at Joshua as a father might his own son, and rightly so, I thought. Joshua, still overcome to the point of being stripped of words, managed to look to Quintus, then to me, and then back to Quintus, embarrassed at the praise and love being aired and expressed, and he not knowing what to say. As he looked for direction to the man who had been his father for so many years, I was surprised to feel no jealousy kindled within me. Instead, I found their bond touching, and comforting.

I left my musings to listen anew to Quintus's tale. "When he was ten, he began learning a trade. He chose metalsmithing and showed promise with the smiths who took him as their apprentice, but when he was in his twelfth year he became ill and was struck with a palsy. His health was never the same after that, but he was a strong boy. I would cry in the dark when the other children would tease him. But he never struck back; I never once heard him complain, even as he became a man."

I looked to the tall strong man sitting with Deborah. There was neither a withered hand nor shaking limbs.

"Two years ago he fell ill again," Quintus continued. "I had never seen such a sickness. I called on the best physicians and wise men in the surrounding country, but they could not help him. Their combined opinion was that death would come quickly, but I refused to accept this."

The memory of his pain was strong enough to bring fresh tears to his eyes.

"I would find a cure," he continued. "I refused to believe that he could not be saved. Your God would not spare him only to let him die now. As you know, Egypt is known for their wisdom and medicine, so I prepared a journey to the banks of the Nile. But then word reached me of a man who was performing miracles, traveling from city to city. Fortune was kind, for I learned that earlier that day he had arrived where I was stationed, in Capernaum. I went immediately to find him. As I pushed through the throng of people surrounding this Jew, I heard strange words. Some called him a holy man, a prophet, while others warned that he deceived the people, that he was possessed of a devil and wrought his acts by an unholy power. But priest or con, prophet or devil, if he could heal my son . . . your son . . . then his name and his god be praised.

"When I reached the streets, he had just passed by. I stretched forth my hand and entreated him to stop, which he did. I was filled with a sensation I had never before had but have felt many times since—a feeling that I was standing on hallowed ground. I dared not ask him to return with me, but told him that I knew if he were to command that Joshua be whole, I could return with that authority and it would be done. He did, and Joshua was whole even before I returned. It was even as if he had never had the childhood palsy. No one could explain it. It was a miracle."

He paused and looked to Joshua and then to me. "Thirty years before I had been commanded to find the child born King of the Jews. That day I finally found Him."

"And today I watched Him die," I said. "How could it be that the very people He had been sent to save would treat Him with such cruelty?" I pondered this for a moment. Then another thought entered my mind and filled my soul with exquisite light, as only truth can. "But even as He was lifted up and crucified, He breathed life into our spirits, lifting our burdens that we each were determined were ours alone to bear."

At the time, I knew the words I had spoken were true, though it would take a lifetime to fully comprehend the miracle that took place that night, both atop Golgotha and within my heart.

We talked long into the night, asking and answering questions and filling in the details of our lives. We shed so many tears that we began to think they would never dry. And each tear that fell washed away part of those many years of pain. As a thick darkness fell like a blanket over the land, so heavy that even our lamps lost their light, we did not fear. A new light warmed us as we spoke and illuminated our vision and our understanding, and together, with Quintus as my brother, our family set out on the long journey toward healing—made possible by the life and love of one man, Jesus, which is called the Christ.

AUTHOR'S NOTE

Lifted Up is a work of fiction. Though based on scriptural accounts, the author has taken creative license and liberty in the telling of the story.

Where the story and characters cross into recorded scriptural accounts, much research and great care was taken to present them accurately. Some of the direct quotes (such as the cry of Matthias, father to Judas Maccabeus, that sparked the Jewish revolution against the Syrians, and the warning words displayed on the ancient Temple balustrade) were taken from *Jesus and His Times*, a publication of Reader's Digest (1987). Other items of historical note, such as the Jewish assault on Herod's Temple to remove the Roman ensign, and the actions of Pilate upon taking office, were taken from the writings of Josephus. Many other events, people, and places are products of the author's imagination and should not be taken as historical fact.

However, the Jewish struggle against the power of the Roman Empire was very real. Zealots, referred to and so called for their zeal and fervor for the Law, were a party among the Jews not afraid to raise swords (if need be) in defense of their country and their God. Zealots were found in every community of Jews scattered throughout the Roman Empire, including Cyrene and Jerusalem. Their feelings toward their foreign oppressors were intense, but many of this story's catalysts (such as the attack on the fictional Roman galley, *Vindicare*, and the plot to rescue Barabbas) simply did not happen as far as we know.

The scriptural accounts and quotes were taken from the King James Version of the New Testament. Additional insight was largely taken from *Jesus the Christ*, by James Talmage. As an additional note, the scriptural passages quoted in the last chapter were taken from Isaiah 53:4–7. Some scripturally based conversations used in this book were adapted slightly to fit the style and voice of the rest of the text, but they remain true to the integrity of their meaning.

ABOUT THE AUTHOR

Lifted Up was the result of the author's own struggle to learn what it meant to freely forgive, and to apply this divine principle in his own life. The scriptural accounts which inspired this work have always occupied a special place in his heart.

Guy M. Galli is a divorce and child custody mediator and is the director of the Third District Court's Co-Parenting Mediation Program. He lives in Draper, Utah, with his wife, Natalie, and their two children, Hannah and Brandon.